CW00427917

Killing Charlie

GRAYSON HARDY

£2.75

EASY P

Copyright © 2020 Grayson Hardy

All rights reserved.

ISBN: 9798623765437 (Paperback)
Illustrations Copyright © 2020 By Grayson Hardy
Design by German Creative

First Edition: April 2020
This Paperback Edition First Published in 2020

The right of Grayson Hardy to be identified as the author of this
work has been asserted by him in accordance with the copyright,
designs and patents act 1988

All rights reserved. No part of this publication may be reproduced,
stored in any retrieval system, or transmitted, in any form or by any
means, electronic, mechanical, photocopying, recording or
otherwise, without the prior permission of the copyright owner.

DEDICATION

For the countless brave men and women who have served their country, some who gave the ultimate sacrifice and are no longer with us. Not least, for those who still carry invisible scars and live with PTSD on a daily basis.

"It is not the critic who counts; not the man who points out how the strong man stumbles, or where the doer of deeds could have done them better. The credit belongs to the man who is actually in the arena, whose face is marred by dust and sweat and blood; who strives valiantly; who errs, who comes short again and again, because there is no effort without error and shortcoming; but who does actually strive to do the deeds; who knows great enthusiasms, the great devotions; who spends himself in a worthy cause; who at the best knows in the end the triumph of high achievement, and who at the worst, if he fails, at least fails while daring greatly, so that his place shall never be with those cold and timid souls who neither know victory nor defeat."

April 23, 1910, Theodore Roosevelt – Paris, Sorbonne

Lest we Forget

PRAISE FOR GRAYSON HARDY

'Fast-Moving, gripping and gritty'
Lloyd Figgins–Author of the Travel Survival Guide

'A high-octane adventure that I couldn't put down'
Adam Liardet–Ex Royal Green Jacket Officer and Rifleman

'Boys own adventure in close up reality from start to finish'
Pete Dodd–Global Security Professional

'With high levels of adrenaline & testosterone it's what every jungle adventure is made of'
Major Martin Bishop–RE (V) RTD

AUTHOR'S NOTE

This is a work of fiction. This novel is part of the John Hart series. The story and characters are entirely fictitious. Geographical places, long-standing institutions, agencies, and public offices are mentioned, but the characters involved are wholly imaginary.

Any resemblance to persons living or dead is coincidental. The opinions expressed are those of the characters and should not be confused with that of the author.

A percentage of all sales from this novel will be donated to my local Royal British Legion branch and other charities working within our communities to support those effected with Post-traumatic stress disorder (PTSD) and other Mental Health issues.

ACKNOWLEDGMENTS

To my children and grandchildren, the most special treasure that a parent can ever have in this world.

Very special thanks to my family for all the support, love and guidance offered whilst writing this fictional adventure, inspired by my own military experiences and the numerous special forces operations across the world. The patience shown during the long hours and hard work has been humbling and beyond words.

Thank you to my mother and late father, brother and sisters. Their support and love over the years has been steadfast and warmly received.

I would like to finally thank all those who I have served with during my time within the regular army and the British special forces, your camaraderie and brotherhood is a debt I cannot repay. We will never forget those friends' who didn't make it and who died in the prime of their lives. RIP.

PROLOGUE

Sergeant JOHN HART had seen many disturbing sights during his time in the armed forces, but the sight of his right-hand trembling uncontrollably was not one of them. Regarded as one of the best marksmen in the SAS, Hart had become something of a reluctant legend within the 'Regiment' during his service with RWW— better known as 'The Wing' by those serving; an elite cadre of hand-picked SAS operators tasked with supporting Secret Intelligence Service (SIS) operations.

Briefly glancing at his trembling hand, Hart could not comprehend why this was happening and why now of all times; what the hell was going on? The sweating and chest pains had become familiar since his return from Afghanistan a month ago, but he'd convinced himself it was just reoccurring symptoms from a virus he'd picked up whilst on some recent overseas op—but the trembling hand. This was new, this was something different and deeply concerned Hart, but now was not the time for concern - the task in hand required his full focus.

Hart was concealed in the thick and thorny hostile undergrowth deep within the Colombian jungle waiting for the

JUNGLA commander's signal. Hart knew that some of his physical reactions were normal in the moments before an attack. His heart rate had increased, his breathing shallow and the adrenalin coursed through his veins. He knew he was experiencing extreme circumstantial stress, but why did it feel so much worse than anything he'd experienced before? If he couldn't get his hand under control, he would be useless in the attack and potentially even compromise the entire operation.

As the seconds ticked by, Hart took long, deep breaths, trying to regulate his body and get it under control. A minute or two later, the pains abated, the sweat pouring down his back turned cold and his right hand finally steadied. Glad of the extra time to recover from the unwelcome sensations, Hart was frustrated with how long he and his team had been waiting in the inhospitable undergrowth. The jungle was host to some of the planet's most feared and venomous species, including the golden poison dart frog, the world's most poisonous animal, carrying enough poison in its skin to kill up to 20 humans just by touch. The oppressive heat and humidity pressed in on Hart's skin making sweat almost pointless. The mosquitos had been exceptionally hostile, feasting on his blood through any exposed skin they could find. Hart had also come under attack from leeches and stinging ants, but the snakes and scorpions had so far thankfully left him alone.

Throughout the night the jungle had been deafening, as countless nocturnal creatures slowly emerged from their day-time slumber to hunt and feast. A rustle, a croak, branches snapping and breaking in the canopy above; the same soundtrack throughout the night. This crescendo of noise had offered welcomed cover for the operation as the teams moved into their final attack positions, now patiently lying in wait for the anticipated attack signal to come. Due to the need for strict radio silence, it had been agreed that the attack signal would be the firing of an M203 grenade round - chosen for its effectiveness at producing multiple casualties and destroying emplacements with a kill radius of five metres.

The signal for the attack should have come just before first light, but dawn had broken some time ago and still nothing. It was critical they ambushed the camp before its occupants were fully awake and the day commenced. "What the fuck's going on?" Hart seethed under his breath.

The SAS team had expertly coordinated the attack's planning phase with their US Special Forces counterparts, and even the local JUNGLA police appeared reasonably competent, so why the delay? This was exactly why Hart wasn't a huge fan of multi-agency operations: too many chiefs and not enough Indians. No matter how well he and his team were rehearsed, they were reluctantly dependent on other's keeping to the meticulous operational timings. The JUNGLA police commander, the diminutive Major Rodriguez, who's most annoying trait was his arrogance, had insisted on leading the operation and giving the attack signal, despite only having attended the final operational briefing moments before the attack force deployed. Hart was furious with this decision, but his objection had been quickly dismissed by the powers above. After all, the British and the Americans were only there in an 'advisory capacity' at the request of the Colombian Government.

Hart was heading up a five-man SAS team and the US 7th Special Forces numbered a team of twenty-five, all of whom were experienced, and battle-hardened. In contrast, the JUNGLA was forty-strong and inexperienced by comparison. Hart and his team knew all too well from experience that a large force meant nothing if they weren't organised properly. They had no choice but to accept they were outnumbered when it came to operational decision making.

Whilst lying in position steeling himself for the imminent attack, Hart couldn't possibly know just how much this operation would push him to the limit, not just as a special forces soldier but also as a human being.

CHAPTER ONE

A LOUD BANG woke John Hart with a start. He leapt to his feet, reaching around for his weapon, frantic for a few moments, before realising where he was. He was no longer in the compound in Afghanistan, he was in a London hotel, just off Neal Street in Covent Garden after being summoned by the Director of Special Forces to attend a Ministry of Defence meeting the previous day to discuss the fallout from the operation in Afghanistan. He'd fallen asleep watching TV; a car must have backfired. Moments ago, he'd been back there again, in Afghanistan, in the recurring dream that replayed the events of that fateful night. He'd had it every single night since his return two weeks ago. Sometimes Paddy made it back to the helicopter, sometimes it was Hart himself, feeling his body ripped apart by enemy fire. Sometimes they got Stern out alive, sometimes Stern died, but every night, every single detail of the boy's face remained the same, down to the exact shape of his face with half his cheek blown off.

The look in his eyes never changed.

Hart felt familiar nausea rising up through his body, clawing at his throat as he tried to force down the bile. He could taste the excess of bitter saliva in his mouth. His stomach kept contracting violently. He just made it to the bathroom, his face was white and chin dripping with bile. He lurched forward and sunk to his knees. The pungent stench invaded his nostrils as he heaved up into the toilet bowl. Only after he'd finished did he realise his clothes were drenched in sweat; when was this going to end?

A number of hours later, Hart had changed and was walking out of his hotel heading towards Piccadilly. He was sure he had enough time to walk to the Mandarin Oriental, near Hyde Park Corner. If not, he'd jump in a cab somewhere along Piccadilly.

Hart thought about his team.

The events surrounding Paddy had been particularly hard on Kav. The Fijian was the newest member of the team; he'd joined them just before they'd been sent on an operation to Iraq and was the youngest member of the team.

By contrast, Paddy McDowell had been endowed with the gregarious, extroverted demeanour that matched both his Irish roots and his chilli-pepper-red hair. A lovable rogue, Paddy had a weakness for leggy blondes, rugby and Jameson's whiskey (not necessarily in that order). He'd joined the 1st Battalion, The Royal Irish Regiment of the British Army at 18. His devout Catholic parents had been intent on Paddy joining the priesthood, but nothing could have been further from the Irishman's mind. A stocky 5' 9" and solid, Paddy had been a natural fighter. He'd made a small fortune bare-knuckle fighting, and also won any verbal match he got into. An expert navigator, Paddy had never got lost, even whilst operating in the most isolated, featureless locations. Hart hoped Paddy was still up on the lay of the land, wherever he was now.

Bob had also taken things particularly badly. Hart and Bob had joined the SAS from 2 Para: the two men passing the same SAS selection course. On the surface, it had always looked as though there was no love lost between Paddy and Bob, but Hart knew that Bob's tough stance with Paddy's behaviour—the drinking, the women, the fighting—was a cover for the fact that he had genuine affection for his teammate. Paddy and Bob were both highly skilled in unarmed combat (although, Bob saved his skills for the battlefield). Standing at only 5' 7", but with the strength of an ox and a fifth Dan black belt in Shotokan karate, Bob was particularly useful in covert operations where weapons could not be used in confined spaces. He could kill swiftly, using only a knife, or even just his bare hands. He was the oldest in the group and was Hart's trusted second in command.

Absorbed in his memories, Hart had been walking at quite a pace. The clouds were beginning to roll back, and the late afternoon sun brought the whole city, shining, into view. He had been oblivious to his surroundings as he'd made his way down Piccadilly, but as he reached Hyde Park Corner, he glanced up at Apsley House. He felt a deep sense of reverence as he passed in front of the historical building that had once been the residence of the first Duke of Wellington, Arthur Wellesley... a military genius.

Distracted, Hart crossed towards Knightsbridge, in the northwest corner of the busy intersection, against the lights and almost being hit by a bus. He jumped back and smiled wryly to himself as he waited with other pedestrians for their turn to cross. How ironic would it be to lose his life like that after everything he'd been through?

He imagined his epitaph:

"In Loving Memory of John Hart: Died 19th June 2007. Fought for his country. Killed terrorists. Got run over by a big red bus!! Shit happens."

That would tickle the SAS boys.

A few minutes later, Hart was standing in the lobby of the Mandarin Oriental looking for his old friend - ex 2 para and former SAS comrade Phil "Geordie" Savage when he felt a hard slap on his back, "Talk about long time no see!" Geordie bellowed.

"Not long enough..." Hart replied turning to greet his with a warm smile.

"Seriously, it's good to see you, John, let's grab an early evening drink," Geordie said as he simultaneously signalled to the bar area.

Having ordered a bottle of cold beer for himself and a rum and coke for Geordie, Hart set the drinks down on the table that Geordie had secured in the corner of the bar.

After a few jovial exchanges between the two of them, mainly about their ages and relationship disasters, the tone changed.

"So how have you really been John?" Geordie asked in a serious tone. Hart was slightly taken aback, "Christ I must look like shit" he thought to himself, although that's how he was feeling on the inside, he thought he'd been hiding it well up until now.

"You know how it is with the regiment at the moment, mate", Hart replied "We're doing back to back ops with little or no downtime in-between, but that's the job and there's no point complaining. Who'd listen anyway? The guys rather it was that way than fuck all happening at all."

"So are the rumours true?" Geordie asked in a low voice. "About Paddy? Don't talk about it if you don't want to, but I heard through Bob. He told me that you and the boys had a screwed-up mission trying to get some spook out of a village over there. Bob said the weather was shit and fucked everything up."

Hart waited until after he'd taken a long slug of his beer before speaking.

"We all did our best. The odds were against us that night," he told Geordie, bluntly. Geordie nodded, taking the hint that Hart wasn't going to discuss it further.

"Still," Geordie said, "You wiped out a good few Al-Qaeda. Great job mate."

Hart couldn't and didn't respond. Yes, he thought, several Al-Qaeda..." and one kid. Great job.

It was good to see Geordie, but Hart really wasn't in the

mood for talking shop or digging up past operational exploits. After having another drink each, Hart bid Geordie a good evening, before heading back to his hotel. It was now 10 pm and as Hart lay down on the king-sized bed reflecting on the earlier conversation with Geordie, he felt the blackness of sleep falling over him. Caught in a carousel of thoughts, his consciousness ebbed, his mind swirled, replaying the events that continued to relentlessly raid and torture his soul. The scene before Hart was always the same. Was it really a nightmare, if it refused to leave his presence when he was awake?

The scorched land shimmered in the intense white rays of the sun. Hart was part of the four-man SAS QRF team stationed with the US 1st Battalion (Airborne) in the Maidan Wardak province of Afghanistan around 50 miles west of Kabul. The local population was scattered sporadically across the mountainous region with many isolated areas, making it an ideal area for the Taliban and Al-Qaeda leaders to hide out in. Many of the locals were also sympathisers of their cause.

Then without warning everything changed, an undercover MI6 officer had just been captured by Al-Qaeda and it was now mission-critical that they got him back safely. Earlier that day the SAS team had been given the signal and authority to locate and extract the MI6 officer.

Hart's team were now minutes' away from the Al-Qaeda convoy, flying low over the deserted eastbound highway, which wound through the Afghan mountains. The vast mountain range soared up towards the sky, dominating the landscape in a great line as if they were the spine belonging to this harsh land.

The predator drone, operated by a member of the American Air Force 17th Reconnaissance Squadron from Creech Air Force base in the Mojave Desert had already confirmed that Jason Stern, the captured MI6 officer, was in the lead car of the convoy. The plan was simple; the Black Hawk pilot would drop as low as possible as they approached the convoy, allowing the door gunners to open fire with their M60Ds and take out the two rear vehicles. Hart and his men would then abseil to the ground whilst the door gunners took out the wheels of the lead car. The SAS men would then engage the three Al-Qaeda men in that car before extracting Jason Stern.

The image-intensifying high- powered cameras fitted to the un-manned drone were, so far, giving Stern a chance of getting out of this situation alive.

As soon as Stern had been captured, the CIA had informed MI6; they had in turn immediately made the call to Hart. Hart was now sitting in the Sikorsky UH-60 Black Hawk helicopter beside his 2IC, Bob King, along with the other members of the QRF team; Paddy McDowell and Kav Rabuka. The helicopter was a state-of-the-art flying machine, employing stealth technology which enabled it to be virtually invisible at night and emit minimal sound from its adapted rotor blades. All the Sikorsky's occupants wore the latest night-vision goggles, making it appear as though outside was still illuminated in daylight and revealing every detail and potential threat from the land below that the darkness attempted to hide from them.

Through their earpieces, Hart's team and the US pilots received a running commentary from the drone operator at Creech. The Al- Qaeda convoy had left the highway that ran between Kabul and Ghazni and was now heading towards the town of Behsud. The US QRF platoon was on its way from Kabul to provide the outer security cordon and was also receiving regular updates from the drone operator—who was now telling the combined rescue mission that the convoy had reached the Chahar Qal'eh area of the highway and had turned off down a narrow dirt track, heading towards a small remote village: around twelve small houses within a walled compound.

The mobile ambush was off.

They'd have to make their attack on the ground where the kidnappers would presumably be taking their hostage to some sort of safe house.

Hopefully, the SAS team would get there before the Al-Qaeda interrogator could begin sadistically subjecting Stern to unimaginable torture.

There was no time for a formal briefing; they'd have to run with the unfolding events as best they could. Hart began to issue his men with a set of snap orders.

"Okay, guys, we've got one shot at this. We have to go in blind and roll with the punches," Hart warned them before addressing the pilots. "Stay low. If you can get us down to 50 feet, perfect."

"Shouldn't be a problem. There are no obstacles on the approach," the chief pilot assured him.

The drone operator at Creech informed everyone that the convoy had now arrived at the walled compound. The three Al-Qaeda men in the lead car had just dragged Stern, who remained hooded, from the car before unceremoniously pushing him towards a small two-storey building at the far end of the compound; the Al-Qaeda safe house set slightly apart from the other buildings within the compound.

"Drop us on a nearby roof if you can," Hart instructed him before turning back to his men. "We'll exit using fast ropes. Bob, you stay in position on the roof and place covering fire into the compound. Kav, Paddy and I will move from the roof and make our way towards the safe house." Hart turned back to the aircrew to give them his next instructions.

"Once we're clear, take her back up to get some height, then get the door guns firing at full capacity. We need lots of fucking *lead hornets* downrange. I want you to hose down the compound and give us as much covering fire as you can."

To his men, Hart ordered, "Keep to the edge of the buildings. I don't want any fucking blue-on-blue. Paddy, when we get to the safe house, you drop off and cover the main entrance and staircase to the upper floors. Kav and I will clear the bottom floor. If we can't locate our guy on that floor, we'll move back towards the main door and move past Paddy, heading upstairs clearing the upper level. As soon as we have our man, we'll radio all call signs that we're exiting the building and ready for extraction."

Hart turned back to the aircrew. "This will also be your signal to land in the compound. Once you're down, we'll exit the building and get on board. When I've got my headcount, I'll give the signal to take off and we'll get the fuck out of there. Any questions?"

"If there's a comms problem," asked the chief pilot, "How long do we remain hovering and providing covering fire before extracting?"

"I'm hoping you'll have a direct line of sight with Bob, and comms will be good. Barring the possibility, the compound's positioned in one fucking huge comms dead spot," Hart replied. "If you can't see any of us, or you don't hear us on the net after ten minutes, from the time we hit the ground, then pull out and get the fuck out of there. Presume we're all 'man down' and head straight back to Bagram airbase."

"Affirmative," the pilot assured Hart. "We'll stay in the hover for ten minutes before we go into emergency EVAC."

Before Hart could speak again, word came through from the drone operator that the US outer security cordon was now in place around the village.

"Okay, if there are no other question's and everyone's happy, let's carry out last-minute checks and get ready to deploy in figures five," The men nodded their acknowledgement and an eerie silence descended upon them all as they flew towards the mountain range. It was the calm before the storm; Hart felt the adrenalin kick in.

The Black Hawk was now travelling at its maximum attack speed of 183 mph and at a height of 55 feet. Night had fallen an hour ago and thanks to slowly thickening cloud cover there was no moonlight to warn the occupants within the compound of their imminent approach. The blackness now offered the SAS team and helicopter crew a blanket of protection. The usual friendly scattering of stars was now partially obscured by cloud cover. The few guards positioned around the compound's perimeter looked up in utter bewilderment as the Black Hawk suddenly appeared out of the night sky, hovering over one of the low buildings.

Within seconds, Hart and his men had disembarked. As instructed, the pilot took the Black Hawk up to 150 feet and the door gunners opened fire, obliterating any of the guards who had been caught out in the open.

Bob King stayed in position on the rooftop they'd hovered over, covering Hart, Kav, and Paddy as they hurtled down the outside stone staircase of the building and made their way towards the Al-Qaeda two-story safe house that had been identified by the drone. They stuck close to the walls of the buildings, staying in the shadows, out of the way of the door gunners' fire, and on full alert in case some Al- Qaeda men had escaped the initial barrage of gunfire and could now also be hiding in the shadows or inside the buildings.

Within seconds, the three-man team had reached the safe house. With his M16 colt firmly in his shoulder and at the ready, Hart stepped over the bodies of the guards who had been stood by the entrance to the house just seconds before. They lay on the ground riddled by gunfire, limbs at awkward angles, a look of surprise still etched on their faces. They had been totally outmatched by the speed and swiftness of the attack.

Leaving Paddy at the main entrance, covering the stairwell and downstairs corridor, Hart took Kav and moved further into the seemingly deserted building, down a long dimly lit corridor that stretched out in front of them, the walls made of the same rock and dirt they stood on. Halfway along, they stopped and listened for a few seconds. There was a faint, muffled sound coming from the rear of the building on the ground floor. They continued down the corridor with caution, weapons trained and ready, Hart in the lead. The corridor led to what appeared to be a small kitchen, with two closed doors at either side of it.

Hart silently indicated to Kav that he was going to try the right-hand door first. They lined up on either side of the door, which was scratched and dented. Against the poor light, Hart could see the door was crumbling, as were the walls either side of it.

Hart took out his 9mm Sig pistol and made sure the safety was off. He then swung his M16 colt rifle around onto his back, out of the way, but ready to use at a moment's notice if he needed it. Kav kept his M16 to hand and readied a flash-bang grenade, specifically designed to stun rather than kill.

Holding the Sig in his right hand, adrenalin pumping, Hart reached for the door handle. He nodded to Kav, who nodded back to indicate that he was ready to throw the flash-bang into the room as soon as Hart opened the door.

Hart slowly turned the handle and gently pushed the door; it was locked. They exhaled little of the tension they'd been holding in and Hart placed his ear to the door and listened. There was no noise from the other side. Suddenly, the muffled sound they'd heard occurred once again, but this time it was clear that it had come from directly behind them. Both looked up sharply and scanned the corridor. There was still no one in sight, so the noise must have come from the other room. The sound was more distinct this time, identifiable as the sound of shuffling feet.

Hart took the lead again and both men stacked up either side of the other door, apprehensive, yet unafraid. Hart's left hand on the handle, his right on his Sig, waiting for Kav's signal that he was ready. Kav nodded at him, and Hart slowly turned the handle and gave a small push. This time the door opened. Hart pushed it just wide enough to allow Kav to throw the live flash-bang grenade into the room. The second Kav's hand was out of the way, Hart firmly held the door to prevent it from opening and exposing them. In the next moment, the stun grenade exploded with a series of bangs and flashes. Hart threw the door wide open and entered the room with Kav, staying low and driving forward. In the split second before the occupants recovered from the grenade's explosion and started firing,

Hart spotted that there were four guards standing around a hooded man tied to an old metal-framed chair. Hart and Kav instinctively fired on the guards. Their aim was true, their rounds effortlessly finding their intended targets with extreme precision whilst their empty ammunition cases now began to cover the floor of the room. All four guards succumbed to the inevitable and hit the ground almost instantly. The two SAS men reached the casualties with lightning speed and fired two more rounds into each guard's head, ensuring they were dead and wouldn't be re-joining this particular action-packed evening any time soon.

The seated man moaned. Kav covered the entranceway whilst Hart dealt with the hostage. He removed the hood, identified Jason Stern, and started to cut him free from the ropes binding him to the old metal-framed chair. Stern had been badly beaten and was now moaning incoherently. Hart spoke calm reassuring words to the MI6 officer, telling him he was now safe, and that they were going to get him out of there. The man was clearly in a great deal of pain but was just able to alert Hart to the fact that he'd overheard his abductors talking on the radio to another Al-Qaeda team due to join them shortly. Hart radioed the other call-signs, updating them with this vital piece of information and telling them that they had secured the hostage and were now entering the extraction phase of the operation. He asked the American cordon team and helicopter crew for a sitrep. He particularly wanted to know if there was any sign of the second Al-Qaeda team. Both confirmed that the Al-Qaeda reinforcements hadn't been spotted yet.

Hart helped Stern to his feet and Kav moved from the door to come and help support Stern, whose legs had almost given way. His pain was now his constant companion. Hart replaced his Sig in its holster and grabbed his M16 from his back before leading them to the doorway.

As Hart reached the doorway, he suddenly noticed that the door to the locked room was now fully open. He instinctively hit the floor and rolled out of the way just as a barrage of bullet rounds flew into the room, travelling at supersonic speed. Kav pushed Stern back against the wall, out of immediate danger and the direct line of fire. Hart scrambled to his feet and readied two grenades—one the flash-bang grenade and the other, the more deadly L2A2 HE fragmentation grenade, whilst the gunman continued to empty his deadly magazine into the room. Hart pulled the pins from both grenades and steadied himself. As soon as the gunman stopped firing to reload, Hart threw the grenades through the open door into the dimly lit corridor.

Seconds later, there was an almighty explosion, ripping the already fragile wooden door off its hinges and illuminating the corridor and the opposite room in a bright cacophony of intense light for a vital few seconds. Hart pressed home his advantage, diving into the corridor ready to finish off the Al-Qaeda gunman, but it wasn't a man who faced Hart in the doorway of the open room, it was a young skinny boy; no older than 13 years old!!

The boy was on his knees, his upper body upright and rigid, an AK47 on the floor beside him, having just fallen from his hands. There was a hole in the boy's chest, a piece of grenade shrapnel had pierced him and ripped through his lungs. The boy made a deathly rasping noise as he struggled to breathe. Blood flowed from his open mouth and out of the hole in his face where another piece of shrapnel had ripped away most of the boy's right cheekbone and teeth, making his already scrawny physique look almost skeletal. Hart had watched many men die from hideous wounds, but he'd never seen anything this gruesome. Far worse than the sight of the disfigured remains of the boy's face and body, was the look in his eyes.

Hart had seen that look before, and in eyes not much older than these: that look of intense fear and confusion, of an adolescent on the brink of death. Too old to be in any doubt that death was imminent and too young to have truly contemplated this moment before now.

Hart knew the boy had barely a minute of life left in him. Suddenly, the boy began to move his right hand slowly behind his back. Hart took no chances; he fired his M16 colt with a standard double-tap. The two rounds pushing through the air and penetrating the boy's skull, killing him instantly.

Hart bellowed to Kav over his shoulder that another enemy combatant had been successfully eliminated.

"X-ray down! Let's get the fuck out of here!"
Moving slowly, helping Stern who was struggling to walk as a result of the countless blows he'd taken to the kneecaps, Hart and Kav made their way down the corridor.

"Hold your fire!" Hart shouted to Paddy who was still covering the stairwell and corridor, "We have one friendly. Moving towards your position now!"

Just as they reached the main entrance to the building, Bob King's voice screamed down the radio, "Contact! All call signs. We have at least thirty X rays all over the fucking place, approaching from the gorge to the North."

The new insurgents had arrived without being detected by the drone above.

The continuous build-up of cloud cover in the local area during the evening hadn't just assisted Hart and his team, it had also assisted the Al-Qaeda team, allowing them to remain undetected by the drone and reach the compound without encountering any opposition. They had also managed to slip past the outer cordon by choosing to travel along a track that naturally followed a steep gorge. This formed part of the nearby rocky foothills just north of the compound. A route that was often favoured by the local goat herders and despite the cloud cover, one that offered natural cover from above, helping to avoid the unwanted attention from any foreign prying eyes that may be operating in the dark skies above.

Hart was furious. How had the cordon troops failed to spot or contain them? This development was potentially fatal to his team. They were really up against it now; if the insurgents were equipped with an RPG or Stinger missile system, they were screwed. Hart heard the M60D guns open up again. He didn't know whether the Black Hawk was on the ground or in the air. He hoped it was on the ground: they had no time to lose, they had to get out of there, fast.

A quick look outside told him that the Black Hawk was now on the ground and waiting for the extraction team, as was Bob King, who was covering them from a nearby building, beckoning them to hurry. Hart helped Kav get the barely conscious Stern across his shoulders as they slipped along the sides of the building approaching the waiting helicopter with Paddy covering them from the rear. Hart reached the Black Hawk first and helped Kav lift Stern on board. Bob King reached them a moment later and joined Kav and Stern on board. Hart turned to ensure Paddy was right behind him, whipping his head around just in time to see Paddy's body fly into the air as it was riddled with a thick barrage of bullet rounds delivered by an assortment of varying weapons!! The bullet wounds were too numerous to count. There was no chance of survival.

"I'll go with you!" Bob shouted to Hart above the din of the M60D's, still doing their best to keep any collateral damage to the helicopter at bay, assuming that Hart was going to retrieve Paddy's body according to SOP's.

"No!" shouted Hart, blocking Bob from disembarking again, and hauling himself into the Black Hawk. "Take her up! Go!" he yelled at the pilot, who immediately took the helicopter up to 1,500 feet before swinging her due east towards Kabul. Hart slumped back against the side panel of the helicopter. His men stared at him, stunned. "I had no choice," he said, "I wasn't prepared to lose another man."

The team fell silent, out of respect to Paddy.
Hart's mobile phone rang on the bedside table. It was 5 am. He was suddenly awake, his eyes flung wide open; every terrible thought engrained in high definition within his head. Salty sweat droplets flowed down his face, dripping on to the hotel bed like a spreading map of perspiration. Hart sat up to regain his breath and answered the call.

It was Hereford.

CHAPTER TWO

THE ROUTE Hart drove to take him to the SAS headquarters in Credenhill took about fifteen minutes longer than the fastest possible route. Both were picturesque, but the northern route left the M4 at Swindon and headed north along the A419 towards Cirencester, before then following the A417 around Gloucester. This was less dramatic than the southern route. Hart preferred to stay on the M4 motorway until he crossed the Severn Bridge (which was well worth the £5.10 toll for the views in his opinion) and then headed north along the Welsh border and through the Wye Valley. This route offered exceptional views, curving and changing, no two parts the same. Occasionally there was a wood that separated the fields, or a barn, or farmhouse. The countryside stretched before Hart like a giant quilt of green, golden and brown shapes held together by the thick green stitching of hedgerows. It rose and fell like a ship on a gentle ocean. He could glimpse Chepstow Castle and then the Forest of Dean as he passed through Monmouth, before approaching Hereford from the South when he would eagerly anticipate his first sighting of the Hereford Cathedral. In their majesty and beauty, these sights were always a welcome calm before whatever hellish situation he was about to be briefed on when he arrived at "the Kremlin", the RHQ of 22 SAS, as it was colloquially known.

Hart had set off from London just after receiving the call from Hereford, hoping to avoid any major morning traffic around the Reading area of the M4. He'd used the journey time to reflect and consider his life, a life that had been mostly nomadic and chaotic. Negative actions had created negative chaos, and Hart knew, negative chaos was destructive.

No wonder at 37 years old, he was still single.
There was no denying that Hart was exceptionally handsome, strong spirited and highly intelligent, but he was also fiercely independent and prone to boredom and mild depression when not challenged. Hart knew he had issues, which was why he never seemed to be able to commit to any long-lasting relationship, preferring instead short-term sexual recreation.

Even his normal recreational pursuits tended to be solitary: running, skiing, hiking, and climbing, which he supposed was his way of seeking solace and comfort. Hart was never one to be nostalgic, instead choosing to live firmly in the present. He had only vague notions and thoughts about old age and retirement but felt sure he would never live long enough to experience it. Hart enjoyed pushing himself to the limit, both mentally and physically; his stress levels dropping when the stakes became high. He was goal-oriented, and because of his self-sufficiency and independence, he had become an incredible tactician.

He wondered if things might have worked out differently had he made solid and wise life choices. He knew good choices were made not on the journey, but in a moment, at a fork in the road, impacted by circumstance and surrounding events.

Hart's thoughts drifted back in time to the 5th May 1980, a pivotal moment in the life of the young 10-year-old John Hart. Along with his 11-year-old sister Louise, Hart had sat in his grandmother's lounge just outside the city-centre of Glasgow, utterly engrossed in the unfolding events displayed on the television, both children absolutely mesmerised watching the black-clad figures detonating explosives on a first-floor window of the Iranian Embassy in central London, as well as abseiling from the roof at the rear of the building, detonating explosives to gain entry through the second-floor windows. The SAS raid had been codenamed "Operation Nimrod" and was viewed by millions of people. It was destined to become a major defining moment in Hart's young life.

The previous day, Hart's mother Sandra had taken the children from the family home in Dennistoun's Craigpark Estate in the east end of Glasgow, to her mother's tenement flat in Gourlay Street, Springburn, just to the north of Glasgow's city centre. She had taken this decision following another of her husband's drunken attacks, but this time it was different. George Hart had returned in the early hours from an all too familiar drinking binge, later that morning waking up still intoxicated. This time John had found himself on the receiving end of George's temper, resulting in him being thrown and kicked across the kitchen by his father, before being dragged by his hair up to his bedroom. George kicked the bedroom door wide open, his rage heightened further on seeing the mess that greeted him—clothes, books, toys, and muddy shoes lay across the floor. He threw John down on to the small single unmade bed below the window, narrowly avoiding smashing John's head against the windowsill above.

George bellowed at his son. "Get this fucking room tidied up now! Do you hear me you little shit? I'll deal with you later. You're grounded for a month you little bastard!"

George turned and slammed the door behind him, staggering downstairs to continue his barrage of verbal and physical abuse at Sandra. A terrified Louise who had been hiding under her bed covers in her bedroom next door, crept into John's room in tears and sat with him on his bed utterly terrified. Whilst in his own shock and pain, John put a comforting arm around Louise as they listened to the dreadful commotion carrying on downstairs in the kitchen.

"I'm going to get help." John whispered to Louise.

"No, don't leave me! Please don't leave me, John," Louise pleaded.

"I promise I won't be long. I've got to try and get the police, otherwise, he's going to kill mum if I don't."

He knelt up on the bed and opened the brittle framed window as quietly as he could. He peered out of the window looking at the significant drop to the flat roof of the porch below, which was just to his left. Deciding to attempt the jump from the window to the porch, he crouched upon his knees on top of the windowsill and sat perched on the edge not even contemplating whether the flat roof of the porch would take his weight, knowing he just had to somehow find help. Suddenly, from below, the front door slammed. John had to hold onto the fragile window frame to steady himself as the whole house seemed to shake with the force. He watched his father stagger out from the porch below and down the road, totally oblivious to his young son who was perilously perched on the outside of the bedroom window above.

Almost at the same time, their mother burst into John's bedroom, blood pouring from a cut above her eye, screaming at John to get down from the window. John hurriedly got back inside the room, only to be told by his mother that they were leaving and there was no time to pack anything. Sandra Hart was leaving with her children now and she didn't care about anything else, this was their chance to finally escape the physical and mental abuse.

As Sandra drove the battered Morris Austin 1800 and headed to her mother's small tenement flat in nearby Springburn, the cut above her eye had, at last, stopped bleeding. She gazed straight ahead, only half-aware of a world outside the claustrophobic interior, she nervously stroked the wheel and turned her tear and blood-stained face to John, who was sat next to her in the passenger seat and smiled. John knew this was a smile of relief and freedom. He turned to Louise, who was sat behind her mother. Her eyes were fixed on the road, wilder than a deer caught in a car's headlights. Her breathing faster than usual. Her head shook gently from side to side almost too slight to notice. Then suddenly, her bottom lip buckled upward, and tears began. John let her cry, and said nothing, but sat with her hand in his warm and easy clasp.

Everything was going to be OK.

John Hart vowed to himself at that very moment, he would never let anyone hurt him or his family again. In the years that followed, times were often hard, and money was short, but they were happy. The three of them continued to live with Sandra's mother in her cramped tenement flat. The living room was usually dimly lit due to thick velvet curtains obscuring the window, just leaving a shy peak of the light beyond. A worn sofa stood on a poorly hand-woven rug in front of a fairly new colour TV; one of the few modern objects present throughout the entire flat.

Over time, Sandra's confidence eventually returned, having secured a part-time job in a local care home, something the controlling George Hart would never have allowed. Despite the upheaval, both John and Louise settled well into their new schools. They remained living with their mother and grandmother until they both followed their respective career choices. Aged only sixteen, John visited the local army recruitment office in Glasgow's city centre with Sandra reluctantly in tow and signed up to the parachute regiment. On his passing out parade at Browning Barracks - the Parachute Regiment & Airborne Forces Depot in Aldershot, his mother, sister, and Grandmother, who by then was frail but determined to see her Grandson in all his finery, all attended the event with pride.

After joining the army, John Hart never saw his father again, and many years later, when he learned of George Hart's death, he felt absolutely nothing.

Hart's thoughts returned to the present; he was now at last approaching Hereford. At 9.30 am Hart was nodding, cordially, at the heavily armed MoD officer who was waving him through the entrance to the camp. After finding a convenient parking space close to the main building, Hart casually strolled up to the main door of RHQ where he was greeted by an anxious-looking young admin assistant, whom he assumed was one of the Colonel's aides.

"Sergeant John Hart?" the lad enquired. He was probably in his early twenties but, standing at around 5' 7", looking like he weighed no more than 60kg, and with a face riddled with acne and a nervous disposition; one would be forgiven for placing him closer to sixteen.

"Yes," confirmed Hart. "I've got a briefing at 10:00 am with the Colonel."

"You better follow me, quickly," said the aide, his voice sounding as though it had broken only last week. He set off at a pace and Hart followed him down a long brightly lit corridor, passing numerous hanging pictures on both walls, depicting past SAS operations from almost every location around the world. There were doors to various offices on either side, leading towards the imposing set of double doors at the very end of the corridor.

"He thought you might have come up last night. He had to bring the meeting forward by 30 minutes. It was a last-minute change. He asked me to call you to make sure you got the message and weren't late. I tried to call you again after calling you first thing this morning, but I couldn't get through."

"Sorry, the signal is useless from the M4 through to Ross on Wye." Hart looked sideways at the nervous soldier, casting his mind back to his own early army days.

"What's your name?" enquired Hart

"Lance-corporal Collins. Mark Collins."

"First week on the job?" Hart smiled.

"First day, sergeant," Collins mumbled back.

"Don't let the Colonel bully you," Hart warned him. "Don't show any weakness from the get-go and he'll soon back off."

Collins nodded, dutifully, but didn't look particularly reassured as he pushed open the double doors and came to a stop at the next office door on the right, which read "Lt. Colonel Andrew Williams".

Collins knocked on the door, which cued an impatient "Yes!" from within. He opened the door, making a conscious effort to stand an inch or two taller and announced Hart's arrival. Hart walked past Collins into the office.

"Sergeant John Hart, sir," Collins informed the Colonel, who was sitting behind his desk.

"Immediately, clearly doesn't mean what it meant in my day," Andrew Williams boomed at Hart as Collins gratefully scurried from the room, closing the doors behind him. Hart smiled, calmly, at his superior, who was a tall, medium built man in his early 50's with strawberry blonde thinning hair and a blotched complexion—the result of his love of real ale, which also accounted for the beginnings of a middle-aged spread, making his uniform look a size too small for him.

"Sorry, boss," Hart replied, calmly, "I was told 10:00 am, I thought I'd have plenty of time to—"

"I'm joking, man!" Williams interrupted, jumping up and towering over Hart as he shook his hand and slapped him on the back.

"Great to see you... and excellent job in Afghanistan. Though I heard the weather didn't do us any favours. I'm told it restricted the overhead drone spotting the Al Quada reinforcements who turned up."

To be fair, the weather should have been factored in during the planning stage, boss," Hart offered. "Given the situation though, we didn't really have a lot of time to consider the visibility restrictions the drone might encounter due to poor weather. Everything was a bit fluid and last minute. So, I guess it just couldn't be avoided."

"Yes, yes, well the main thing is that MI6 was damned impressed, and that's why you're here. They've specifically requested that RWW, and you in particular, head up this next mission. I wanted you here early this morning so I could brief you on some of the more delicate details before we're joined by our Ambassador to Colombia." Williams indicated that Hart should take a seat, then sat back down behind his desk and pressed an intercom button on his phone, leaning forward to speak into the microphone.

"Two teas, please, Doreen," he said in a softer tone before glancing up at Hart. "How do you take it?"

"Milk. Two sugars, please, boss" Hart replied, trying to get comfortable in the highly uncomfortable leather armchair he'd been offered.

"Did you get that, Doreen? Milk and two sugars for Hart and of course you know how I like mine."

"Yes, Colonel, came Doreen's weary voice over the intercom.

"Oh, and some milk chocolate Hob Nobs with that, please, Doreen," Williams added before settling back in his chair.

"So, what are we dealing with in Colombia, boss," Hart asked, keen to get the meeting started.
Williams frowned and stretched his hands out, flat on his desk, inspecting them studiously, the way a woman might whilst pondering whether she needs a manicure.

"We have a serious problem in Colombia," Williams stated. He took a long pause, which Hart mistakenly took to be his cue.

"Yes, boss, I'm aware of the issues in Colombia. I came across the FARC during a team job out there a few years back." Williams looked up at him, sharply, and carried on impatiently, as if irritated at having his chain of thought broken.

"Yes, yes, Hart," he muttered. "But there are developments, relating to the FARC's side business, and unfortunately, it's all got a little too personal for us Brits."

At this point, Williams's secretary, Doreen knocked lightly on the door and entered, carrying a tray with two mugs and a plate on it. A short, plump Welsh woman in her late 40s, she spoke rapidly, almost excessively cheerfully, as she set the mugs down in front of first Williams and then Hart.

"There we go, sir. The Ambassador's PA just called from her mobile. They're a few minutes away." As she said this, Doreen placed the plate down in the middle of the desk so that it was within reach of the two men; on it sat a selection of rather unappetising crackers.

"What are these?" Collins asked, mournfully, staring at the

crackers. "Where are my Hob Nobs?" Doreen looked at him, meekly.

"Sorry, sir. These are the Weight Watchers crackers that your wife asked me to give you. She gave me strict instructions not to buy any more Hob Nobs." Blushing slightly, as she received a warm smile from Hart, Doreen hurried out of the room, closing the door behind her.

"No pleasures left in life," sighed Williams, picking up a cracker, inspecting it and then placing it back on the plate with disdain. "She's also got me off the ale during the week, but still, who can tell when one's going to have a horrendous day in the office and needs a pick-me-up on the way home. Still not married, yourself, Hart?"

Hart shook his head.

"Wise man," sighed Williams, shaking his head slowly. "Dodged a bullet there, I assure you. Now, where were we?"

"The FARC's side business, boss," Hart reminded him. "You said something about it getting personal for the Brits."

"Ah, yes," Williams exclaimed, in a tone belying the nature of the information he was about to impart. "It involves the PM's son, Jonathan Hughes."

"The one who died?" asked Hart, curious as to what the connection to Colombia could possibly be.

"Yes," Williams confirmed gravely, before leaning forward, planting his elbows on the desk, clasping his hands together and resting his chin on them, still eyeing up the low-calorie crackers with disgust.

He raised his eyes to Hart's. "Now, what I'm about to tell you is classified information at the highest level," he began, slowly and seriously. "Top secret, understand."

"Yes, boss," replied Hart, dutifully, adding, "Terrible story."

"Indeed," mused Williams. "I'm not a Hughes supporter myself, I find the woman rather dull, if I'm honest, but I have to confess I felt for her when I heard the news. You don't have children, Hart, so you can't fully understand. I've got three of them. Drive me bloody bonkers most of the time, but I don't know what I'd do if anything ever happened to one of them. Anyway, you can't help feeling sorry for her, can you? No matter what you think of her and her politics." Williams paused for a moment and cracked a knowing smile at Hart. "I suspect you hate her. SNP man, are you? You probably welcome the new leader of the SNP; I believe he just took over last month?"

"Not particularly, sir," Hart replied patiently, taking a quick sip of his still steaming tea. "I'm a cynic when it comes to politics. I think they're all as bad as each other and can't be trusted. How does the old saying go - climb the greasy pole to Downing Street and weep?"

"Anyway, to get back to the death of her son, you saw all the news reports about the cause of death," continued Williams.

"Heart failure, wasn't it?" Hart offered up. "Didn't he have an undetected aneurism?"

"That was the story circulated to the media," Williams explained, lowering his voice considerably. "The real story is that he did have a heart attack, but it was directly related to ingesting a drug... thought to be cocaine. His flatmates at Oxford surrendered the rest of the stash to the police and had gagging orders slapped on them so that if they so much as breath a word to a soul, they'll find themselves behind bars for intent to supply Class A drugs instantly. The spooks have been in and bought the silence of the hospital staff and paramedics. They're also monitoring social media vigilantly for any leaks, and the government got a swift super-injunction granted. So, so far, so good, but the story's bound to get out in the end. Either way, we've got to be seen to be doing something to get to the bottom of where the killer drug came from and close down production sharpish."

"And this is why I'm off to Colombia?" Hart surmised.

Williams nodded. "Intelligence has led us to a specific FARC camp."

The British Ambassador was recalled to London to attend a COBRA meeting that ended last night with the decision to send you and a team in. He'll be here any minute now to brief us further on the situation over there."

Moments later, there was a knock on the door. "Come in," Williams said. Collins entered, and introduced the British Ambassador to Colombia.

Hart was immediately struck by the fact that the Ambassador looked far more native to Latin America than his home country. He cut an imposing figure. Whilst not too tall coming close to Hart's own 5' 11" stature, Nigel Massel made up for any lack of height in his width. His shoulders were wide; even his head seemed to be unusually wide. His jet-black hair, accompanied by a thick moustache and beard, made him look as if he could have been Castro's brother in another life, rendering the juxtaposition of his voice, which was surprisingly high-pitched with a lingering Yorkshire accent.

"Good morning Colonel," he started, offering his hand to Williams who shook it heartily. "Sorry for the tardiness. We hit a bit of traffic around Oxford."

"School-boy error, sir," ventured Hart, somewhat brazenly, as he stood up. "Regular visitors soon discover it's always best to come down the M4 corridor and cut up along the Welsh border." He offered his hand to Masell. "John Hart, sir."
Massel shook Hart's offered hand but without much warmth.

"Well I'm sure it's six of one and half a dozen of the other," he mumbled "There's no telling what traffic will do these days."

"How did it go with the PM?" asked Williams, indicating that everyone should take a seat.

"Lovely woman," Massel began, placing himself, gingerly, in the Chesterfield to the right of Williams's desk. "Third time I've met her, actually. The wife and I were invited to Chequers for a supper party last summer. Terrible business with the son. I've got a twenty-year-old myself. Emily. She's at York University. Under strict instructions not to mix with the wrong sort, of course. Ted, my boy, is seventeen, in his final year at Rugby? Father was a Rugby man, so...

well." He broke off, suddenly aware that Williams's upper lip was starting to twitch with impatience. "Yes, so, coming back to the situation in Colombia," he went on, quickly. "The decision's been made to go in and shut them down once and for all."

"Who exactly is 'them', Ambassador?" Hart enquired.

The FARC front responsible for making the drug that killed Jonathan Hughes," Massel sharply informed Hart. "It's similar to cocaine but has a different chemical composition and more alarming side effects. Our moles have discovered that the FARC has been messing around with the coca plant. Backed by a Ukrainian group they've developed a kind of GM version of the plant. It's been found in other autopsies around the world. Several high-profile deaths have also been linked to it, unofficially of course. They're calling it 'Russian' on the streets because taking it's like playing Russian Roulette. It will kill one in three or four users the first time they take it. Cocaine can do this, too, of course, but there's some kind of daredevil hype surrounding this new drug. Most users get an effect like an exaggeration of what they feel when they take cocaine, but not everyone's body can actually tolerate it. Goodness knows why anyone would take it when there's a chance they'd die instantly, but there it is. Could never stand the blokes I knew who did cocaine... turned them into right cocky bastards."

"It was called Charlie in my day," Williams mused.

"Then killing Charlie will now be our new priority, gentlemen! What transpired from the interviews with the other Oxford students," Massel continued, "Is that users think it's an urban myth, that the 'Russian' moniker is an exaggeration. All they believe is that it's the new super drug, justifying its price tag of around four times the price of cocaine, making it a sort of status symbol. Obviously, the PM ordered a swift investigation into the origins of the drug. It was a joint effort by MI6 and other intelligence agencies around the world where deaths from the drug have been reported, which led them to a production facility run by a FARC commander deep in the Colombian jungle. Not too much of a surprise there, of course. The

CIA was involved in the investigation right from the start, so now the Americans are sending in the 7th Special Forces. I'm told you had some brief experience with the FARC forces a few years ago, so you seemed like the best man for the job."

Hart chose his next words carefully.

"Thank you, Ambassador. Could you tell me more about the FARC front that's producing this drug, Ambassador? How much information do we have on them at this point? Who are the key figures?"

Hart noticed Massel throw Williams a foreboding look before he continued. "The key figures. Yes, indeed," Massel started. "Well, of course, there are the usual suspects in Colombia, the FARC bloc commander and his minions. However, it's the international figures involved who also interests us, one, in particular, a British fella. Well, technically a Brit, now based in Ukraine. Someone you'll be familiar with if you cast your mind back." Hart looked at Massel and then Williams. He shook his head. "Not aware of any specific Ukrainians in my past, sir."

Williams leaned forward and spoke with a hint of apology in his voice. "I'm sad to say he was one of us, Hart. British Army. Do you remember your old platoon commander in the parachute regiment, Captain Max Chaplain?"

John caught his breath. He hadn't heard that name uttered in years. The very sound of it sent shivers down his spine. Did he remember Max Chaplain? How could he forget him? The man was a true psychopath who had made the lives of John and his fellow soldiers' hell for several years. Finally, his actions had caught up with him.

Whilst on exercise in Kenya in 1992, Chaplain had been arrested on suspicion of abducting and raping two local 14-year-old girls. He was charged and found guilty. He was stripped of his commission and sentenced to fifteen years. The first two years being served in Colchester's military prison before then being transferred to serve the rest of his sentence in HMP Belmarsh – one of the UK's maximum-security prisons. That was the last John had ever heard of Max Chaplain until now.

Massel cleared his throat, breaking Hart's reverie.

"Yes, I remember Chaplain," Hart informed the men. "He was a nasty piece of work. How the hell has he ended up in bed with the FARC? Last I heard he was banged up for the shit he pulled in Kenya."

"He got out of prison in 2002," Williams explained. "After serving ten years of his fifteen-year sentence. He's been enjoying liberty for five years now. He disappeared for a while but then he reappeared on MI6's radar a couple of years ago in the summer of 2005. He was involved with some arms dealing between Russia and Ukraine. He bought his way out of it with the Ukrainians, but we kept him under surveillance. Seems he fancies himself as the Al Capone of Kiev and becoming a head honcho in the Ukrainian mafia. He and the head of the Russian mafia—nasty piece of work also, called Alexei Chernavsky, a Ukrainian born actually, who's been on the FBI's ten most wanted list for the past two years—have got their sights on controlling the supply of the new drug to the entire European Union. Chaplain and Chernavsky supply arms to this FARC officer in exchange for exclusive distribution rights of this 'Russian'."

"Ironically," Hart commented, swiftly.

"Our informants within the FARC group also found out that it was Chaplain and Chernavsky who funded all the genetic research and experiments that enabled them to produce the drug," Massel explained. "They were trying to grow a new coca plant that produced twice as much paste as existing varieties. Well, they succeeded in that, but it also increased the potency four-fold."

"Those Ruski bastards must have thought they'd hit the jackpot," Williams commented.

Hart turned to Massel. "Ambassador, what's the official line from the Colombians? Are the JUNGLA forces involved?"

"Indeed, they are," Massel confirmed. "But how far they can be trusted is anyone's guess. There's too much cross-contamination between the FARC and JUNGLA to know for sure whether you're dealing with loyal officers. I can say that your official role, and the Americans know this applies to them also, is an advisory one. President Santos has been particularly vocal about that. On paper, only the JUNGLA forces are authorised to storm the FARC camps, make the arrests and destroy the crystallisation equipment. In reality, well..."

"Hart knows what to do," Williams reassured the Ambassador.

"The exact location of the lab is believed to be in a clearing near the jungle village of Pogue. It's a notoriously inhospitable area of the jungle that's hard to penetrate. Chosen, we have to assume, for this very fact. The Bloc's commanded by a Juan Carlos Rodriguez Gomez, who goes by the alias of Fernando Márquez. Márquez handed the construction and overseeing of the lab to his 57th Front Commander, Jose Posada Zamora. The head of the FARC since January has been Miguel Iván Escobar, but Zamora's the one who deals with Chaplain directly as he controls the growing of the plant and the subsequent production of the drug. We've also recently received strong Intelligence indicating that the New IRA has a play in all of this. We've been reliably informed they've been sniffing around this particular drug operation, although it's not yet clear how far and to what extent their involvement reaches."

"Sounds like there are a few players with serious skin in the game, all feeding off the north-western Bloc of FARC. As you pointed out, I had some dealings with them when I was last out there," Hart interjected.

"Indeed," concurred Massel. "The problem is, whilst President Santos doesn't want any official direct international involvement, he hasn't got many choices. The JUNGLA is only prepared to go so far. Until recently they were denying the existence of this particular lab altogether, despite the fact that our FARC informants had provided evidence to the contrary that was clear as a bell. Anyway, now we know exactly where everyone is and what our official and unofficial lines are the PM's keen for you to put a team together and get out there without delay. Of course, the primary mission is to ensure that the crystallisation lab producing this stuff is destroyed immediately. That will send a clear message, but we also need to find out how they're making this stuff, otherwise, they'll just find another bunch of lackeys to start up production again. We must ensure we nail Chaplain and his men, and whoever else is involved. We want to take out every part of the supply chain until there's no one left in this particular racket. We'll give you all the support you need at the embassy in Bogotá. Do you have any questions at this point?"

Massel leaned back in his chair, indicating that he had concluded his briefing.

Whilst Hart's head was full of questions, he knew most of them concerned operational details and logistics that would be taken care of in due course. He was curious, however, about one aspect of the mission.

"Overcoming the FARC and closing down this production line, I'm clear on," stated Hart. "But how are we expected to secure the information to pin the whole thing on Chaplain and his people? I'd assume that would be MI6's job."

"Good question," Massel remarked, with a glance at Williams. "Of course, you'll be briefed in more detail on the ground, but we have a particularly delicate rescue mission that we'd like you to oversee personally."

Massel stroked his beard and then continued. "A senior FARC officer, with the code name Phoenix, has passed on some particularly interesting information to an undercover British customs officer. Zamora, the 57th Front's commander has a daughter by one of his female officers, a woman called Paola Sanchez. The officers repeatedly rape the female soldiers, and whilst they're soldiers, if they get pregnant, they're then forced to have terminations, but if they become officers, they're allowed to keep the babies. Sanchez wormed her way into Zamora's affections after he began raping her when she was a teenager. The third time she got pregnant, he made her an officer and let her keep a baby girl. Phoenix reports that Sanchez has secretly managed to obtain vital information from Zamora, who has unknowingly drip-fed her the information over the years; names and account numbers, security codes passwords, perhaps even the very formula for producing this new drug. Because she knows what would happen to her if Zamora ever suspected her of possessing this information, she has apparently taught everything she knows to her ten-year-old daughter, Valentina.

Personally, I find it hard to believe that a child of ten could memorise such complex information, but Phoenix is closely related to Sanchez and insists that this is true. Sanchez won't work with us directly, but she wants us to get her daughter out of the camp and away from Zamora, in exchange for the information that the daughter will give us. I imagine she's trying to save the girl from being forced into working for the FARC, as are most of the children born into the organisation. She wants us to get the girl out and protect her. Then we'll get everything we need to put Chaplain and his sidekick away, as well as plenty of senior corrupt foreign officials who are apparently mixed up in the whole messy business."

"If the woman is to be trusted," Williams interjected, "This little girl's a gold mine of information. If the FARC knew how much she knows; I doubt she'd stand much chance of seeing her next birthday. Like I say, Hart, you can't know what it feels like to be a parent, but believe me, you'd put your neck on the line to save your kid's life. That's what this woman's doing—although she's taking a mighty big risk. She knows the only way we'll prioritise getting the girl out is because of what she's worth to us... but what a position to put a kid in! What do you reckon, Hart? You think you're up to extracting the girl?"

As long as you don't think my childless status compromises my skills in this situation, boss," said Hart, without even attempting to disguise the wry contempt in his voice; he was sure he noticed Massel suppress a small smile behind his beard.

CHAPTER THREE

DIANA BROOKS hung up on Colonel Williams and released her vice-like grip on the phone. She was fuming. Her jaw was clenched, and she was grinding her teeth rapidly, from side to side. She quickly rummaged around in her desk for the small red case, opened it, took out the plastic bite plate and popped it into her mouth where she slotted it into place over her lower teeth with her tongue. On her last visit to the dentist in Brighton six months ago, he'd told her that her teeth had the wear and tear he'd expect in a seventy-year-old, and if she didn't wear a bite plate every night as well as frequently during the day (like now— during particularly stressful times), she'd be looking at needing dental caps before she turned forty.

After today she wondered if her teeth would actually make it to the end of the year without being ground down to stumps.

In what world did she take orders from the head of the SAS? If London had decided they needed to challenge her authority and close down the FARC camp before she felt they'd gathered all the intelligence they needed, then she expected a call from Owen Bennett himself.

Owen was the recently appointed Head of MI6 and Diana's old bête noire from Cambridge. He'd been a twenty-six-year-old PhD student in Political Science at Caius College, University of Cambridge when she'd arrived to read law a week before her eighteenth birthday. He led a first-year tutorial group in basic International Law. She'd fallen madly in love with him, but her love had remained not only unrequited but also ridiculed. When Owen had got wind of her infatuation, he had made a sport out of toying with her and tying her up in logistical knots in tutorials.

When Diane first met him, Owen was already practically married to Charlotte Goodwin, holder of every economics prize available, currently the Treasury's key advisor and tipped to become the first female Head of the Bank of England. Owen and Charlotte were the perfect couple as far as Diana could see, with the perfect marriage and perfect children. They had everything that Diana had given up on ever having. She'd had a string of disastrous relationships; she was a manic-depressive magnet, although only the last boyfriend had actually managed to succeed in killing himself. That was a few years ago now and had been the impetus for her taking the posting to Bogotá. She'd gone to Owen, by that time her boss in London, and begged him to post her as far away from the UK as possible. He'd offered her Bogotá, asking her if she'd be prepared to take over the Head of Station position when Ian Duggan's contract finished.

With no illusions as to the fact that Owen was probably dangling a promise over her that he had no intention of keeping, especially when she met Nick Hammond, whose eye was definitely on the top job, Diana had gratefully taken the job. She had subsequently been astonished when, three months ago, Owen had come good on his promise and appointed her Station Head, much to the infuriation of Hammond. The promotion had made Diana, at thirty-six years old, officially the youngest MI6 station head.

However, she had never fully settled into the role. She couldn't help but suspect that Owen might have ulterior motives.

Was this latest affront Owen's idea of having a little fun with her again, subjecting her to the orders of this pompous SAS Colonel? Also, why was Hammond walking around looking fairly smug these days, instead of the black looks he'd thrown around when he'd first found out he'd been passed up for promotion. Was something going on behind her back? Was she being set up to take the flack for some fuck up that was about to be uncovered?

Were they preparing to throw her under the proverbial bus? Diana couldn't work it out, she just knew she had better be on her guard and exceptionally vigilant.

Now, how should she play this out with Hammond? To save face she wanted to claim the decision to bring in the SAS had been hers alone, but if Hammond was in cahoots with Owen, he'd know she was lying. If she admitted she was out of the loop with London, she'd lose face with everyone, and if Hammond was in on it, he'd only get a kick out of watching her discomfort. The latter seemed like a lose-lose situation. Her only option was to lie to her Head of Operations and claim she'd made the decision herself.

Diana called Hammond's extension. No answer. Next, she called Sarah Smith, their newest Junior Intelligence Officer, who she could see, through the glass door of her office, sitting in the open-plan office. "Sarah, where's Hammond?"

"He went with Carter to the airport to interview a detainee."

"Let him know I need him—both of them actually—back here ASAP."

"Will do," Sarah said and was about to hang up when Diana came back with,

"Oh, Sarah, I need to brief you on this, too, could you step in here for a moment."

"Of course," Sarah assured her boss. She grabbed her notepad and phone and got up, typing a text to Hammond as she walked the short distance to Diana's office. Her skirt was a little shorter and her shirt a little tighter than was appropriate for the office environment, but she didn't care. She got off on causing a stir wherever she went, especially with these over-sexed Latin men. Aware that all their eyes were on her, she ran her hand around the back of her neck and lifted her long blonde hair off her shoulders, letting it fall gracefully down her back, before entering Diana's office.

As Diana Brooks was briefing Sarah Smith on her duties regarding the impending arrival of the SAS team, a C-130 Hercules touched down to refuel in the small Canadian town of Gander in Newfoundland. The four-engine turboprop aircraft had left RAF Lyneham at 4 pm local time and from Gander was bound for Fort Bragg in North Carolina, where the crew would stay overnight before flying on to the US Air Force base at Elgin, Florida, on Thursday. At Elgin, the RAF aircraft's cargo would be off-loaded and then loaded onto a US C-130 to continue on to Bogotá the following day, where Hart and his team would collect their equipment and weapons from the US Embassy.

As the RAF C-130 was landing in Florida, the SAS team was waiting in the transit lounge at Madrid's international airport, ready to board their Iberia flight bound for Bogotá. Given the urgency and importance of the mission, along with the fact, there was no direct flight service to Bogotá from London, Hart's team was offered two flight options: Depart from London to Bogotá via Madrid by a commercial flight on a business class ticket, or alternatively, leave a few days earlier and hitch a ride in the back of a noisy RAF C-130 whilst lying in a swinging hammock, wearing ear protection and surrounded by numerous cargo boxes. Madrid won!

By the Thursday evening, Diana Brooks was more convinced than ever that something was going on behind her back.

Hammond and Carter had not reappeared until 6 pm, despite Diana's best efforts to contact them. They had claimed they'd been taken to an off-site holding cell that immigration used when they were over-stretched at the airport, but she still wanted to know why they hadn't responded to texts. They were too focused on their interrogation, they'd said, and the phone signal was patchy.

When she finally had them in front of her, she'd briefed them on the SAS team's imminent arrival. Then she'd given them instructions to pick up their FARC informant, the Dutchman, Hans Borgman, and get him to the safe house so that, as soon as the SAS team arrived, she could give their leader the chance to interview Borgman to secure as much detail about the camp as possible.

Hammond had been hesitant when discussing their surveillance of Borgman. He didn't seem to know exactly where to locate the Dutchman that evening. Hammond's lame explanation was that Borgman could usually be found at one of the local high-class brothels he regularly frequented, but because they were numerous and he always switched off his phone when visiting, they could never be sure where to find him. Diana was alarmed by this and had made it patently clear that they were to find him and bring him in immediately – no excuses. Even if it took all night and they had to visit every single brothel.

Diana had only received the confirmation that Borgman was safely contained in the safe house just after 10 pm; she had a long few days ahead of her. She would head over to the safe house and meet the SAS team commander shortly.

When Hart set eyes on the stunning, leggy, blue-eyed blonde waiting for them at Bogotá airport, he felt something stir himself, not because he fancied her—but because it made him think of Paddy. He knew that, if Paddy had been there, the Irishman's eyes would have been popping out on stalks.

Sarah Smith correctly singled Hart out as the leader of the group, sashayed towards him, noting how exceptionally handsome he was. She held out her hand and said, in honeyed home counties tones, "John Hart? I'm Sarah Smith. I'll be looking after you." Hart didn't miss the insinuation behind Sarah's "looking after you" and again, thought of the banter Paddy would have immediately struck up with this beautiful woman. He gave her a perfunctory greeting and introduced the team. They all perked up considerably as they eagerly shook hands with Sarah; all of them except Kav, who was still in the honeymoon phase after recently marrying a local Hereford girl.

Hart had chosen to bring a five-man team for this mission. He had kept his core men—Bob King as his 2IC and Kav Rabuka, whose expertise as a tracker would be invaluable out in the jungle— and had replaced Paddy with Mike Lewes. The thirty-four-year-old Rhodesian (as he corrected anyone who called him Zimbabwean) was also, an incorrigible skirt chaser, and standing at 6' 4", with a permanent tan and a light dusting of almost white-blonde hair, it wasn't hard to see how he pulled it off. Mike had begun his military career in the 1st Battalion the Royal Green Jackets, a British army light infantry unit, before becoming the 2nd Battalion the Rifles earlier that year on the 1st of February 2007. Having passed SAS selection, he had an almost immediate interest in becoming a demolition specialist, which suited his earth-shattering laugh. When Mike Lewes laughed, the ground beneath you reverberated, conversations in pubs paused as people turned their heads, and glasses rattled on nearby tables. He was one of the "Chosen Men" and had a huge personality. Hart was counting on him to keep up group morale on this mission.

The fifth man was Jock Asher. Hart's fellow Scotsman hailed from Edinburgh and came from a family with a long history in the Armed Forces. Jock's father and brother had been in the RAF and on his mother's side, there were Royal Marines and Wrens. Jock was a natural-born fighter and a weapons specialist, so he'd signed up for The Royal Scots. With his credentials and years in the SAS, Jock should have held a senior position to Hart, but he'd been hauled up in front of the C.O. more than once on account of his drinking. He wouldn't touch a drop on the job, but off duty, Jock had a problem with booze.

On the journey to the hotel, Hart sat silently in the British Embassy's people carrier, he had vomited during the flight and whilst the men bombarded Sarah with questions—not all of them strictly about Colombia; Hart was just looking forward to getting into his hotel room and resting before they deployed in the days ahead. It was only 10 pm local time, but the time difference told Hart's body it was 3 am and he knew it would take its toll... on all of them. A degree of anxiety about his physical state was bubbling up inside him. He'd never experienced airsickness before. Even though that was what he was calling it, he knew it was the same thing that had struck him every day since returning from Afghanistan, even Geordie could see something wasn't right when they had met in London. It was unlike anything he'd ever experienced. Without warning, a wave of nausea would overwhelm him almost immediately followed by him vomiting. Afterwards, he always felt fine. He hadn't reported it because what precipitated every incident was the sight of the boy's face after the grenade had ripped half of it away, and he wasn't ready to talk about that, or Paddy, whose face was also haunting him every night when he fell asleep.

Once she'd checked the men into the Casa Medina Hotel, a four-star hotel located in the Chapinero Norte district of Bogotá; Sarah turned to Hart.

"Do you want to freshen up? I can wait here in the lobby for you," she offered with a charming smile. "We're on a tight schedule. Diana Brooks is waiting for you at a safe house where she's holding an informant for you to question. I'll brief you on the journey," she said in a discreet tone.

"I'll be down in ten minutes," Hart told her, wearily.

"I'll be waiting for you at my safe house," Mike ventured, sidling closer to Sarah. "Safe house room 209."
The young, ambitious intelligence officer took it well, laughing with the boys and assuring them she'd be back in a couple of hours to take them to dinner.

Forty minutes later, Hart was sitting with Diana Brooks, Nick Hammond, and the HMRC officer, Joe Carter, in a small room in the safe house. It was decorated tastefully in a corporate way - nothing that would cause offence no matter what a person's design preferences might be. Hart was listening intently to all they could tell him about Borgman, who was sat in an adjoining room, waiting to be interrogated.

This room was different in every possible way. The walls were shaded grey, from washed-out concrete to clear steel blue. Every line was straight, and every corner sharp. The interview room was like a prison cell, with a bare bulb hanging from the ceiling and a one-way privacy glass window built into the back wall. In the centre of the room, where Borgman now patiently sat waiting, was a small black metal table surrounded by six metal folding chairs looking as comfortable as a metal train station bench. The surface of the table displayed two metal D-rings that had been expertly welded into place. Also, an unremarkable desk-top spot lamp stood on the table, throwing a bright beam of light across the unwelcoming room, casting silhouettes and dark shadows on the nearby walls. The table was devoid of any other objects. Borgman knew all too well the small D-rings were used to shackle and handcuff those detainees who unwisely decided to become uncooperative. This only added to Borman's tenseness and worry.

Hans Borgman was a 46-year-old Dutchman who masqueraded as a rental car business owner; his real business enterprise was drug smuggling and he was extremely successful at it. Over the past five years, he had become responsible for half of the cocaine trade Colombia and into Europe.

Growing up in Hoofddorp in Holland, Borgman, like many of his contemporaries who had dropped out of high school, had gained employment at Amsterdam's international airport, Schiphol. Over the years, he had become involved with a group of men, corrupt officials, who were responsible for getting illegal goods into Europe through the Netherlands. He'd been a small-time drug dealer on the side but after turning thirty and celebrating with his partner Britt, the birth of their daughter Sanne, he'd tried to clean up his act. He'd left the airport and got a security job in Haarlem. Although money was tight, Hans appreciated the absence of fear that had dominated his life when he'd been involved with drug runners and bent airport officials.

He focused on raising his daughter and keeping Britt, a primary school teacher, happy. Then tragedy struck. On his thirty-ninth birthday, Hans had been involved in a near-fatal motorcycle accident. He'd been laid off work for six months whilst undergoing countless operations to repair his back and right leg. There were times when the doctors doubted that he would ever walk again properly. This had sent Hans into a terrible downward spiral and he experienced bouts of extreme rage and depression, which in turn put an enormous strain on his relationship with both Britt and Sanne.

Eventually, relations broke down entirely. When Sanne turned thirteen she stopped speaking to her father altogether and Britt asked him to move out of the family home. Hans moved back to Hoofddorp, where he met the men who introduced him to the Ukrainians. Borgman's physical stature and menacing demeanour helped him quickly work his way up the chain of command. When he was offered the opportunity to move to Colombia and set up a car rental business as a front for a massive cocaine smuggling operation, he felt he had nothing to lose and everything to gain. Three years later, power had gone to Borgman's head. He felt invincible.

That had all changed when six months ago, on the outskirts of Cartagena, the JUNGLA had intercepted a shipment of the new drug that was bound for the Netherlands and the UK via an exploratory route through Mauritania in West Africa. Borgman had been arrested and interrogated by Joe Carter from British HMRC and Nick Hammond from MI6. He had offered up essential information about the production of Russian, in exchange for his release. After heated negotiations with the Colombian authorities, Ian Duggan, Diana's predecessor had agreed, and this led to the discovery of the FARC camp where the drug was produced. Whilst the British had guaranteed Borgman immunity, the Colombians had no intention of keeping to their end of the bargain. Major Rodriguez, of the JUNGLA group, couldn't wait to throw Borgman into jail once they successfully wiped out this particular FARC camp.

Borgman was too smart to be unaware of this and had double-crossed everyone approaching the Medellin cartel, the biggest Colombian drug cartel, with the offer of stealing the formula for producing the new drug and selling it to them in exchange for protection. This was a fly in the ointment that neither the British or the Colombian authorities were aware of, or indeed had anticipated, and threatened to scupper their plans to eradicate the existence of this new deadly drug.

Only two people knew the exact formula for altering the coca plant seeds that eventually produced the new drug: the camp's commander, Zamora, and the Ukrainian Mafia boss, Chaplain. Borgman knew the clock was ticking. He had to get that formula from Zamora before the British helped the JUNGLA destroy the camp. He thought he had more time. When Hammond and Carter picked him up and took him to the safe house to await interrogation, he knew he was almost out of time. He had to get to Zamora without delay.

Diana Brooks had made quite an impression on Hart. He saw the determination in her eyes... and the pain; something he identified with. What had she been through? What was she burying? In different circumstances he would have liked to have sat down with her, over dinner perhaps, digging deep in conversation. She was exactly the type of woman he preferred to get together with these days, and they were few and far between. He couldn't risk any more relationships with the likes of Sarah Smith; her type, the young ones always got attached. They started to want more. No matter how many times he explained that he was not the marrying kind, that he did not want a family, the questions would start up around six months into the relationship. "Where is this going?" "Can we have a talk about the future?" "You know you'd make such a great dad." Nothing terrified Hart more than the idea of being a father. His own hadn't exactly been a role model. The very word "father" brought more negative associations with it than some of the atrocities that Hart had seen in the field.

"Any questions?" Diana asked, snapping his attention back into the room.

"No," Hart replied softly, with a brief smile.

Maybe, he thought... maybe after the mission was over. It had been too long since he'd been with a woman, over six months since the American CIA woman who'd briefed him in Nicosia before they'd flown on to Baghdad.

Nick Hammond led the way into the small interview room where Borgman was being held. The tall Dutchman sat up abruptly as the team entered and sat down in one of the metal chairs surrounding the interview table.

"Okay, how long is this going to take? I have no new information; you know everything I know. I had meetings arranged for tonight, and a business to run." He addressed his question to Hammond, but Diana answered.

"Your meetings will wait, those girls don't exactly shut up shop at midnight, your business runs itself, and since you are only a free man at our discretion, we'll hold you here for as long as we want."

Hart was impressed. Diana's tone was perfectly pitched: authoritative, with a pinch of condescension and the hint of a threat. He normally had no time for spooks, but she was different. Whilst there was rock-solid confidence about her, and the suggestion of a ruthless streak, there was no ego. No wonder she was running this ship in Bogotá.

"This is Alex," Diana continued, indicating Hart who was sat in the furthest chair. "He's a security official from the UK government.
He's just arrived from London to help us with our operation. We need you to tell him everything you can about the layout of the camp and its operation, including positions and the movements of any security sentries."

Borgman raised an eyebrow at Diana. "So, this is it? You're

closing them down, finally?"

Diana smiled at him. "This is how our arrangement works," she told Borgman, patiently. "I get to know everything you know, and you get to know nothing of what I know. So, please, just answer all of Alex's questions."

Borgman narrowed his eyes at Diana. Nothing irritated him more than a woman trying to do a man's job, but he wasn't exactly in an advantageous position at this particular point in time, so he turned his attention to Hart.

"What do you want to know, Alex?"

Hart began by asking Borgman some basic questions about the terrain surrounding the region, about the weather and the thickness of the jungle around the camp. Then he moved on to forces-oriented questions, about the numbers of FARC soldiers working inside the camp, their activities and defences, living arrangements, any children living in the camp, and of course, about the number and types of weapons they possessed.

When Hart was satisfied, he had all the information he needed, he stood up. Diana, Hammond, and Carter followed suit.

"That will be all for now, Mr Borgman," she said, plainly. "You will be held here for a few days in case we need you."

"What?!" Borgman exclaimed, leaping to his feet. "No way! I have a business to run. You can't keep me here. Hey, that's not our deal."

Diana ignored him and swept out of the room with Hart, Hammond and Carter following close behind.

CHAPTER FOUR

B Y THE TIME Hart got back to his hotel room, it was after 1 am local time, and 6 am by his body clock, still on UK time. He'd turned down Diana's offer of nightcap in the hotel bar, saying he'd prefer to turn in and would order room service if he was hungry. He had briefly considered accepting the offer as he was sure he'd enjoy her company, but he desperately needed to sleep and focus only on the upcoming operation. He'd noted that Diana was not wearing a wedding ring, and a couple of things she'd said had hinted at the fact that she lived alone, so perhaps after the mission was over, he could ask her to join him for a celebratory drink. For now, it was all he could do to get his shoes off before lying back on the bed and falling into a deep sleep.

Hart woke at 3 am in a cold sweat; jet lag and the lingering memory of his recurring nightmares put paid to anymore sleep. He switched on the TV and watched a soap opera with the subtitles on to brush up on his Spanish before it was time to get dressed and meet in the lobby at 6.30 am local time, to be taken to their breakfast and operational briefing at the American Embassy.

At the US Embassy, a Warrant Officer Paul Parsons

introduced himself to the SAS team. He was a tall, good- looking Native American man, who told them to call him Chief because "...everyone else does... wouldn't answer to Paul these days if it was my own Mom yelling it!"

Chief led them into a large briefing room where they met another twenty or so members of the 7th Special Forces Group, all of whom had bleached white teeth and sun-kissed hair. This set them apart from the JUNGLA representative from the anti-narcotics jungle group of the Policía Nacional de Colombia. He was introduced as Colonel Gilberto de la Bernardo, who informed them all that the ground commander of the operation, Major Rodriguez, was running late and would join them as soon as possible. Not the best start when the ground commander can't even turn up on time for his own operational briefing thought Hart.

As the briefing got underway, Hart felt a wave of nausea rise up inside him. He willed it to go away and focused hard on what was being discussed. He was not best pleased with the fact that after Major Rodriguez had finally decided to make an appearance and grace them with his presence, he'd insisted on assuming complete control over every aspect of the entire operation; there seemed to be no talking him down. The JUNGLA commander came across as a jumped-up arrogant dictator. It was his way or the highway. Hart immediately disliked him, but they hadn't come all this way to abort the mission on the grounds of an impasse on the operational procedure. Especially as all other planning aspects of the operation were satisfactory to Hart.

The JUNGLA would provide 40 officers for the ambush whilst the 7th Special Forces Group would deploy the 25 US soldiers present to act as the outer security cordon for the operation; they would completely encircle the FARC camp from 300 metres out.

Not a moment too soon, the meeting ended. Hart made a beeline for the bathroom where he dry-wretched. His stomach contracted so violently that Hart thought he had pulled a muscle with the exertion. Thankfully he hadn't had the stomach for the American breakfast they'd been offered. Pancakes and waffles with bacon; everything smothered in maple syrup. What was it with Americans and their sugar obsession? His grandmother had made porridge with milk and a pinch of salt. They were allowed half a teaspoon of sugar sprinkled over it; they would watch this dissolve slowly into the stodgy substance. He knew he should be eating well today because they would be on limited rations once they entered the jungle, but with his stomach behaving the way it was, he preferred to leave it fairly empty. He resolved to find somewhere to have a steak dinner that night.

The team's freight had arrived at the US Embassy earlier that morning, couriered from the airport after it had been offloaded from the C-130. Before they left the embassy, the men checked through all their equipment, carried out weapons checks and packed up their individual kits, leaving them prepped and ready to be collected at the embassy before they were flown out to the jungle the next day.

When they finally got back to the hotel at 5 pm, Hart and his team stood around in the lobby discussing their evening plans with Sarah who was suggesting restaurants.

Hart had lost his appetite and knew he had to catch up on his sleep so excused himself and went to his room. A decision he somewhat regretted the next morning when he saw the state of Mike and Jock.

He should have stayed with them and supervised. From the look of Sarah Smith's botched make-up job, and the fact that she was wearing the same outfit she'd been wearing the day before, Hart correctly deduced that she hadn't been home, and Mike was avoiding all eye contact... with anyone. Jock was clearly hungover. No one said more than three words on the journey to the U.S. embassy. Hart was livid and would have shaken them all with well-chosen words telling them to sharpen up, but he was feeling fragile himself, for other reasons.

The Sikorsky UH-60L Black Hawk hovered over the Embassy gardens on schedule at 9 am. The blades beating the air had much the same effect as a small tornado on the manicured lawn below. As it came lower, Hart covered his ears, held his breath and closed his eyes until he heard the slowing of the blades. Hart and his team loaded their Bergens into the back and climbed aboard, Hart noticing Mike's sideward glance towards the vehicle Sarah Smith had accompanied them in, that now headed off.

The pilot took them up and another three Black Hawks took their turn to land and pick up the US Special Forces cordon team. They then collectively headed north-west for the 220-mile journey that was scheduled to take just over an hour. On the outskirts of Bogotá, they were joined by the other eight Black Hawks carrying the rest of the attack force and the convoy continued to make its way to the insertion point, approximately 10 kilometres from the FARC camp. They were due to be dropped off on the other side of a mountain away from the camp so that the inhabitants of the FARC camp wouldn't hear the Black Hawks approaching.

As they flew low over the vast emerald canopy of the Colombian jungle, Hart looked down and absorbed the beauty of it all. The towering trees slanted and appeared to consume the land below as far as the eye could see. As the morning light became more brilliant, fragments of cloud began to appear on the distant horizon, scattering as if painted by the delicate inflexions of an artist's brush layering white and grey upon an emerald canvas, warning of the rain that would inevitably fall later that day on the jungle canopy below. It seemed incredible that a place that looked so peaceful and natural could be the setting for one of the bloodiest and longest-running insurgencies in South America. This was further soured by the fact that the insurgency organisation had become nothing more than a mafia, running a lucrative cocaine business, filling its leaders' pockets with millions—if not billions—of US dollars. It was almost impossible to contemplate this when looking down at the apparent tranquillity below. The jungle literally stretched to the horizon, seemingly to infinity and beyond.

When they reached the planned insertion point, each helicopter took its turn to hover over the chosen area and drop off its human cargo. As soon as their pilot got the helicopter into position, the Black Hawk door gunners threw the thick ropes out of the side doors, allowing Hart and his men to carry out a fast-rope insertion into the hostile rainforest below.

Within ten minutes, the insertion was complete and the attack force of nearly 70 men began to navigate through the jungle towards the FARC camp. The 7th Special Forces Group took the lead with Chief in command. They expertly navigated through the primary jungle, stopping at RV (rendezvous) points along the way to allow the attack force to rest a few moments and rehydrate, before moving on to the next RV. The humidity was incredible; the sweat literally ran into their eyes, occasionally blurring their vision. It literally felt like they had just stepped into a health and leisure centre's sauna fully clothed. Their new surrounding offered a sensory overload. There was more life in the jungle per square metre than anywhere else on the planet. So many insects, mammals, and birds. The noise was incredible, thousands of noises crashed over the men. It was now impossible to see the colour of the sky - under the canopy there were only different shades of green, and the men now felt fully detached and separated from the outside world.

As the group drew closer to the FARC camp, their pace slowed, and vigilance became more of a priority than speed.

By late afternoon, after moving through 12 separate RV stops, the group found themselves less than 1km away from the FARC camp. Chief decided to locate the FRV/FUP (final rendezvous/form-up position) by a small dried-up stream and waited for the troops that followed him to form up in a circle around the chosen spot, offering the group all-round defence. Once they had formed a circle and each man had taken off his Bergen, they laid down on their fronts, facing outwards and linking legs to ensure there were no gaps in the circle. They kept their weapons aimed, remaining on high alert for any signs of FARC troops that may be patrolling through the area.

As darkness fell, Hart met Chief and Major Rodriguez at the centre of the FRV/FUP circle to go over, once more, the details for the most difficult and dangerous part of the mission: moving into their final positions and readying themselves for the attack. This was a good final opportunity for commanders to run through things once again, especially given the JUNGLA commander had turned up late for the operational deployment briefing the previous day. Two JUNGLA police commandos were nominated to remain in the FRV position to guard the Bergens and any equipment that would not be required at the start-line of the attack. The plan was for Hart's team to proceed, with the JUNGLA troops, to the attack start-line - south of the FARC camp on the edge of the jungle clearance. They would take one 7th Special Forces Group soldier with them as a runner to act as a link between Major Rodriguez and Chief due to the operational necessity for complete radio silence throughout. Under the cover of darkness, each man in the attack force would reach his designated position and lie down, waiting until just before dawn to launch the attack on the camp. Major Rodriguez would place himself at the centre of the attack start-line, with the rest of the attack troops fanning out either side of him in an extended line.

Chief would lead the 7th Special Forces Group troops from the FRV/FUP and slowly encircle the camp, forming a secure cordon to stop any hopeful escapees once the attack got underway.

A few hours later, after moving from the FRV and finally getting into position on the attack start-line, Hart saw that Borgman had been right about the festivities in the camp that evening. In the small clearing, the FARC camp occupants were clearly celebrating. He could hear the loud singing and beating of drums. The combined noise from the camp and the jungle's wildlife was a welcome cover whilst the attack teams got into position.

There was nothing more to do now except wait.

CHAPTER FIVE

PAOLA SANCHEZ knelt over her sleeping daughter and took a few moments to marvel at her growing beauty, before waking her with a kiss on the forehead. These days she never knew when she would next get to do this, so she savoured every precious moment with her little girl.

Dawn had still not broken. The jungle beyond the camp was unusually quiet and still.

"Good morning my beautiful bird of paradise," Paola whispered in her daughter's ear as Valentina's eyes fluttered open, faintly batting against her lids when she blinked. Giving her a moment to shed the sleep from her brain and allowing the visions of the night to give way to the day. Her dream ending abruptly, as she was gently shaken back into reality.

"You sleep well, Chiquita?" Valentina nodded. "Come on, now, let me hear your prayers and then we'll eat," Paola suggested.

Valentina pulled her body up off the bed and swung her legs beneath her, so she was kneeling up, facing her mother, who sat on the jungle floor beside the low bed inside their small canvas tent. Living a nomadic existence, there was no silken mattress to rub her fingers along, or velvet pillows to press her cheek against. For as long as Valentina could remember she had slept on a camp bed with only an old threadbare blanket to keep her warm at night.

Together they recited a string of words and numbers that certainly bore no resemblance to the standard prayers of any regular religion. They spoke under their breath; their voices, barely whispers in the morning air. Even a person standing a few feet away could not have distinguished what they were saying.

By the time they were finished, dawn was on the verge of breaking. Peering out of the tent, Paola could see that the eastern sky above the jungle clearing was beginning to fill with blended tones of rosy pinks and sandy yellows. A subtle way to welcome a new day, perhaps even a new beginning. Whilst Valentina washed and dressed, Paola prepared a small plate with some fruit, nuts, and rice on it. Several times she dropped the knife whilst cutting the papaya; she was unusually nervous. Paola refused to allow herself to think about what was due to take place any day now. She had been informed that the British had agreed to her proposed plan and that it would take place this week, but she did not know exactly when. Paola knew her hours with Valentina were numbered but she wanted to ensure that nothing disrupted her little girl's routine, so that Valentina would only have positive lasting memories of her mother.

In her heart, Paola wanted to scream and cry at the injustice of Valentina having been born into a life of such conflict and violence, but she knew this would only be a waste of energy. There was no one to hear her prayers. She had long since given up the fantastical notion of a "God", which was discouraged by the FARC's ideology anyway. No God would allow such suffering to continue in the world without intervening. All Paola believed was that everyone, at some point in their life, had to suffer; some for longer than others.

As a child, she had watched a snake swallow a baby crocodile whole, and a puma tear a raccoon from limb to limb. Both times, Paola had felt no pity for the prey. Simply, she had resolved that all living things have one thing in common, that one day they will die. What they can do between the day they are born and the day they meet their demise is partly up to them and partly down to what chance serves up for them. Within the limitations of their circumstances, every living being makes choices, whether driven by instinct, desire or emotion; and whether calculated or impulsive, those choices will shape our lives.

This was how Paola had survived the early years of Zamora's attacks. She had chosen not to feel the pain; she had chosen to call the feeling "pleasure". This had unnerved Zamora, and in the end, Paola had won him over and had secured his respect and trust. She did not love him—indeed Valentina was the only living soul she loved—but she had skilfully affected behaviour that convinced Zamora that she had feelings for him, and she knew he genuinely felt emotionally connected to her because his actions had changed over the years. In time, Paola knew she had the upper hand, she knew she had control over Zamora, even though—to the outside world—it looked the other way around. He trusted her implicitly; she had access to anything she wanted. She made him drunk on wine, high on oxytocin, then raided his brain.

Two months ago, Paola had made a calculated choice, driven by the intense love she felt for her child and the hatred for Zamora. She had chosen to spare her beautiful daughter the fate of a life inside the FARC. Even if that meant that Paola herself could not survive.

Paola's choice to join the FARC when she found herself an orphan at the age of 13, was one driven by sheer survival instinct. Her loving parents had died within six weeks of each other after an outbreak of yellow fever within their village had killed most of the inhabitants. Paola was one of several orphaned children targeted by FARC recruiting officers who promised them food and shelter, as well as a small wage. Basic food and shelter were, as promised, provided, but there was no wage forthcoming and when Paola began asking her fellow recruits about the money owed to them, word finally came back that their wages had been held by the central administration and used to pay for their basic needs; it was slavery dressed up as communism.

Within a week, Paola was being given basic firearms training, learning how to use AK-47s and M16 rifles as well as mortar units. She was lucky, she was taller and stronger than most of the other girls, some of whom were barely able to lift the weapons offered to them. The basic military training lasted two months. Of the forty potential recruits, ten (seven children and three adults) disappeared after they failed to complete certain tasks; they were never seen again. This kept the others on edge, fighting for their lives as they clung on to their resolve to complete the assault courses, dig the designated trenches, construct the bunkers, and finish the swimming endurance tests in precarious jungle rivers and small lakes.

Unfortunately, Paola's relative maturity also made her a target for many of the male officers looking to satiate their carnal desires. Her virginity was taken from her during the second week of training, raped by a man old enough to be her grandfather.

There was something almost ritualistic about the occasion. The girls in the camp were lined up and an officer, who was being rewarded for his part in a brave and brutal attack on a counter-guerrilla unit dispatched by the Colombian army, walked along the line, sizing them up. He asked each girl in turn if they were virgins.

Paola didn't catch on in time; she was too busy registering her amazement that every single girl in the line answered "no". Too late she answered, truthfully, "yes", and found herself being dragged off to the officer's tent where she experienced more physical pain than she could ever have imagined possible. She didn't allow herself to cry and afterwards she rationalised the whole experience, deciding that it was simply a part of the experience of living. She decided to view the incident as neither a good thing nor a bad thing; it was simply something that had happened.

Paola couldn't change the fact that she stood out from the pack. She was strikingly beautiful even with her hair cropped short, as was the FARC's requirement.

She'd inherited her mother's curvaceous hourglass figure and no amount of binding her breasts down or bulking out her uniform around her waist seemed to hide it.

All recruits were forced to play soccer during their recreational time; men and alike were expected to play. The training officers insisted that it provided the necessary mental relaxation. On this point and on this point only, Paola agreed with them. She loved playing soccer and in the rare moments when she allowed herself to daydream, she imagined how—if her life had turned out differently—she might have had a chance to qualify and travel to Germany with the women's national team in four years' time, representing Colombia in the Women's World Cup for the very first time.

There were regular classes to teach new recruits about the FARC's official doctrine. They were taught basic Marxist theory as well as Marxism-Leninism. They studied the Cuban revolution and the life of Che Guevara. Every recruit was made to take a vow, swearing allegiance to the cause, to the fight to establish "social justice" in Colombia. They did this beneath the FARC's flag, which depicted a book and two rifles in the middle of a map of Colombia, signifying followers would "learn and fight for Colombia". This highlighted the importance the FARC put on ideological education, in an attempt to prove that they were not simply a rebel militia group, but a viable political movement. The three colours on the flag's background—yellow, blue and red—reflected the colours of the flags of Ecuador, Venezuela and Colombia, indicating the region's shared past and identity under Bolívar's Greater Colombia.

Paola found she absorbed information quickly and easily. She had no opinion on the ideology she was being spoon-fed, she simply learned it and repeated it back to the trainers to their satisfaction. Again, as much as Paola was aware of the importance to blend in—from a strategic standpoint—she couldn't help but stand out. She was a star recruit.

Halfway through the training course, a couple of new instructors arrived. White men. One looked like he was pushing sixty, with a shock of grey hair and matching beard, and the other was clearly much younger, in his mid-thirties perhaps, handsome, with long reddish-brown hair, which he wore greased back into a ponytail. These men turned out to be members of a group calling itself the New Irish Republican Army, an Irish paramilitary organisation that Paola had never heard of until now. The two men were there to lead specialist training in explosives and demolitions. They were experts in explosives—in particular car bombs, mortars and roadside bombs. They had brought a Spanish translator with them. By carefully listening to the translations, Paola got her first lessons in speaking English—or Irish, as the men would have it. She also managed to use a small Spanish-English dictionary that one of the men had left lying around during a training session.

She instinctively knew that the ability to speak two languages would, one day, serve her well. Paola also ensured she was close to the officers and IRA men around mealtimes, which is how she overheard conversations that explained the nature of the relationship between the FARC and the New IRA.

The New IRA was assisting the FARC in setting up a new European route to market in exchange for quality cocaine at a reduced price. Every few months, a couple of IRA men would visit the camp and give the recruits some specialist training. Paola used these visits to practice her English by offering to assist the men during their stay. Her language skills would one day make her indispensable to Jose Zamora.

The first time Paola crossed paths with Jose Zamora, was when he came to speak to Paola and her fellow soldiers in the summer of 1996. She knew immediately that his mind was poisoned; he knew immediately that he was going to possess her. Paola was eighteen and had been in the FARC for five years. She was still a soldier. Zamora, on the other hand, thanks to a massively successful assignment, in which he managed to kill fourteen police officers, was now—at twenty—the youngest officer in the FARC, after only four years' service.

The soldiers in Paola's division had been assembled in the middle of the camp to listen to the story that was going to be told by the FARC's youngest and newest most celebrated appointed officer.

As Jose Zamora started to speak, he glanced around the group and did a double take when he saw Paola staring at him. As usual, Paola focused all of her attention on the subject ahead of her, unlike most of her fellow female soldiers who, at times, allowed their minds to drift into daydreams. Paola always had her wits about her. She naturally memorised every detail of Zamora's story and impressed him regularly over the following years by recalling details better than he could.

She also extracted from him the parts of his life story he had shared with no one.

Exactly one week after his sixteenth birthday Jose Posada Zamora found himself standing over the body of the man who, until two minutes earlier, had been his living, breathing, drunk, abusive father. His mother's screams had quickly been silenced by the high-pitched whining noise inside Zamora's head. What was that noise? It had started moments earlier, like a siren, announcing to the world that another evil man was dead, and it was safe to come out of hiding, like at the end of an air raid. Zamora's hands were shaking, his hands scarlet and sticky, his father's blood flowed thickly over his fingers like caramel over an apple, only brilliant red instead of golden browns. His eyes watched each finger move, entranced by the new colour of his skin. The body beneath him had thirty or so stab wounds. Zamora had stopped counting at fifteen. He was sure he'd killed his father by then, but he wanted to be absolutely certain.

Knowing that the man would never again lay a finger on him had made Zamora feel a sense of elation that was unprecedented. The ringing in his ears suddenly increased in volume and Zamora became aware that his mother was pulling him away from his father's body and pushing him into the bathroom. There, she held his bloody hands under running water until every spot of blood was washed away. She pulled his clothes off him and urged him to dress into clean ones. Zamora complied obediently. The noise in his ears was deafening but he was peaceful... because the monster was gone.

Within the hour, Zamora's maternal uncle arrived to take him to Medellin. Zamora himself had to be led to his uncle's car, like a well-trained dog. He later discovered that his mother had told the police there had been an attempted burglary. She said her husband had disturbed an intruder who had stabbed him to death and then escaped.

Somewhere in his psyche, Zamora had believed that if he killed the man who was torturing him, he would stop torturing other beings and become a kinder person. He had long been breaking the neck of stray cats, pulling the legs off insects and dissecting live lizards as a way of dealing with the abuse his father had inflicted upon him. Alas, this turned out not to be the case. If anything, the killing of his father turned him into an even bigger monster than his father had been.

Fifteen years on, Jose Zamora was one of the most feared FARC commanders in the Colombian jungle. He had killed at least fifty men and women and was the FARC's 'go-to' man when they needed to torture the truth out of suspected informants. He particularly liked inflicting pain on women, especially when in doing so he could get his own sexual gratification. After graduating as, the top soldier in his basic training course, Zamora had been introduced to the 57th Front, which was composed of around 250 combatants, operating mostly in the Chocó Department. The 57th Front formed part of the north-western bloc of the FARC and historically had a strong influence in the Medellin and Antioquia regions.

The north-western bloc had been targeted by the Colombian President's defence plan. The subsequent attacks mounted by the Colombian military and police had forced the FARC to retreat to more remote areas and, as a result, they had lost some of the dominance they once had in the area.

The specific divisions of the FARC group were somewhat blurred, in part due to the number of attacks they had endured, but the 57th Front remained intact and was growing ever stronger.

Not long after joining the 57th Front, Zamora took part in a raid near the town of Juradó, on Colombia's north-west Pacific coastline. The beach town of Juradó was around 12 miles from the border with Panama and was extremely remote and difficult to reach. It was exactly because of these key attributes that the town had become a popular magnet with cocaine producers, who used Juradó as a launch-pad to ship their product through Colombia and up into Panama City.

As a result, the local police began thwarting the efforts of cocaine producers as they tried to move their product through the town. In direct response, the 57th Front planned an attack on the local police base that would send a strong convincing message and hopefully force them to back off.

The story had become legendary and was what Zamora had regaled Paola and the other FARC members with when she first saw him.

Zamora explained that his specific task was to ensure a hole was cut in the security fence that surrounded the police compound in order to allow the main attack force to enter the base un-hindered. He had strict orders to wait by the fence line and shoot any police officers that tried to escape.

During a reconnaissance mission the night before the planned attack, he had cut a hole in the fence with wire cutters so that his task on the night of the attack would be a simple and silent one.

Once he had created a hole large enough for the entire attack team to crawl through, he had tied the pieces of the fence together with some thread, ensuring that if any of the police officers inside the base carried out a perimeter check, the fence would appear to be intact.

On the night of the attack, he returned to the area along the fence line where he'd made the hole and hid a few metres away in the low undergrowth, waiting for the command to open it up. As the moment approached for him to complete his task, he felt immense excitement. Of course, he was nervous—he said—one false move could have sabotaged the entire operation, but the knowledge of how important his role was to the ultimate success of the attack had kept him calm and focused.

On schedule, the mortar support team that was stationed about 300 metres up the hill from the perimeter fence, unleashed rounds from a military 81mm mortar they'd previously captured: now turning the weapon on its previous owners. Moments later, the fire support team, positioned further down the hill, fired their RPG-7 rocket-propelled grenades into the cluster of police buildings that were quickly becoming silhouettes against the backdrop of blinding flashes from the mortar explosions as they took direct hits. After their rocket attack, the same team opened up with their two NSV 12.7mm Calibre heavy machine guns at indiscriminate targets ahead of them.

Anything or anybody moving around the compound and caught out in the open was almost instantly obliterated. Gun barrels glowed fiery red in the darkness of the night from the maximum rate of fire, 650-750 rounds per minute, spitting out bullet rounds at 2,800 feet per second. These weapons were at the highest end of the destructive scale.

Zamora lay motionless on the ground, as the constant barrage of bullet rounds, whistled narrowly passed his head, appearing to strike their targets with frightening precision. The heavy calibre machine guns effortlessly tore through soft human tissue and rapidly began scattering the corpses of policemen caught out in the open and unprotected, across the floor of the police compound.

The excitement of watching this pyrotechnic display inspired Zamora as he readied himself for his next move. The place Zamora had carefully chosen to make his hole in the fence was not only strategically well-positioned for the attack force to reach the buildings in the near distance unimpeded, but it was also around 50 metres from the rear entrance to the compound. He had anticipated that any surviving policemen trying to escape would assume they had a better chance of survival by heading for the dimly lit rear gate, rather than the main entrance that would be illuminated by the main searchlights belonging to the base.

Zamora waited until the supporting fire began to lift from the police compound before crawling forward and opening his expertly placed hole in the perimeter fence. He then signalled two flashes of his red-filtered torch to let his commander know that their entryway into the compound was now open. The men, who had been waiting patiently a few metres behind him, hidden in the treeline, now surged forward and made their way through the fence and into the combat zone. After the last man had passed Zamora, he stayed, waiting and observing. A young hunter waiting for his unsuspecting prey to run towards him.

Zamora described to his audience what it felt like to breathe in the acrid smell of burnt nitro-glycerine and sulphur created by exploded ordnance. How, whilst it irritated his eyes, burnt his nasal cavities, and made his mouth and throat unbearably dry, it also excited him because he knew this was his first real taste of the battlefield. Nothing, he said, you experience in training will ever prepare you for the reality of battle, the true sounds, tastes and smells of the battlefield.

He paused for a moment and savoured his own description. He locked eyes with Paola before looking away and continuing the story. Soon came Zamora's crowning moment. Through the thick smoke, he made out figures hurrying towards the fence where he lay in wait. Policemen trying to escape but unwittingly running blindly towards the waiting shadow of death. He counted them as best he could in the dim light and smoky night air. There were ten at least, maybe eleven or twelve; survivors of the devastating attack running directly towards him. He lay on his front, disguised by the dark mud that he had disturbed and wiped across his face.

Suddenly, the night sky was lit up from the blast of an explosion inside one of the buildings. Zamora used this to his advantage, taking aim with his AK47 at the running figures, who had almost reached the rear gate and were no more than 30 yards from his concealed position.

Without a moment's hesitation, he fired a quick succession of three-round bursts. The bullet rounds glowed red in the night air. One by one his targets fell to the ground. The first policeman was hit directly in the chest, propelling him backwards in an awkward cartwheel. Zamora was now up and moving fast, closing with his victims. The most dangerous enemy is the one you leave wounded he explained to the young soldiers. Finding two policemen groaning on the ground, not quite dead, Zamora took his machete and finished them off in a frenzied attack. The machete meeting soft flesh, making a satisfying sound as it sank deep enough to make both victims scream out in tortured agony. Zamora continued to swing the machete, each time sinking it deeper and deeper. The skin of both men being torn apart in shreds, the sound of their muscles and nerves being brutally ripped apart grew louder with every frenzied blow. Zamora eventually stopped, he was physically exhausted and covered head to toe in the blood of his victims.

Privately, the fact that it mirrored the attack on his own father a few years earlier was not lost on Zamora. He gained huge pleasure from repeating the stabbing actions as if every plunge of the knife into flesh made his father that little bit more dead to him.

The FARC assault team had now started to withdraw back towards the fence. They had about four minutes to get out of the police compound before the mortars started up again, giving them covering fire during their extraction from the police base. As the men made their way back through the opening in the fence, the team commander, Sergio, spotted the group of corpses lying close to the fence, nearby the rear gate. Zamora proudly reported that he alone was responsible for this massacre. The commander was astonished that a raw recruit had pulled off such a feat.

As Zamora crept through the undergrowth along with the other men in the attack force, his skin prickled with pride and excitement. He knew this was going to be a huge story. The intelligence report from the FARC informant, a cleaner at the police base, had reported approximately sixty or seventy policemen operated from the base. Assuming this was correct, it would mean that Zamora alone had been responsible for around one-fifth of the total fatalities.

The FARC attack force made their way clear of the compound just as the next round of mortar fire landed.

As Zamora explained to his enthralled audience, it was always prudent to cover your escape with a further round of mortar fire, to ensure protection from an unwelcomed counterattack.

After the successful attack on the police base at Juradó, word had spread fast. Jose Zamora's name was heard throughout the entire FARC organisation. Whilst police morale fell to an all-time low, the 57th FARC Front had regained the initiative, bolstered by their successful operation. Their product was once again moving freely across the border into Panama, completely unhindered by the local Colombian police.

No one told the story about the momentous night without mentioning the name of Jose Posada Zamora. Of course, as time went by, the number of policemen he had killed single-handedly rose. At some point, it was over thirty men that Zamora had finished off on that legendary night. The FARC leaders did not care how far the story was embellished; it was serving the purpose of boosting confidence amongst the troops. They were only too happy to put Zamora on a pedestal and revel in his glory. The story of the ruthless soldier, who had prevented the escape of so many police officers and turned the night into the FARC's biggest triumph in years, was too good to worry about details. Recruitment figures had never been higher. Times were good.

Jose Zamora soon found himself taken out of active duty, whilst at the same time, being rapidly promoted to the rank of squad commander, the equivalent of a full corporal in the regular army. He was escorted from village to village throughout the departments of Chocó, Antioquia, and Cordoba and even up to the department of Sucre where he would tell the locals of his life's journey, from a small-town boy to being recruited into the FARC, and the benefits that this had brought him financially. FARC recruits were paid far more than the Colombian military. The FARC recruitment body relied heavily on the promise of financial incentives to secure recruits, despite later holding back the promised financial incentive to help cover training and other incidental costs. FARC recruits would eventually receive the promised pay upon successfully completing the basic training programme – which would normally last 12 weeks or longer. This vital piece of information was something Zamora conveniently decided to hold back from his audience during his recruitment drive.

Zamora would always wrap up a village visit by re-telling his story of the police compound attack at Juradó. If there were any potential recruits still undecided, they would always jump forward once having heard this story. It was a game-changer and the FARC recruitment chiefs knew it. Zamora was also often brought into camps to help boost the morale of soldiers who had not yet seen any real action, hoping to inspire them and keep them focused, which is how he came to be speaking to Paola and her fellow soldiers during the summer of 1996.

As the soldiers started to disperse, Paola's instincts told her to disappear into the crowd, but Zamora was one step ahead of her. He had already indicated to one of the camp's officers that he wanted Paola brought to his tent. She had reached the entrance to her sleeping quarters when a senior soldier took her rifle from her and marched her back to where Zamora's tent was erected. Zamora was waiting at the entrance for her. His eyes narrowed at her as she approached.

Zamora ordered her to go inside the tent. Paola knew exactly what to do, how to maintain some control whilst seeming to be compliant. She made direct eye contact with Zamora, giving him a blank look of indifference, and then entered the tent, which was big enough to stand fully upright in but looked somewhat dishevelled. The ropes that should have been tight, showed plenty of give in them and the bottom of the tent should have been pulled tighter when Zamora had pegged it, making it appear that it could potentially collapse at any moment.

Zamora followed her inside, ordering the soldiers to stand guard. He started to remove his uniform and ordered Paola to do the same and strip. She obeyed, keeping eye contact with him the whole time. This irritated him and once he was naked, he put his hands on her shoulders and roughly pushed to her knees, forcing himself into her mouth, pulling her head onto him to prevent her from recoiling. Paola had long since learned to control her gag reflexes and complied without making a sound. She kept turning her head to one side to look up at him.

Seeing her gaze up at him unnerved Zamora; suddenly he was afraid he was about to lose his erection. On impulse, he pulled himself out of her mouth, pushed her away and ordered her to turn around and put her hands on the floor. Paola obeyed and, reassured by the sight of her bare buttocks in place of her steely eyes, Zamora grabbed her hips and entered her from behind, thrusting into her with the same intensity with which he liked to thrust a knife into a man's abdomen. Paola still made no sound. Zamora resorted to hitting the side of Paola's head several times, trying to produce a reaction. He dug his nails hard into her back, but she still showed no reaction and any outward signs of feeling any pain. He leaned forward and bit her shoulder as he came, sinking his teeth into her hard enough to draw blood. Finally, when he was satisfied, Zamora threw Paola's clothes at her and ordered her to go. She paused at the opening of the tent and turned to face her rapist, who was licking Paola's blood off his upper lip. Standing in the entranceway of the tent, her clothes held casually in her hands at her sides, making no effort to cover her nakedness, Paola.

"You are welcome," she said to him, calmly and politely, in English. Zamora didn't understand the words but knew that, whatever she had said, she had shown him her superiority by speaking to him in a foreign language. Then she left.

Zamora sat in his tent, naked and fuming. Whilst he was physically satisfied, on an emotional level, it was the most unsatisfactory experience he had ever had. Whenever he had women, whenever he killed men, he had control; he had them in his power. He took their lives, or he took their dignity. This woman had given him nothing.

He was furious.

Before he left camp, Zamora tried to break Paola five more times.

Short of killing her, which would defeat the object, he couldn't find a way of making her suffer. Paola Sanchez was the ultimate downfall for Jose Zamora. She was his weakness.

Over the course of the next eleven years, he would become obsessed with her. He came back to the camp again and again, and when he was promoted to the rank of FARC commander, he ensured that Paola was transferred with him. He raped other women regularly, but never with the same intensity that he unleashed on Paola.

Eventually, over time, when their daughter Valentina was born, his violence reduced. Something fundamentally had changed in Zamora. The intense hatred he had felt towards his father, that he had harboured inside over the years, turned into the love he felt for his daughter. In turn, his emotional connection to Paola intensified and he became vulnerable when he was with her, which confused and angered him. He was also in Paola's debt. Not only had she given him Valentina, but she had also eventually taught him to speak English. This had made him the natural choice to deal with the Ukrainians and had ultimately inflated his position within the FARC. The coca crop that they had developed together, and the crystallisation lab built to process it, were Zamora's pet projects. He was making the FARC wealthier than anyone could have ever hoped for, and subsequently, more powerful as every year passed. He was also rising through the ranks, with his sights set on the top position.

CHAPTER SIX

A MOVEMENT to Hart's right startled him. Christ! He was jumpy. A split second later, Hart saw someone crawling towards him through the dense undergrowth. He assumed it was an officer from the line of JUNGLA troops lying concealed just a few metres to his right, but soon the face of Bob King came into view. Hart increased the pressure of his grip on his M16 in case his right hand trembled again.

"What the fuck's happening? Why hasn't Rodriguez given the signal to attack?" Hart hissed at his 2IC. "Those bastards in the camp will be awake soon; we'll lose our advantage."

"I've got a sitrep for you" King hissed back. "The runner has just reported to Rodriguez that the troops on the cordon believe there's a bunch of sentry positions dotted around the perimeter; north, south, east and west; all fucking well-hidden. Nothing more specific than that reference their location. Fucking amateur hour! Anyway, Rodriguez wants us to take them out."

"Christ! Borgman, the useless twat! He told me the perimeter was clear!" Half of the planning for the operation had been based on the information Hart had gathered from the Dutchman, Hans Borgman, back in Bogotá. Now Hart felt partly responsible for this setback.

"You said you thought that prick was a slippery fucker," King whispered, hurriedly. Hart nodded, ruefully.

"Okay," Hart whispered, urgently. He knew he had precious little time to give out a set of snap orders. "Tell Mike to go east, Jock goes north, and you take the south. I'll head west. Tell Kav to stick with Rodriguez and get ready to use the M134 in overtime mode. Also, get the runner to inform the cordon we'll be crawling around the perimeter trying to locate these fucking positions. We don't want any blue-on-blue at this stage. I still don't forget the American Hornet attacking the trench filled with Royal Marines in Helmand last December. Usual SOP's apply. As soon as we're all firm in our assault positions, each of us will give one long click on the radio Pressel. Once we've heard all four single clicks, you go first, then Mike. Jock will be next and then me. Only go noisy if there's no way to avoid it. Deliberate, spaced out double clicks on the Pressel when your target is down. When I give the fourth double click, we'll know the perimeter's clear. Make it crystal clear to Rodriguez that he's not to fire the M203 and send a fucking grenade into the camp until he's heard all four double clicks. Kav needs to keep an eye on the dickhead and make sure he doesn't fuck up and give the order too early, or we'll all be going home in body bags."

Hart added, "Once the attack starts, tell the boys to regroup and join the JUNGLA's main attack force. All going well they should be pushing through the camp by that stage, clearing northwards. Kav should be working overtime with the M134; we're going to fucking need it!"

The M134 was a 7.62x51 mm NATO-approved machine gun with six-barrels and a high rate of firepower (2,000 to 6,000 rounds per minute); featuring Gatling-style rotating barrels with an external electric power source that could wipe out a platoon of 30 men in seconds. It was a beast of a weapon that needed a man of Kav's build and stature to control it.

Kavekini Rabuka was a tall, good-looking muscular man, and

an expert soldier like his father. One of the SAS's best trackers, he was also an excellent medic. He had followed a deep-rooted Fijian tradition of coming to the UK to join the British Army, entering into the Royal Engineers. He'd completed his SAS training at 23, becoming one of the youngest men ever to do so.

"At this rate, the FARC will have time for coffee and a leisurely shit before we get started on them; the fucking place will be swarming with them. So much for an ambush whilst they're sleeping." Hart shook his head, exasperated.

He had no time for regrets and reflection now. "If it all goes tits up," he continued, "It's straight to the ERV at the southern edge of the clearing."
Bob King gave Hart a thumbs-up signal and started to crawl back through the jungle.

Hart took a moment to double-check his stripped-down belt equipment. It contained the bare minimum: eight magazines of 5.56mm ammunition, his combat knife, a machete blade, water bottle, small PRC patrol radio and a basic medical pack. Hart was relieved that his right hand now appeared to be steady. He moved off in search of the sentry position he was charged with taking out, crawling silently through the undergrowth in a westerly direction.

If he'd stayed in position a few moments longer, he would have seen the children.

The FARC camp bordered a small clearing between the Río Atrato, which flowed from south to north through the departments of Chocó and Antioquia, and the small jungle village of Pogue. It was surrounded by ancient trees as tall as a small skyscraper, with a strange green light shimmering through their vast canopy of leaves. Valentina and her friend ran towards the centre of the clearing and out into the early morning sunshine, oblivious to the concealed armed soldiers surrounding them. They chased each other for a couple of minutes, weaving in and out of the treeline that encircled the clearing and then stopped to play a game of catch with an old baseball.

Like most of the occupants of the camp, their ethnic mix was part Spanish, part *Emberá Indian*. The boy's pudding- bowl hairstyle was typical of his particular tribe; Valentina's jet-black straight hair fell to her shoulders. As they threw the ball to each other, daring each other to get further and further apart, they dodged the remnants of the previous night's activities in the clearing: a dozen or so burnt-out campfires—some still smouldering—and a number of empty wooden beer kegs.

Beyond the children's makeshift baseball field, to the north, evidence of a temporary camp that had been their home for the past six months could be glimpsed through gaps in the dense jungle foliage. There were several tents and some small, hastily constructed wooden huts. Well concealed beyond these primitive structures, however, lay some significantly larger and more structurally sound buildings with thick wooden walls and corrugated iron roofs covered with camouflaged netting to prevent them from being spotted by the military aircraft that had recently started flying over this part of the jungle. Alongside these larger buildings were several long wooden tables nestled under extensive plastic awnings that had been hung from tall wooden posts. Alongside the tables stood a number of large, light-green metal drums and an assortment of large clear plastic containers containing acetone solvent, ethyl acetate and hydrochloric acid... all the substances required for the crystallisation process to produce cocaine.

After crawling 60 metres through the jungle undergrowth for about twenty minutes, with trees almost blocking his motion in every direction. Every view appearing to be the same in whatever direction he looked, Hart finally spotted the camp's western sentry position. It was well concealed and had been built with sandbags with a thin sheet of plastic with jungle foliage placed over it.

To Hart's relief, the sentry looked like he was asleep. The man was sitting, almost upright, in a death-like slumber that, for the moment at least, was not perturbed by the presence of Hart. He was propped up against some sandbags with his head bent slightly forward, looking reasonably comfortable. Hart heard the unmistakable sound of snoring. The guard had a typical South American handlebar moustache. He looked to be in his late 30s, but he was also dirty and unkempt, which might have aged him. Hart stopped himself having any more thoughts about the man who lay metres from him, thoughts that could lead to sentiment, which could compromise his ability to act.

Keeping his eyes trained on the sleeping Colombian, Hart inched forward and crawled into his final assault position and waited. Barely a minute later, through his earpiece, Hart heard a single Pressel click over the radio airwaves, quickly followed by another single click and then another. All three SAS soldiers were now in their FAPs, ready to strike with clinical efficiency. Pressing down on his radio Pressel, Hart gave his own signal that he was now also in position and ready. Willing the sentry in his sight not to wake up, Hart waited with increasing impatience for the next signal. Finally, Bob King gave the signal that the first sentry was down. Two minutes later came Mike's double click. Hart glanced up at the sky. The sun was continuing its morning ascent, sending a canopy of golden light and shimmering rays across the jungle. Were they going to complete this mission? Doubt began to creep in. Finally, Jock's signal came. The sentries positioned to the north, south and east of the camp's perimeter had now been successfully and silently eliminated. Now it was Hart's turn.

Hart's adrenalin level peaked and his heart hammered inside his head. In similar situations in the past, the cacophony of jungle wildlife, in particular, the chattering of the birds and primates would usually cover any noise he made during his final approach.

On this morning, however, the jungle had become unusually still and quiet, as if the animals had pre-empted the attack and were waiting, silently, watching it unfold. This was the moment when all emotions had to be switched off, when fear had to be suppressed and man had to become machine. The act of killing a man by cutting his throat was messy. He pictured it without the blood. He forced

himself to believe that he could do it. That was the only way; that was
how he detached himself, by thinking through the physical motions
and not the result of the act itself.

Hart finally reached the sentry position and prepared to strike;
a single shriek rang out across the jungle. He whipped his head to the
right and saw through the trees, for the first time, the heads of the
two children playing at the centre of the jungle clearing. He stared at
the girl, who was laughing now. Hart's pulse throbbed in his temples.
Was that her? It had to be her! According to Borgman she was the
only child in the camp. So, who was the boy? The Dutchman hadn't
informed them about the perimeter sentries and now the boy. A
movement in front of Hart snapped his attention back towards the
sentry. The girl's shriek had woken the sentry who was stirring from
his sleep. Hart had no time to lose. He had to make his move now.

Taking the greatest care not to make a sound, Hart adopted a
low crouching position and raised the knife he had pulled from its
sheath moments earlier. He had bought the Webster Marble
Trailmaker himself, a few years earlier. The knife had a hardwood
handle, with a dual ten-inch, high-carbon steel blade, cut with great
precision. Everything about it was precise. Having used the knife on
previous occasions, he had great confidence in its efficiency. Without
taking his eyes off the man in front of him, Hart moved forward,
quickly and silently, striking the oblivious sentry from behind with
lightning speed, covering his mouth and pulling the sentry back
towards him. Hart now lay backwards, his legs wrapped around the
sentry's body in a vice-like grip to immobilise him. With all the
strength he could muster, Hart thrust his knife, at an almost vertical
angle, into the back of the man's neck, into the space at the top of the
spine just below the base of his skull. Hart felt the adrenalin
anaesthetise all human feeling in his own body whilst he felt every
part of the sentry's body instantly stiffen, tightening with the shock.
Hart tightened his grip as the sentry's arms flayed desperately,
reaching back, trying in vain to grab at his attacker. Hart shook the
10-inch blade from side to side as forcefully as he could, pivoting the

knife handle back and forth until the blade broke through the front of the sentry's neck, now almost half severed.

Hart lay back even further, with his left hand still covering the sentry's mouth and nose to ensure there was no chance of the man omitting any noise. Blood was spraying in thick droplets, spattering the jungle floor and Hart in equal measure. It quickly began to blacken as it encountered the heat of the jungle. The blood that flowed so freely from the sentry's neck now began to form on the ground in large pools around both men. It smelled like an abattoir. Hart was covered in it and he knew from experience that the blood would continue to pump for some time after the man lost consciousness.

Within seconds, the muscle spasms ceased, and the FARC sentry's body finally came to rest. When he was sure the man was dead, Hart rolled the sentry's body off his own. He took a few seconds to compose himself and then pressed his radio Pressel twice to signal that the western sentry position was now neutralised and the potential threat from all four sentry positions had been effectively closed down.

Hart quickly wiped the blood off his knife and replaced it in its sheath. There was no time to think or feel anything about what he had done; the attack on the camp was imminent, but as he looked down, he saw that both his hands were now shaking uncontrollably. What the hell was wrong with him? The question consumed him only for the next few seconds.

CHAPTER SEVEN

V ALENTINA asked, "Mamá, is my Papa a bad man?" whilst she waited patiently for her mother to finish braiding her hair.

"Why do you ask this?" Paola started to weave some rags into the end of the braid, which she would use to tie the end of it.

"Alejandro heard his Mamá say my Papa is a bad man." Paola thought for a moment about how to answer the question. In the end, she told the truth, or what she believed to be the truth.

"There are no bad people, only people who do bad things." Valentina was too young to understand this statement but thought about it for a moment.

"Alejandro did a bad thing" Valentina continued, "He made a fire and caught a frog and was cooking it to eat it. His Mamá found him and told him it was a poisoned frog. She made him throw it into the fire. If he had eaten it, he would be dead now."

Paola smiled to herself as she finished tying her daughter's braid. "Alejandro is a lucky boy," she said. Valentina turned to face her mother and put her hands upon Paola's shoulders, gently stroking the myriad of scars and bruises that were dotted all over them.

"Am I a lucky girl, Mamá?"

Paola gazed into her little girl's eyes, innocent eyes that were the colour of hazelnuts. She was using every ounce of strength she possessed to keep her emotions in check.

"Yes, Valentina," Paola said, steadily. "I believe you are a lucky girl. I believe you are the luckiest girl alive. I believe that whatever happens, luck will always be on your side. You are a good person."

Valentina contemplated her mother's face for a minute then said, decisively, "No, Mamá. I am just a person who does good things."

Paola pulled her daughter tight into her chest and hugged her, aware that any hug could be the last one they ever had.

On the other side of the camp, Zamora opened his eyes and quickly closed them again. The pain in his head felt like a red-hot poker searing the inside of his skull. He felt like he had a balloon under his cranium, slowly being inflated, the pressure continuing to mount. Zamora was more aware of his thumping headache than the layer of dehydrated saliva that coated his cracked lips. Once on his feet, the tent swayed almost causing him to lose balance and he reached out for his bed. The tent swirled before becoming stationary again. It had been a long time since he'd drunk like that, but there had been two causes for celebration. Not only had it been the annual Feast of Saints Peter and Paul, but Hans Borgman had unexpectedly arrived in the camp around late afternoon to say that his Ukrainian partner was making an order for a supply of 'Russian', five times the size of the last shipment. The last batch had moved through the global marketplace like a wildfire burning everyone it touched with addiction or death. Despite the risks, the feedback from the world's elite junkies was good. They wanted more and they wanted it soon.

With the deal done, and Zamora obliviously unaware that less than just 24 hours earlier, Borgman had been an unwilling detainee within an MI6 safe house in Bogotá, having only just barely escaped after offering the poorly paid Colombian night-shift worker almost $2 million Colombian Pesos, nearly $1000 USD, to 'accidentally' leave the door to Borgman's room unlocked, as well as the back door that led out into the rear courtyard and freedom. This had allowed Borgman to make good his escape into the night, disappearing like a ghost, only to turn up again, some 14 hours later, in the remote and inhospitable jungle of the Chocó Department.

Both men had celebrated by drinking the Irish whiskey that Borgman had brought with him. Zamora had consumed plenty of beer beforehand and remembered drinking even more after all the whiskey was gone, so no wonder his head felt like it was filled with lead. He remembered Borgman asking a lot of questions about the formula. Had he said too much? Zamora couldn't remember. At some point he'd lost sight of Borgman; he hadn't been able to locate him anywhere. Zamora just assumed that Borgman had gone and passed out somewhere, but this wasn't his usual behaviour. The tall Dutchman could usually drink any of the Colombian men under the table. Maybe he needed to keep a clear head because he had to leave early the next morning. Zamora didn't care; it had been an exceptionally good night. His success would surely put him in good favour with Ramon and the FARC's Secretariat. His would surely be the most profitable operation they had ever known within the FARC.

Shaun O'Conner, the IRA man, had also joined in with the celebrations. He'd been part of the camp on and off over the past 18 months, teaching advanced demolitions and brushing the FARC soldiers up on their shooting skills. He had a presence in the camp, similar to that of Zamora's, an aura of utter and sheer ruthlessness. Zamora had seen first-hand the man's capabilities. Shaun O'Connor was one of the very few people Zamora had a wary respect for. During the previous night's festivities, Zamora had caught O'Connor not for the first time, looking at Paola with his intense, unnerving large green eyes. He knew what O'Connor wanted, he well understood Paola's allure, but was he really ready to share her? Well, maybe. O'Connor had proved himself loyal and ruthless time and time again. Perhaps he should let him have one night with Paola.

However, at this thought, the sickness that stirred inside his body was not simply due to overindulging in alcohol and *bandeja paisa*, it was jealousy. It was rage!

Zamora decided to return to bed and try to get back to sleep for another hour or so. It seemed light outside, but it couldn't be dawn yet as there was so little sound.

Usually, by dawn, there was a general buzz coming from the distance as the jungle's dayshift woke up. His head pounded and he couldn't get the image of Paola with O'Connor out of his mind.

As a young man, Zamora had taken great care never to allow himself to feel any emotions, for fear they might jeopardise his actions. He was only too aware that sentimental men were the first to die, but Paola had got under his skin. After eleven years of trying, Zamora had discovered that he could not break her. She would not cry. She was tough, tough as a man. She was made of stuff that even Zamora, himself, was envious of. So, after the third time, he made her pregnant in under a year, and the second abortion had failed to make her sterile (as it had with most of the female soldiers), he made Paola an officer and let her keep the baby. That baby had turned into his beautiful daughter, Valentina. If any man ever laid a finger on his daughter, Zamora knew he would literally rip the man's head off without a second thought. This love, this huge pool of emotion he felt, for both Paola and Valentina, made Zamora feel vulnerable.

If Zamora had known what a threat his own daughter posed to him, the dilemma over how to handle the situation would have completely destroyed him.

Suddenly something seemed to explode inside his head. For a split second, Zamora blamed the hangover, but a moment later he realised that the explosions ringing in his ears were not coming from inside his dehydrated brain; they were coming from just outside his tent.

The camp was under attack!

***

As Hart waited for the JUNGLA commander's imminent signal, he turned his attention back to the children who were still playing in the centre of the clearing about 70 metres from his position.

Now he had a clear visual of her face, he quickly did a double-check against the J2 intelligence picture he carried in the top right-hand pocket of his camouflage jungle top.

"Shit!" Hart said to himself, yes it was Valentina, but what about the boy?

This was the part of the operation that Hart had been unable to share with anyone, not even his own men, whom he trusted with his life. He'd been secretly charged with bringing in this girl to the British Intelligence Services. According to gathered intelligence, the girl possessed invaluable information that could help MI6 bring down a major international drug trafficking ring.

The attack was imminent and there was no way Hart could leave the boy, knowing the camp and its occupants were about to be destroyed. He would have to extract the boy out of the camp along with Valentina. Serious doubts had begun to manifest in Hart's mind. Where had this intelligence come from? Why would a child be entrusted with such high-value information? After the discovery of the four concealed sentry positions only moments before and now the boy, Hart was now acutely suspicious. Why hadn't the informer Hans Borgman known about the sentries on the perimeter of the camp? Or if he had known, why hadn't he told Hart? Was he really on their side? Had he turned or not? If not, how soon would Hart be able to relay his concerns and a warning back to HQ? As these questions bounced about in his head, the morning silence was abruptly broken by the sound of an M203 grenade round landing on one of the nearby FARC accommodation tents. The attack had begun!

The two children froze in shock and turned their heads

towards where they thought the noise had come from. Fear instantly curled up inside them and clung to their ribs. Pure terror surged through their veins, sending icy daggers straight to their hearts. Suddenly, all around them, uniformed JUNGLA police troops sprang out of the jungle, shouting and screaming, firing their weapons. Hart was relieved that Rodriguez had waited until he and his team had eliminated the sentries, but he had no time to get to the children.

A barrage of gunfire started. Hart was barely on his feet, though he recognised the familiar sound of the M134 in Kav's hands. The FARC had mobilised quickly. All hell was breaking loose around him.

The children stood rooted to the spot in absolute terror. Hart kept his eyes on the young girl as she whipped her head from side to side, watching the onslaught of emerging JUNGLA troops. Hart acted instinctively, breaking cover and running towards the children with adrenalin-fuelled speed. He would soon be in the centre of the clearing.

"Get down! Get down! Bajar! Tanto de bajar, ahora! Bajar!" he screamed at them as he approached. The children spun around in his direction and stared in horror at the wild-looking Extranjero (foreigner) quickly approaching them.

A bullet round whizzed past Hart's head, then a second and a third, missing him by what felt like millimetres.

Hart's heart was pounding, his throat rasping, his legs suddenly feeling very heavy. He knew he had to keep running forward. Another round whizzed past dangerously closer than the last. Suddenly, a dull metal thud filled the air around him. He was knocked sideways by the force of something hitting him hard, almost forcing him to the ground. He didn't have time to check where he'd been hit, although he couldn't yet feel the dull pain that immediately comes from being shot. He couldn't stop for anything. He had to keep going.

He heard the crack of a nearby rifle as more bullet rounds flew past, travelling faster than the speed of sound, and only just inches away from his head. As he raced towards the children, he desperately tried to identify where the bullet rounds were coming from. After more rounds of fire, and with a huge surge of relief, Hart finally spotted the concealed position over to his forward right, roughly two o'clock from his current position.

Hart's would-be killer was firing at him from the base of a tree on the edge of the clearing. He was almost completely hidden from view, lying in the deep undergrowth. His large, bald head had helped to give his position away. As Hart drew closer with every desperate step, he could see that his would-be killer looked more like a South American Vin Diesel. The skin across his skull was now shining brightly in the early morning sun.

Two more bullet rounds, referred to as *lead hornets* by Hart, whizzed narrowly passed his left ear, far too close for comfort. His enemy's aim was improving with every shot.

Hart estimated that he had, at best, roughly ten seconds to get to the boy and girl and make good his escape before Vin Diesel finally homed in on him. Through the trees, Hart noticed that the FARC soldiers were beginning to properly organise themselves. They were now starting to lay down effective and organised suppressing fire; they were holding their own and hindering the advance of the JUNGLA police force.

The two children were still rooted to the spot in the middle of the clearing, like two small deer caught in the headlights of an oncoming car. Hart was a split second from reaching now, when suddenly the young boy's forehead erupted in front of him, blown into hundreds of fragments of blood-soaked brain matter that splattered across Valentina's face. The boy had been shot through the back of the head; a bullet round that had been intended for Hart had instead exited from the boy's forehead. He wasn't even aware that he had been hit. Just for a split second, the boy wore a look of complete surprise across his face, then his legs gave way, his lifeless body slumped towards the ground.

Valentina screamed and threw herself forward, trying to catch her friend's dead and crumpled body as it fell. Hart threw himself on top of the boy's dead body and the now hysterical Valentina, who crouched beside him. She screamed, frantically trying to push Hart away, but he pushed down on her with as much weight as he could whilst he returned rapid-fire towards the large tree. His aim was accurate enough to force the man to shift his position.

As Hart continued to fire, help came to hand. A section of the jungle suddenly disintegrated; it was Kav on the M134, blasting away. Vin Diesel didn't stand a chance.

Moments later, two JUNGLA officers with light machine guns (LMGs), who had been positioned at the edge of the jungle clearing, took out four more FARC soldiers who had moved into position to take aim at Hart.

Aware that he could not remain stationary for much longer, and acutely aware of the now almost catatonic girl pinned down underneath him, Hart planned his next move. He had to consider every angle of his vulnerable position. The JUNGLA officers were beginning to hurl grenades into the camp with nothing like the skilled aim of the US and UK trained Special Forces; indeed, as their fear escalated, the grenades began to rain down like confetti.

Hart lay as still as he could, exposed in the jungle clearing, returning fire towards the FARC soldiers. Kav's M134 was in overdrive, firing rapidly, almost 1000 rounds per minute. After only twenty seconds, the target area was almost completely decimated, devoid of any remaining vegetation. Any surviving FARC soldiers were now attempting to seek refuge by retreating into the deeper jungle. Kav ceased fire.

Hart took advantage of this lull in the fighting. He had spotted a large tree directly to his right. It stood ghost-like, the silent observer of the death and destruction below. Hart dragged Valentina up, carrying her full weight under his left arm as if she was a rag doll. As soon as he began running, the enemy fire started up again. Hart retaliated immediately by firing his M16 colt from the hip as he ran for cover, but before he could reach the sanctuary of the wide trunked tree, he felt a sudden sharp pain to his right shoulder. The pain was almost unbearable and sent an immediate burning sensation to his very core. He resisted the urge to stop and forced himself to keep running, aiming for the cover and protection of the tree.

Moments later, and against all the odds, Hart reached the tree. The tree was even larger than he'd thought, with the added advantage of having a deep natural hollow dip behind it; it was the perfect shelter. Throwing Valentina into the dip, he followed her and held her down with both hands. From their vantage point, Hart could see that many of the tents and cabins were now on fire. He could still hear screaming, but the sound of gunfire had subsided slightly. The main JUNGLA attack force had now moved well into the main camp, which meant that the operation would soon be over. The clean-up operation would then begin. This would be carried out by the clean-up troops who were already standing by, waiting to be airlifted into the camp.

They would bury the bodies and clean up the camp. Once the operation was over, the entire JUNGLA force, along with their joint US and UK support teams would call for an extraction from the jungle by the same Black Hawk helicopters that had dropped the attack force off the previous morning. The JUNGLA would leave the destroyed FARC camp behind them as if nothing had ever happened and return to civilization for a full debrief. Hart knew that with this type of JUNGLA mission—a 'search and destroy' operation—they would leave no one alive to tell the tale of what had happened; it didn't matter whether they were FARC soldiers or civilians, the JUNGLA would ensure there were no survivors.

Trying to ignore the excruciating pain in his shoulder, Hart was struggling to contain the Valentina, who was still kicking and screaming. He had to restrain her, but at the same time, he was afraid of hurting her by gripping her too tightly. Hart tried to gather his thoughts—despite the heat, his head felt icy cold.

Keeping one hand firmly on Valentina's upper arm, Hart looked at her and saw that she was staring at his shoulder. He looked down and saw that his camouflaged shirt was soaked in blood; the bloodstain was growing larger by the minute. Valentina was crying now.

"Valentina," Hart whispered, in a quiet and calm voice, despite the concern he was feeling inside. The girl immediately became still and silent upon hearing her name, stunned that her captor knew it.

"I'm going to let go of your arm, but you mustn't run. You'll be killed if you run. You speak English, right? Do you understand?"

Too startled to speak, Valentina simply looked up into Hart's mud-smeared face and nodded slowly.

"My name is John. I'm a British soldier and I've been sent by your mother to take you away from here. It's not safe here."

CHAPTER EIGHT

IN THE NEXT few vital moments, Zamora threw some clothes on, grabbed his AK47 and belt-kit and scrambled out of his tent. Outside was utter chaos; the air was filled with the sounds of gunfire, mingled with the shouts of soldiers on the run and the screams from those who had been hit and mortality injured.

As Zamora moved quickly towards the back of the camp where he had told Borgman to pitch his tent the previous afternoon, memories of the night before came flooding back to him. He remembered; he had told Borgman the formula. If that formula got into the wrong hands Zamora was dead. Why was the camp under attack now? How had they been discovered? Had they been spotted by the C-26 surveillance plane flying over the area a few months earlier? If that were so, then why had nothing happened after it had flown overhead, despite a week of fearful anticipation; he had assumed their camouflaged camp had not been spotted.

Upon reaching the spot where Borgman always erected his tent, Zamora cursed aloud. The Dutchman was gone! The bastard must have double-crossed them; the minute he'd got the formula, Borgman had fled the camp. How could he have been so stupid and blind? Borgman had turned on them. He had gone to the JUNGLA and planned to have Zamora taken out. So, who was Borgan going to sell the formula to? If Zamora survived this raid, the FARC secretariat would destroy him. If Zamora managed to escape from Colombia, he would never be safe. He would be on the run from the FARC and Ukrainians for as long as he walked this earth and breathed air.

Zamora spun around on the spot, searching for... who? His first thought was Valentina. Where was his daughter? He needed to find her. They would be lucky to get out of the camp alive. Paola could look after herself. He had feelings for her, but there would always be others if she died. For the first time, he fully understood the power of a blood tie to another human being. When he'd killed his father, he had cut off the bond with his mother, too. Even when Valentina was a baby, he was indifferent to her, but since she had become a little walking, talking person with a personality, with an attitude, his love for her had been overwhelming. Where was she?

Running towards him with O'Connor was his 2IC, Juan, together with Diego and Cesar. Other soldiers were beginning to emerge from their tents, frightened and in disarray. Through the trees, near the clearing and close to the crystallisation laboratory, Zamora could see small explosions from the grenades being thrown. There were bodies all around him on the ground. Despite guaranteed death, he went to running towards the centre of the clearing, shouting for Valentina.

Juan grabbed his arm. "No, Patrón, it's too late, we must go this way to get the guns."

"My daughter," Zamora shouted.

"She's gone," Juan told him, plainly. "The white soldier took her!"

Everything swam in front of Zamora's eyes for a moment. Then he was aware of O'Connor dragging him back towards the ammunition store at the rear of the camp.

"We're outnumbered," O'Connor was saying. "We have to get to the cave; let's hope it's inside whatever cordon the attackers will have probably set up."

When they had set up camp in this location, Zamora had given Juan the task of finding a remote hiding place. Being an expert tracker, Juan had found a cave that had probably once been the lair of a jungle predator. It was located about 150 metres from the camp. It was extremely difficult to spot by anyone who wasn't specifically looking for it. Apart from Juan, Zamora had shared the information with O'Connor, Paola and his three most senior officers. He had hidden provisions and weapons inside. It was their bunker to hide out in if ever the necessity arose.

Assuming Paola would make her own way there if she survived, and still reeling from the information that Valentina had been taken captive by whoever was assisting the JUNGLA, Zamora followed O'Connor and the others to the cave. They would have to hide out there until at least nightfall, when the JUNGLA forces would probably leave after clearing the camp... leaving no survivors.

The cave was halfway up a small hill next to a dried-up ancient gorge, its entrance concealed by a fallen tree. Zamora sent nineteen-year-old Diego inside to check for snakes. He was the youngest and newest recruit and had tagged along with them as they made their way to the cave. As soon as Diego gave the all-clear, the small group slid under the tree trunk and into the cave mouth of impenetrable damp blackness. There was little space, but comfort was the last thing on anyone's mind.

This was survival.

Once they were inside the cave, Cesar told Zamora he was fairly sure he saw Paola lying dead in a ditch.
Zamora spent the next hour whittling a groove into the side of the cave wall with his knife, imagining it was the gut of the man who had shot Paola.

***

Valentina took a moment to process what Hart was telling her and then a word sprang to her lips.

"Mamá," she whispered, trembling from head to toe.

Hart shook his head. "I'm sorry, we can't save your mother now. Hopefully, she will find her own way to safety and then come and find you." Hart tried to sound convincing, despite knowing any chance of Valentina's mother living through this attack was slim at best. "For now, you stay with me and do everything I tell you to do. Do you understand?"

"Yes," Valentina replied, her eyes filled with tears and confusion.

Hart released his grip on Valentina's arm. She immediately made a break for it and started to scramble out of the hollow. She got halfway up the slope before Hart caught her ankle and dragged her back. She screamed and tried to kick him.

"Valentina, no!" Hart warned her, holding her with both hands, ignoring the searing pain in his right shoulder. "You have to stay here and listen to me, or you will die. Do you understand? You will die."

The little girl narrowed her eyes, staring at Hart defiantly.

"You killed my friend Alejandro," she hissed, angrily. Hart shook his head emphatically.

"I didn't kill your friend. You saw me. I came to save you both."

"Then who killed Alejandro?" Valentina continued angrily "One of your friends, I think."

"No, Valentina. No chance. My men would never kill a child. He was shot by one of the soldiers inside the camp. You have to trust me, Valentina."

Valentina frowned at him. "How do you know my name?" she asked.

Staring deep into her eyes, Hart sensed that there was no point in telling her any half-truths. He didn't have much experience with children, so the best approach was to treat Valentina as if she was an adult. He didn't know how to speak kid language.

"Your mother is Paola Sanchez. She contacted my boss through some people who were helping her. She wanted us to get you out of the camp. She knew there would be an attack on the camp, and she asked us to make sure we got you out safely." Hart watched Valentina's face closely. Suddenly something seemed to dawn on her. Her demeanour changed, she immediately seemed calmer and more resolved to her situation. She nodded her head slowly.

"My mamá said one day I would have to be very brave and help some people by telling them everything she taught me. What is going to happen now?"

Hart didn't know, but he didn't want to admit that, so he stalled for time by turning his attention to his injury. He opened his shirt for a closer inspection. A bullet round had torn effortlessly through the soft tissue and buried itself into the back of Hart's right shoulder. There was now a sizable coating of blood on the jungle floor where he knelt, a slick, thick liquid. Hart's blood. Considering the sprint across the open ground he had just made; it was a miracle that was the only injury he had sustained. Although there appeared to be no exit wound, Hart prayed that the round hadn't lodged itself too deeply in his shoulder. Hart knew the bullet round was domed, shaped to fly fast and enter the human body to achieve maximum damage. Each one was fashioned to kill. Thankfully that hadn't happened just yet, but even so, out here in the jungle he knew his chances of survival were slim at best if the wound became infected. He could only try to stem the blood flow and hope to be extracted out of the jungle as soon as possible. Hart knew that he needed to come up with an action plan, and fast. He had to figure out how to get himself and Valentina back to his SAS team. His unavoidable dash to save the girl had caused him to become dangerously exposed on the right flank of the attack. Furthermore, Hart could no longer hear the distinctive noise of the M134; his team was probably now part of the main attack force and well and truly in the thick of things.

***

Paola was, in fact, far from dead. After witnessing her daughter being scooped up by the British agent as planned, she had run for her life. She knew that the deal she'd made with the British was a huge risk for them, mainly because the plan to rescue Valentina had to be kept secret from both the JUNGLA and the Americans. Paola had not been able to make any kind of similar deal with the British assuring her own protection, so now she was well and truly on her own. Her plan was to head for the jungle village of Pogue and await news. If she made it, there was a chance she'd see Valentina again. This was enough to boost her survival instinct.

She now headed towards the ditch located roughly 100 metres from the camp. She had prepared it the previous week without Zamora's knowledge. She'd made it deep and covered it with vegetation, under which she could hopefully remain hidden until the attack was over. She was aware that her chances of survival were slim at best, but at least Valentina was hopefully now safe.

Paola was only about 20 metres away from the ditch when a huge force careered into her, throwing her on to the ground and knocking her AK-47 from her hands. Lying face down in the dirt, the air knocked from her lungs, she felt the body of a huge man pressing down on top of her, pinning her to the ground. There was a tightness in her throat. She could not get air into her lungs; it was as if they were surrounded by metal bands. With all her strength she tried to wriggle out from under the man on top of her, but he was too heavy. He had clamped a massive hand over her mouth. She tried to reach back and scratch at him, but he grabbed her arm with his other spare hand before she could reach him.

"Relax! Relax, Paola. It's me, Borgman." a voice hissed at her.

Paola allowed her body to go limp and Borgman released his hold on her. She turned to look up at him. He was now kneeling over her on all fours. His face was contorted; he was clearly in great pain.

"What's wrong with you?" she asked, urgently.

"My ankle!" he whispered in pain. I've twisted it badly. He rolled over onto his back and lay on the ground. Paola looked up and around them, for signs of anyone who might have spotted or heard them.

"We can't stay here," she said, urgently. "It's too open. We will be spotted. I have a hiding place. Don't make too much noise. Follow me."

She picked up her AK-47 and its full magazine of bullet rounds that had detached itself from the rifle after hitting the ground. She then helped Borgman to his feet, who limped along beside her, leaning on her shoulder until they reached the ditch. Only when they were there and concealed did, she speak to him again.

"We have to stay here until nightfall and until the JUNGLA completely destroy the camp and leave."

"Where is your daughter?" Borgman asked her.

"Dead," Paola replied, instinctively. She knew that no one connected to Zamora could ever know about Valentina's true whereabouts and the knowledge she held. Borgman stared at her, shocked, and fell silent for a moment, as a mark of respect.

"Zamora, too, I assume," Borgman finally said.

"Maybe," said Paola. "Or maybe he made it to the cave."

Borgman looked visibly shocked. "What cave?" he mouthed at her.

"He prepared a place where he and some of his trusted inner circle could hide... in case of an attack like this," Paola whispered back.

"Do you know where this cave is?" Borgman asked, urgently.

"Yes, of course, but it's too dangerous to go there. Listen, this is my chance to escape from him. I hate him. I'm heading for Pogue. I will be safe there. I will hide there for a while. Even if he survives the attack, I don't believe he will come looking for me there."

Borgman took Paola by the arms, quite forcefully.

"Paola, listen to me," he said, urgently. "You have to show me where the cave is. If Zamora lives, he will find me and kill me."

"Why?" Paola asked, surprised at this news. Borgman paused a moment before speaking.

"Paola... I can't explain everything to you but...I've not always been loyal to Zamora. He will know this by now. If he survives, he will stop at nothing until he kills me. He has information, and that information can't get into the wrong hands. It's vital that I confirm if he's dead. We must go to this cave and make certain. You know how to track in the jungle, I just can't do it without you."

Whilst Paola was well aware of most of these facts, Borgman's involvement was news to her. Why hadn't she been informed that he was part of the operation? Perhaps he wasn't telling her the whole truth. She thought it best to play dumb for the time being. She stared at him, wide-eyed and he assumed her look was due to the shock of finding out that he had betrayed Zamora. In fact, the look on Paola's face was also prompted by something else.

Something Borgman had said had highlighted a major problem that she had overlooked. How had she been so stupid? What if Zamora had survived the attack? She should have found him during the attack and killed him herself to ensure he died rather than leave it to chance, even if that had put her own life in jeopardy. If Zamora was alive, Borgman was not the only life that would be in mortal danger. She had to help Borgman. Together they would have to ensure Zamora was dead and if not, kill him themselves. It had not been part of the original plan, but now she saw she had no choice. She and Valentina would never be left to live in peace if Zamora was not dead.

***

Hart held the radio handset and attempted to contact Bob for an urgent update. "Sierra One Zero Alpha, Sierra Zero Alpha, request urgent sitrep, over," Hart repeated the radio call a few more times, with no response received. Although he knew communications were patchy and poor at best, the usual static noise from across the radio airways was distinctly absent. Hart peered down at the small AN/PRC-152 patrol radio he carried on his belt-kit and inspected it. He could now clearly see that the radio had taken a direct hit, and as a result, it had inadvertently saved his life. The dull metal sounding noise he had heard earlier whilst running across the clearing must have been from a stray bullet round smashing into his patrol radio. Hart had no doubt that had it not been for his radio, he would have suffered a very slow, agonising, and painful end.

Hart turned his attention back to Valentina. "Before we can move, I've got to take care of this wound," he winced in pain. He had already lost a significant amount of blood and was beginning to feel weak. "Can you help me get my medical pack from this pouch," Hart asked, pointing to a small right-hand pouch on his belt-kit. "I need you to help me patch this mess up," explained Hart. Valentina looked worried, but obediently retrieved the small medical pack Hart urgently needed. Under his instruction, Valentina helped Hart place a dressing and bandage over the wound to help stem the blood flow. Looking at Valentina, Hart wished he could have done more to save this young girl and her friend; his whole life had been dedicated to saving lives— in an attempt to redeem himself for his past mistakes—but he had failed yet again, and now he could potentially end his days here, in the middle of the rotting and stinking hot Colombian jungle.

Valentina kept looking up at him, expectantly. He knew he had to tell her something. Anything.

"Right, Valentina, we'll set off in a minute. Just let me rest here for a moment longer. I just need to close my eyes to think things through properly."

Hart closed his eyes and allowed himself to drift. What a life! Was this it? He had always hoped he'd die with no regrets, but the regrets were stacking up faster than his racing heartbeat. What would become of him? Was death simply the eternal sleep or was there something more? There was no more pain, he felt quite peaceful. Curious even. As he slowly slipped into unconsciousness, the faces that haunted and visited him most nights in the company of his good old friend Jack Daniels, began to swim into his vision: faces from his past with piercing and accusing eyes.

Was it his father's face he saw or was it, Paddy or Kevin's face? All three of them were now dead. Now the image of Kevin running towards the edge of the wooded area forced its way into his blurred vision. This was John Hart's final thought before he blacked out.

***

A week before the end of the deer stag culling season, John Hart and his best friend Kevin Morrison were invited to join six adult members from their local gun club one Saturday morning to attend a shoot being held on the Ormsary Estate—a beautiful 7,500-hectare stretch of land rising from the shore of Loch Coalisport, 560 metres to the central ridge of Knapdale.

When they arrived at the estate (a two-hour drive from Glasgow) the group were briefed by the owners and told that they could only shoot a maximum of eight stags (one each) as long as none of those stags appeared to be too thin. It was John and Kevin's first live shoot and they were determined not to go home empty handed.

The group split into three smaller groups. John and Kevin found themselves accompanied by Dave Allen, one of the key members of the gun club. They received the regulation ammunition for their high-powered rifles (muzzle velocity of 2,450 feet/second and minimum muzzle energy of 1,750-foot-pounds) and set off with instructions to meet back at the main house at 3 pm.

After an hour of walking through the narrow glen and eventually reaching the summit of a hillside, John, Kevin, and Dave got their first sighting of the red deer. The mist rested softly on the mountain peaks like a cloth draped over a pillow. The mountains rose on the horizon, sheer rock striking down from snowy peaks above. The sun tried to break through the gathering of dark grey clouds. There were so many valleys and glens that one could easily become lost. This was the ancient land of the Celts and their presence could almost be felt, as if it surrounded the very fabric of the land they now stood upon.

Down the other side of the hill, and on the edge of some woodland, stood around twenty deer and two large stags. Kevin asked if they should target one of the stags from their current vantage point, but the ever-competitive Dave suggested they had a better chance of shooting both stags if they split up and approached them from three different directions. He told the boys that he'd take out the first stag, the larger one, and then John and Kevin could take their chances with the second one as the herd took flight, startled by the first shot. Dave said it would be great practice for John and Kevin to try to hit a moving, live target.

Kevin offered to go back down the way they had come, then into the nearby woods and around the edge of the wooded area to take a position below the herd. Dave said he would move further along the ridge of the hill and then follow it downwards in order to cover the far side of where the animals were grazing. He told John to stay put and cover the herd from the ridge above.

After about fifteen minutes, John watched Dave take position behind a rocky outcrop below. The day had started out dark and overcast, but now it produced a downpour as heavy as John had ever seen. The thick sheets of rain washed over him and obscured his vision.

The deer moved slowly, grazing as they went. Even with the

rain relentlessly pouring over them, hammering the ground, the slightest foreign noise would cause them to be up and alert, black eyes staring in more directions than any human predator could ever hope to achieve. John raised his rifle and took aim, making sure he had the smaller stag in the crosshair of his scope. About a minute later, a shot rang out. The largest deer fell, and the others bolted. John, compromised by the now-heavy rainfall, suddenly lost his mark on the smaller stag. He looked up and over his rifle to see where the deer were heading; they were running towards the woods. The second stag was almost at the tree line. John lined the stag up in his crosshair again and followed it as it entered the trees. At one point he thought he'd lost it, but then he got it back again; he followed it as it moved between the trees. John knew time was running out and instinctively fired. As the sound of John's shot rang out, another sound mingled with it... an ear-piercing scream. John raced down the hillside and into the woods. Dave approached rapidly from the other direction.

John had shot Kevin in the back!

CHAPTER NINE

ART had slowly regained consciousness and had been helped to his feet by Valentina. He was now moving through the jungle heading east, negotiating the undergrowth as best and as silently as he could. Valentina followed him closely behind, constantly looking back at the clouds of dark smoke and flames that now erupted from the camp, rising up above the jungle's canopy like a huge serpent. The thick grey smoke billowed up into the skies and choked the air, spreading a veil of darkness across the jungle. Hart could recognise the putrid smell of burning wood mixed with human flesh. Suddenly, a huge roar erupted, and Valentina watched helplessly as an enormous plume of fire exploded, covering the buildings connected with drug manufacturing in a deadly fireball. The fire leapt up, picking up speed like a fast-flowing river, the flames rolling outwards and upwards in a mushroom cloud. The heat was oppressive even from just over one hundred metres away and threatened to burn their lungs. This was not just fire. It was death.

Hart had discovered a stray bullet round had smashed into his M16 colt, destroying the plastic covering around its stock before ricocheting into his right shoulder. He hadn't had the opportunity to test the weapon, but he was pretty sure that the damage would compromise the natural aim of the rifle. Fortunately, his Sig Sauer P226 9mm pistol, strapped to his right thigh for easy access, was reasonable back up if his M16 malfunctioned. Hart had also ensured that his knives were easily accessible; he still carried his trusted kukri, the traditional curved Gurkha knife, and his assault knife, the 10-inch Webster Marble Trailmaker, in his belt-kit. Whilst he was grateful that a bullet round had smashed into his patrol radio rather than its intended target—somewhere around Hart's hip or pelvic area—he was now also painfully aware that he and Valentina were completely isolated from the rest of Hart's team with no form of communication. Unless his instincts, combined with a decent dose of good luck, somehow led them to his team, or the Americans on the outer cordon, Hart realised he was pretty much on his own and up shit creek without a paddle.

Calculating that they were located on the far-left flank of the FARC's defence line, which was now in complete disarray, Hart had reasoned that their safest passage was to move due east. Although much of the working business end of the camp was now an inferno, the screaming, gunfire and explosions had started to abate slightly. Experience told Hart that this was only a sign that the enemy troops were reorganising themselves and was not, in any way, a suggestion that they were somehow safer than before.

Valentina's demeanour remained stoic. Since Hart had come around in the dip by the tree with her staring down at him, telling him that they had to move, she had followed his every instruction. If she continued in this vein, at least his efforts wouldn't be too far compromised, Hart surmised, with relief. About ten minutes ago, the challenge of getting a screaming, terrified ten-year-old out of the jungle alive had presented Hart with possibly his hardest task to date. Now it was like having a well-trained dog by his side. She stood still on his command, kept completely silent and followed his instructions.

If only he could feel sufficiently confident in what he was instructing her to do.

Almost an hour later, after battling through the thick and unrelenting jungle undergrowth in an easterly direction without successfully locating the outer cordon, Hart decided his best bet now was to try and locate the cordon troops positioned at the southern edge of the camp. Taking Valentina's hand, he changed their direction and began leading them on a south-west heading. His lungs heaved in air, but it was more like drowning than breathing. The moisture was so thick that sweating had become obsolete, it just ran warmly into Hart's already drenched clothes, only achieving further dehydration.

Hart paused and reached for the water-bottle he carried on his belt-kit, taking a swig of water before then offering a drink of the life-saving liquid to Valentina. He then took out his compass and studied his map and let out a long sigh; he wasn't confident he had pinpointed their current position correctly.

He set off again and after five minutes travelling in the same direction, Hart thought he heard voices ahead of them. It just didn't make sense. The cordon troops were some of the best professional soldiers in the world and would never give their position away by openly talking. He had no way of communicating with them given the recent demise of his patrol radio. They had no choice, they would have to proceed with the caution and move slowly, hoping to avoid being mistaken for escaping FARC and engaged by the outer security cordon.

Hart suddenly stopped in his tracks, causing Valentina to bump into his back. Hart spun around and signalled to Valentina to crouch down and remain absolutely still and quiet. Hart listened intently, trying his best to locate where the voices were coming from up ahead, but he now couldn't hear them anymore. All he could hear was the general distant chatter of birds and monkeys in the trees above. As they crouched in the undergrowth, Hart could make out what looked like a small clearing up ahead of them. The trees were definitely thinning out and there were big pools of sunlight beginning to break through the overhead canopy.

Just as Hart was starting to think he'd imagined the voices and was preparing to give Valentina the signal to move, he heard them once again. This time the sound was clearer. They were probably no more than 40 metres ahead. There was definitely a group of men whispering, and the voices were clear enough to make out a few words.

However, none of them were Spanish... or English. In fact, the longer he listened, the more he was sure that it was not a language he'd ever heard before. Suddenly, he saw movement between the trees ahead of them. He realised whoever it was, must be up ahead in what looked like a small clearing.

Hart looked behind him. Valentina was crouching close to the jungle floor, curled up, as small as she could make herself, just as Hart had instructed her to do if they came across any movements or noises they didn't recognise. She looked up at him. With his hands, he indicated that she should stay there whilst he crept forward to investigate further. To Hart's astonishment, she smiled and stood up. He frantically waved his hands at her, trying to get her to crouch down again, but she simply walked forward. Hart grabbed her arm, but she turned to face him and gave him a look of defiance, whilst slowly shaking her head. Instinctively, he let her go. Their roles reversed, she now indicated to Hart that he should stay still whilst she investigated. He paused for a moment, but as soon as Valentina turned and moved towards the clearing, he followed her, a few paces behind.

Eventually, Hart got a clear view into the clearing where he saw four natives: *Emberá Indian* tribesmen of varying ages crouching on the ground. They were clearly on a hunting trip, each of them holding a huge bow and arrow that they now aimed in the direction of Hart and Valentina. On the ground in front of these men was an array of blowpipes and poison darts, along with a number of deadly looking spears. The surprise of this sight had temporarily taken Hart's focus off Valentina and by the time he realised what was happening, she was walking straight out into the open clearing—it was too late to stop her!

Instinct told Hart to trust that Valentina—a native to these parts and clearly not a naïve girl—knew what she was doing. He stood, partially hidden, and watched.

Valentina walked, calmly but purposefully towards the men. She walked like someone who'd been in the armed services, there was a marching quality to it. She held her shoulders back and upright, with her head steady. When she was a few metres away from the men, she sank to her knees and bowed her head low, in a mark of respect. She eventually looked up and spoke to them, conversing fluently in their language. Hart watched, his heart pounding. The men were dressed only in loincloths, their chests covered with intricate necklaces made of colourful wooden beads. All of them had the traditional bowl haircut. Their bodies were almost completely covered by patterns drawn in black painted dye, giving the men a ferocious look.

Hart reached down his body with his right hand until he located the safety clip belonging to his revolver pouch. He closed his hand around the 9mm Sig pistol, ready to use it if there was any trouble. Valentina seemed to be having a friendly-looking conversation with the men, who had lowered their bows and arrows, but Hart wasn't taking any chances.

After the short discussion, Valentina came back to where Hart was hidden. She stood and looked at Hart's startled expression for a moment before bursting out laughing.

"Mr John, you can't be a soldier and look so scared. You look like a girl. Remember, I am the girl and you are the soldier." Hart replaced his startled look with one of mild irritation. "It's okay. You can come out. Put away your weapon. These men will help us."

"What did you tell them?" Hart asked, edging forward into the clearing, aware of being stared at intently by the Indian men.

"That you are my friend. I told them not to harm you. They are from the *Emberá* tribe. My grandmother came from this tribe, so I learnt their language. I am good at learning languages."

"No kidding," Hart muttered as he now fully emerged from the jungle, blinking in the sharp sunlight that was flooding the clearing, still a little apprehensive of the huntsmen, even though they had lowered their weapons.

"I told them that my family's camp had been attacked by Government troops and my mother had sent a white man to take me to safety. I told them you saved my life and so now they believe you are a good man. They heard the noise of the battle and were getting ready to defend themselves. Because I am from their tribe, they will help me. Because you saved my life, they will help you. They do not like white men, they do not trust them because they steal their land, but they trust me. Come on, they will take us to their village where they will give you medicine for your wound."

Nonplussed, but very warily, Hart continued to follow Valentina. It seemed ominously quiet now. Even the sound of their own footfalls sounded silent, all that could be heard were the sounds of dead, weak trees, creaking at every push of the gentle wind blowing through the jungle clearing.

On closer inspection, the native huntsmen seemed to be smirking at him, as if finding the fact that a ten-year-old local girl issuing instructions to a soldier a highly amusing scenario. Which, Hart had to admit, it was.

The huntsmen looked Hart up and down before collecting their belongings lying on the ground. They motioned to Valentina that she and Hart should follow them, before turning and leading the way out of the clearing. The huntsmen moved swiftly through the primary jungle, moving like ribbons in the gentle wind, flowing in graceful arcs, limbs in constant motion. Elegance at its finest, even though they were carrying their cumbersome weapons; Hart and Valentina struggled to keep up. Whilst he couldn't be sure without taking out his map and compass, Hart had a feeling that they were travelling towards the Río Atrato.

An hour or so later, they reached the next valley. Only when he saw the muddy stream did Hart realise how thirsty he was. Telling Valentina to ask the huntsmen to wait for him, he stopped to refill his water-bottle. The native men looked on with amusement as Hart took a water purification tablet from a pouch on his belt-kit and dissolved it in his water-bottle before drinking its contents a few moments later. He didn't want to take any chances; his body's defence mechanisms were already stretched with his bullet wound. He had no idea how much longer he would be able to hold up; the pain was almost unbearable. He was beginning to feel cold and weak again; it came in waves. He hoped they were going to reach the village soon.

They followed the small stream southwards as it wound its way through the jungle. The water was a turbid brown from the eroding banks it passed by. It was lax by nature and languid in pace, eventually growing wider and deeper as it transformed into a main tributary belonging to the Río Atrato. This gave Hart hope, he knew the river eventually led to the Utría National Park where there was a rangers' station, which was one of the designated alternative ERV's in his team's Escape & Evasion scenario.

After walking for what felt like half a day, they finally picked up an animal trail. The path was lined with thick tree roots. The light that beamed through the tree foliage above was green and warm. The path swerved back and forth unpredictably, remarkably clear for one so rarely travelled within the depths of the Colombian jungle. Mighty trees arched over it. Hart knew this understated path was the only way to secure help and eventual freedom. The jungle foliage was reasonably trampled down and made their progress easier. Hart was aware that he was running out of time. They had to stop a couple of times to rest.

The native Indians shared their dried meat rations with Hart and Valentina. Whilst they rested, Hart asked Valentina to check on the medical dressing and his wound. He was afraid of infection. He had no idea what supplies would be found in the village. He was beginning to feel his chances of survival were becoming slimmer as time went on, but giving up now was not an option, he had been trained to push on until the very end.

He remembered part of the verse by the English novelist, James Elroy Flecker, which the SAS always liked to quote:

"We are the Pilgrims, master; we shall go always a little further."

Finally, they arrived at another clearing. This was where the huntsmen's village was located. Groups of children came running up to the group as they appeared. At first, they were simply happy to see the huntsmen return home, but on sighting Valentina and Hart, their eyes grew wide with fear and awe.

The "village" was a campsite typical of the *Emberá Indians*, who were a nomadic tribe known to move camp three or four times a year, always ensuring they were close to water and wildlife for hunting.

Hart slowly sank to his knees; he could not move another step as his legs simply gave way. He slumped forward onto his hands and held himself off the floor on all fours for a moment before finally giving in to gravity and rolling over to lie on this back.

The last thing Hart remembered staring up into the faces of many mesmerised children.

When Hart later opened his eyes, he found Valentina staring down at him, grinning. "You're alive, Mr John. The medicine man saved your life."

Hart attempted to sit up but the pain in his right shoulder was too great. He slumped back down again on the woven rug he was lying on and looked at his shoulder. It was bound in a bandage of banana leaves, with some foul-smelling paste oozing out of the sides. Valentina brought her hand in front of Hart's face. Between her forefinger and thumb, she was holding a flat-nosed 7.62mm round.

"The medicine man pulled this from your wound. You lost a lot of blood. You're lucky." She paused a moment and her smile slipped. "Me too." Then with pain etched across her face. "I hope my mamá is alive."

"How long have I been asleep?" Hart asked groggily, purposefully changing the subject.

"A very long time," Valentina said in a laboured tone, sounding almost in awe of a man's ability to sleep so long. "Since yesterday afternoon. Without waking up. You had a bad fever."

"Yesterday afternoon?" Hart's mind was swimming as he tried to focus on what his next move needed to be. "What time is it now?"

"The middle of the day." Valentina informed him. "Are you hungry? I can get you something to eat." She leapt up. Hart slowly rolled over, trying once again to pull himself up to a seated position using his good arm. His head was pounding, as he accepted the pain.

"No, we must go. We'll take some food with us."

"No, Mr John," Valentina said sternly. "You are not strong enough yet. We must wait here another day."

Hart looked on the floor around him. He made a mental inventory of his equipment. Everything seemed to be there.

"I have not been apart from you," Valentina said darkly, "Nothing has been taken." She handed him his lightweight camouflage shirt that had seen much better days. It had been washed and dried in the sun. "These are good people."

"Of course, they are," Hart said, getting Valentina to help him pull the shirt over his head. "I'm truly grateful to them, but we must keep moving. We can't afford to stay here any longer."

With a little difficulty, and help form Valentina, Hart got to his feet.

Valentina passed him a cup of water. "Here drink," she instructed.

"Thank you," Hart said quietly before thirstily gulping down the welcomed water. He looked around the hut. It was simple but immaculate and perfectly organised. Two sides of the room were closed in with walls made of bamboo, and two sides were open to allow air to flow through the building, although at this time huge cloth awnings had been hung up to keep the room suitably dark for the wounded Hart. There were two hammocks slung from thick wooden tree trunks, but they were clearly not suitable for a man in Hart's position, which is why he'd been laid out to rest on the floor, on a pile of rugs.

Hart rested a hand on Valentina's shoulder as he drank the tepid water. He felt light-headed and nauseous. At least, for once, there was a logical, physical explanation for this feeling.

Valentina helped Hart up and out of the wooden hut; it was raised off the ground and they had to climb down a large log that had grooves cut in it for foot holes. Once outside, Hart blinked several times in the brilliant strong sunlight. His shoulder felt as though a red-hot poker was being pushed through it, but he didn't want to share this with Valentina. It was imperative that they get moving.

On seeing Hart, a young boy shouted something and came running over. Within seconds, Hart was surrounded by a large number of villagers... mostly women and children. A quick scan of heads told him that there were around forty women and children surrounding him; he correctly deduced that most of the men were out hunting.

The group were visibly excited and were cheering, whooping, clapping, and stamping their feet. There was a palpable excitement buzzing through the charged air, with infectious grins and a spontaneous outpouring of emotion being visibly shown toward Hart. A woman reached out and tugged Hart's shirt. She said something in her native language and then patted her chest. She repeated this a couple of times until Hart realised what she was trying to say.

"You washed my shirt? Thank you, thank you," he said, placing his palms together in a symbol of gratitude and slightly bowing his head to the woman.

Breathing through the pain that was rapidly intensifying, Hart took in his surroundings. The village consisted of around twenty thatched-roofed huts, built on stilts to protect the dwellings from wild animals and flooding. Like the hut he'd woken up in, Hart observed that each abode had only two solid walls, the other two sides having been left open to help circulate the stiflingly hot air. In the centre of the village stood a largish looking building and the only one that was at ground level. Hart assumed that this was a communal space for the tribe's daily activities. It was now out of that building that a relatively tall man now emerged. He was looking to see what all the commotion was about. On seeing Hart, the man walked over quickly, gesturing and speaking rapidly. He wore a brown loincloth and had strings of brightly coloured beads interspersed with carved wooden charms around his neck. He carried a long wooden staff that he used as a walking stick. This was clearly the medicine man and he was not best pleased that his patient was out of bed.

He roughly pushed past the women and children who were surrounding Hart and Valentina and started to speak sternly to Hart. Valentina translated.

"He says you must go back inside and lie down immediately. He has given you very strong medicine. It is working in your body right now and you will be very sick and very sorry if you don't go and lie down right now." Valentina explained rapidly to Hart.

As if on cue, Hart gave in to the excruciating pain that was gripping his entire body. He bent double, threw up and then sank to his knees.

The last thing he saw before passing out for the third time in less than 24 hours was the angry face of the medicine man and the very worried face of Valentina.

CHAPTER TEN

THE ONLY PERSON in the jungle who had possibly experienced a more uncomfortable night than Hart was Jose Posada Zamora. Holed up in the dark, damp cave, with four other men, Zamora had not slept a wink, going over and over in his mind how he had managed to lose everything he cared about in the space of just a few hours.

He looked out at the fallen tree and rocks obscuring the entrance to the cave. Thick green foliage, like shadowy arms, stretched across the mouth of the ancient cave, winding across the fallen tree and helping to conceal the jagged opening of the entrance. On entering the cave, Zamora and the others had immediately been engulfed in chilling blackness. His eyes had eventually become accustomed to the oppressive blanket of darkness. Underfoot the loose stones constantly shifted with every movement, and the noise of disturbed rocks echoed off the dense stone walls. Somewhere ahead in the darkness was the sound of dripping water.

They were certain that the JUNGLA forces would have left by nightfall, but as they would have made very little progress moving back to the remains of the camp in the darkness, and wary of the possibility that the JUNGLA might have left a surprise rear party ambush to catch anyone trying to return, they had decided to wait it out until the morning.

A few hours after they'd reached the cave the day before, they had heard the swooping sound of the Black Hawk helicopter's blades overhead. They had listened closely and speculated as to how many helicopters were above them— seven, maybe eight, they had estimated. The helicopters had hovered for the few minutes it had taken for all the troops to be inserted into the jungle and then the sounds of the powerful blades had faded away. Then had come the wait—it had felt like an eternity but was actually only around four hours—before the Black Hawks had returned to pick up the teams. The extraction had taken no longer than twenty minutes before the noise of the Black Hawks had once again faded away into the distance. A few minutes after that, all had fallen still and silent in the jungle again. The other men had eventually drifted off to sleep, but the thought of sleep was the furthest thing from Zamora's mind.

Now his men were stirring. Zamora had spent the night listening to snoring and farting; he was desperate to get free of this place. He motioned for Diego, to leave the cave and check that the coast was clear. Diego had eagerness where he lacked brains. He was useful in that he was dispensable. He had been born into the FARC, but his mother had died of complications during childbirth and his father, a rather uninspiring officer, had died from malaria when Diego was fifteen. Ever since, he had clung to Zamora, viewing him as some sort of father figure. There was a nervous energy about Diego; he was immature and impulsive.

Diego was back in the cave after about twenty minutes giving the signal that it was all clear. The men gathered the backpacks containing supplies—basic food rations, weapons, ammunition, water and maps—that had been stored in the cave and then crawled out, blinking in the early morning sunlight. They still took care not to make any sound and remained silent and vigilant as they made their way back towards the camp. There was still no guarantee that the area was completely clear of JUNGLA troops.

As soon as they reached the camp's perimeter, they dropped to the ground to carry out their own surveillance, lying side-by-side on their bellies, watching for any signs of movement.

The camp had been gutted. The tents had all been torn down, the constructed wooden huts—that had once housed the crystallisation laboratory and the preparation rooms—had been burnt to the ground, and all the drums that had contained acetone solvent and hydrochloric acid lay on their sides, empty. What suddenly felt odd was that there were no dead bodies.

The JUNGLA clean-up team had been exceptionally thorough in their remit to sanitise the place. What had they actually done with the bodies? Zamora was trying to push the image of Paola's dead body from his mind. At least there was a chance Valentina was still alive. If the white soldier had harmed her in any way, Zamora vowed to subject the man to a drawn-out and exceptionally painful death.

After watching the camp for almost twenty minutes, Zamora was satisfied that it was as deserted as it looked. It had less charm than a city graveyard, at least those places were built out of sentimentality and love. This place had been built through supply and demand and sheer ambition. It had been brutally abandoned by the JUNGLA without a backwards glance.

As they got up and moved towards the smouldering remains of their old home, they remained vigilant. There was an eerie silence as if the animals had also deserted this place of death and destruction. The air was still, and the only noise came from the crackling of wood as it disintegrated in the smoking embers. Zamora shook from head to toe with rage. Here were six months of hard work destroyed in a matter of hours.

The men fanned out to search the camp and after another ten minutes, Cesar, who had been searching the north-west perimeter of the camp gave the call to signal he had found something. This was a native call designed to sound exactly like a birdcall; the native Indians used them all the time. Some sounded like other animal sounds, such as monkeys screeching, but they all had a particular purpose. The call Cesar gave told the others that he had found something of interest, and it didn't look good.

Zamora, Diego and Colm soon joined Cesar on the edge of the clearing where they saw with their own eyes what could only be described as a makeshift burial ground. It was clear that the ground had recently been disturbed to accommodate a large pit. There were probably more than fifty bodies buried under there. Had anyone else escaped? Zamora was half thinking of digging up the bodies and identifying them, mostly wanting to see Paola one last time, when Juan arrived at the scene.

"Patrón, I've found something. Come and see," he said to Zamora. Not only was Juan the 2IC of the camp, but he was also an expert tracker. Zamora had tasked him with finding any tracks that might tell him what had become of the white soldier and his daughter. Were they lifted out of the jungle or did they escape on foot?

Juan, who had seen the soldier take Valentina, insisted that the man had looked in pretty bad shape. He looked like he had been wounded during yesterday's gun battle. What if Valentina was on her own or, worse, had been killed by the clean-up team? Zamora pictured his daughter's body lying at the top of the pile of corpses as dirt was shovelled back into the pit. The thought of this tortured Zamora as he followed Juan to a large tree on the edge of the clearing.

"What can you see, Juan?" Zamora asked, climbing into the large hole after Juan, who crouched down at the base of the tree.

"There, Patrón," Juan said, pointing to something on the ground.

Although they were now a day old, the footprints were clear, even to an untrained eye. The moss covering the tree trunk was bright green, except for a large patch that was covered in a dried brown substance. Juan picked some off and rubbed it between his fingers.

He smelt it.

"The soldier's blood for sure," he said, looking at Zamora, whose heart was beating hard in his chest now.

Juan pointed east into the depths of the jungle. "The *rastro* they have left goes that way. They are moving slowly. As I thought, the solider appears to be badly injured. There is a lot of blood, here, too." He pointed to the ground where there were obvious signs of dried blood mingled with the mud and undergrowth. Zamora looked in the direction that Juan had indicated the soldier had taken his daughter. His heart leapt. She was alive! If they were on foot, perhaps they had avoided the JUNGLA troops.

"We will follow you, Juan. Lead the way. Come, we must move fast, there is no time to waste! I want to find this *soldado sangriento* and make him pay. We must get my daughter!" He looked around the group. "Juan you lead, and I will follow you. Then Diego and Cesar. Colm you bring up the rear." The men nodded their agreement and quickly set off in their given order of march, Zamora praying that they might yet be able to close the gap.

Juan moved as quickly as he could, making sure he did not lose the *rastro*. He had been taught how to track by his grandfather. When, as a young boy, Juan had shown an interest in tracking, his grandfather had taught him everything possible about the native art. Juan had an expert eye; no detail escaped him. He could tell, from the shape and depth of a footprint, the exact size and shape of a person or animal, and even whether they walked with a limp.

Secretly, Juan wished that one of the other members of the group knew how to track. Several times he had suggested training some of the younger FARC soldiers, but this idea usually fell on deaf ears. Although, there had been one FARC soldier who had shown an eagerness to learn the skills of tracking. She had proven to be a natural, becoming a competent tracker in no time. Juan suspected though, like the many others from the camp, she had probably found her fateful end at the bottom of the large burial pit.

This was going to be hard work to accomplish on his own, especially as midday quickly approached and the lack of shadow would make it harder to see the depth of the imprints. Juan broke off a nearby branch to use as a pointer, to be used when he wanted to point out parts of the trail to Zamora. His leader was impatient, but Juan could not track any faster. To pick up some pace, at some points he ignored the *rastro* at his feet and tracked ahead where possible, listening for bird or animal alarms that might indicate movement or presence of humans up ahead. Where the trail was faint, Juan used every possible indicator he could find, such as sand on rocks and upturned leaves— indicating that it had been deposited there by an animal or person. The other men followed dutifully behind him, remaining on high alert.

Juan remained vigilant for the possibility of trickery and deception. In the past he had come across men who had turned towards the water to cover their trail and those who had climbed into the jungle canopy above, moving from tree to tree in the opposite direction from the trail they had been following. Some had hidden underwater or underground in a wild animal's burrow. Some had even tried wearing shoes that had been tied on backwards; others had walked backwards or on the sides of their feet. One group he had tracked had tried to outsmart him by tying cattle hooves onto their feet. In his experience, unless the men were highly experienced trackers themselves and understood where the weaknesses in tracking lay, these attempts at deception only served to mark the trail even more clearly.

For an hour or so they made good progress. They had covered around 500 metres fairly easily, which, considering the terrain, was quite an accomplishment.

Juan stooped to point out a place where the *soldado sangriento* had sat down to rest and assured Zamora that a smaller body had sat down beside him. Somewhat reassured by this, Zamora allowed the group to rest for a few minutes. They then continued to follow the trail for another 200 metres before the direction changed abruptly and they found themselves moving south-west through the much denser secondary jungle. Although their progress was slowed, Juan explained that he knew of a major animal trail just up ahead that would parallel the direction of the trail they currently followed; it would allow them to close the gap considerably. Zamora's heart began to race. Perhaps, by the end of the day, he would have his daughter back, and one foreign soldier would be dead, helping avenge the destruction of his camp.

Two hours later, as the humidity of the jungle continued to increase and the heat of the sun beat down sapping them all of strength, they came out into a small clearing.

Juan stopped and studied the ground for an unusually long time before looking up at Zamora, frowning. "This is not good. This is confusing me," he said.

"Why? What is it? What do you see?" Zamora came back at him, frustrated and anxious.

"I am sure this is still their trail," Juan told him. "But now there are four more men with them. The four men are barefooted, so they are Indians. They went that way," Juan pointed in a southerly direction out of the clearing. "The Indians are leading and travelling at speed."

"If they have help, they could be out of our reach by now!" Zamora exclaimed.

"No, I do not think so," said Juan. "These men will be *Emberá*. If they hunt in this part of the jungle, the village will not be too far away. Maybe they offered to help the *soldado sangriento*."

"Okay, okay! This sounds better. Quick, we must find it before nightfall!" Zamora ushered his men in the direction that Juan was pointing, his spirits picking up again considerably. Colm caught Zamora on the arm. The IRA man's face was bright red. He was unused to spending this much time moving through the sweltering jungle.

"The men need to rest. We are running low on water, we need to find water," he suggested, appealing to Zamora.

"No!" Zamora snapped back at Colm. "We cannot afford to lose any more time. We carry on." Zamora turned from Colm and headed after Juan.

An hour later, Paola and Borgman stood in the very same clearing. They were both feeling extremely tired and weary. They craved rest and sleep; they had changed their original plan to leave the concealed ditch back at the FARC camp as soon as the JUNGLA had departed. Instead, to ensure the coast was absolutely clear, they had spent an uncomfortable night hidden in the ditch. As soon as first light had broken, they had left the protection of the ditch and headed towards the cave. Luckily, and unbeknown to them both, they had narrowly missed bumping into Zamora and his men as they moved back towards the camp in search of survivors from the attack. Had Paola and Borgman remained hidden in the ditch, they would have almost certainly been discovered, something that wouldn't have improved Borgman's chances of survival.

As they made their way towards the cave, Borgman had spotted a discarded AK47, although the previous owner was nowhere in sight. Borgman had picked up the weapon, ensuring that it was still serviceable, before being helped by Paola through the thick jungle foliage. Arriving at the cave, they had both watched the entrance for some time before deciding to approach with caution. There had been no noise coming from inside the cave, and as they approached and drew closer, to their dismay, Paola had spotted recent tracks that appeared to lead back in the direction towards the camp. They had been too late. Zamora and his men had already left the safety of the cave. Nevertheless, they had decided to search inside, entering with weapons raised and ready to dispatch anybody who may still be hiding inside. The cave had been empty, apart from a few spare supplies and backpacks. They had quickly placed the supplies of food, water and ammunition into two small backpacks before leaving the dark, damp cave and following Zamora's tracks back towards the camp.

Now Paola once again crouched staring at the ground, working out which direction the group had gone... because Juan had succeeded in training at least one member of the camp who had been very keen to learn the art of tracking. Juan had taught Paola everything he knew. Now the student was tracking the master.

CHAPTER ELEVEN

O N RETURNING to the U.S. Embassy on late Sunday morning, Bob King and the SAS team he was now commanding, attended the de-briefing with the 7th Special Forces Group and JUNGLA commanders; in whose minds the attack had been a resounding success. The camp had been completely destroyed. Bob drew their attention to all the failings. The intelligence on the area had proved to be inaccurate in places and the camp was larger than originally thought. This had meant the 7th Special Forces Group's cordon hadn't been able to surround the camp tightly enough. There had been too many gaps in the cordon and there was a good chance some FARC soldiers had escaped through those gaps. However, the body count had been 53—more than they'd believed to be in the camp in the first place, so they were fairly certain they had caught most of the occupants.

The success of the operation had come at a high price for the JUNGLA forces. Eleven men had been injured and five killed. Two of the 7th Special Forces Group's men had been injured by the retreating FARC and Bob also pointed out that the SAS team had lost their leader, John Hart.

Bob couldn't help but feel responsible for Hart being MIA.

He pushed hard for permission to re-deploy into the jungle to search for Hart. The American 7th Special Forces Group had been very happy to support a re-deployment to help assist with locating Hart, but the JUNGLA couldn't have been less interested. The mission had been a success as far as they were concerned, and they weren't prepared to lose any more men searching for one lone British soldier, who in their opinion, was probably dead by now. The jungle, as Major Rodriguez explained, was an inhospitable environment even for the most experienced men, and the chances of a British soldier, most likely compromised by an injury or loss of equipment being able to survive alone for more than a day or so, was remote at best.

Bob's only option was to try and use all available diplomatic channels and hope MI6 would agree to them going back in with the Americans providing transportation. Whilst the SAS, in the opinion of most, was one of the best, if not the best special forces organisation in the world because of the amount of autonomy they were given and the lack of red tape that could seriously hold up and compromise missions, the Americans had far superior financial investment and the latest equipment, so there was always a constant trade-off when it came to joint-operations.

Later that afternoon, at the British Embassy, Bob King waited for his debrief with Diana Brooks. He sat outside her large office whilst she finished off a phone call. Her office was painted white, the doorway joined to a floor-to-ceiling glass wall, allowing Diana to keep a constant eye on the staff working nearby in the main open office area. There was a large privacy glass window directly opposite the door to her office that offered incredible panoramic views across the city of Bogotá. On the grey desk sat a desktop computer, a notebook lying open, and a stack of papers sitting under an oval-shaped paperweight. In a corner, the air conditioner was blasting at medium, and there was a swivel chair in the middle of the office. A large whiteboard stood behind Diana Brooks, showing countless pieces of operational information and photos.

He watched Sarah Smith slowly cross and uncross her legs,

purposely seated at an angle to her desk, ensuring that she was in the eye line of several men in the room.

Finally, Diana came out of her office.

"Sorry about that," she said to Bob, "That was a tricky call. Related to you. I'll explain. Do please come in and take a seat." She looked over at Sarah. "Sarah, where are Hammond and Carter, I want them in my office immediately."

"I know they're in the building," Sarah replied, hastily shoving her long, bare legs back under her desk. She stood up. "I'll go and find them now."

"Please do," Diana said, wearily, as she ushered Bob into her office. The first thing Bob noticed as he sat down and took a closer look at the large whiteboard, there was already a picture of Hart stuck to it with "MIA" written in large red letters across it.

"You've heard," Bob said, nodding his head at Hart's picture.

"Yes," replied Diana, grimly. "I was on the phone just now to the head of the CIA. They don't seem to hold out much hope he's alive. They're not prepared to lend any manpower to go and look for Hart, but they'll take you back in and get you—and anyone you recover—back out."

Bob exhaled audibly, thoroughly relieved. "Thank you, ma'am. I couldn't live with myself if I didn't do everything possible to get John out of there. I've got a good team with me. Kav Rabuka is a highly skilled tracker. If anyone can figure out which way John went and track him down, then it's Kav." Diana frowned.

"How exactly did this happen? How did you lose radio contact with him?" she asked.

"It's one big comms dead spot around there," Bob explained. We had no way of communicating clearly. Also, if he got hit, which I'm assuming he did, otherwise he would have got back to the extraction point, it's possible his radio went down."

Diana gave him a small, sympathetic smile and then looked up to see that Hammond and Carter were approaching her office. She walked to the glass door and held it open, ushering them in. "Bob

King," she gestured, doing the formal introductions. "Nick Hammond. Joe Carter. Nick is one of ours and Joe's HMRC. They're holding an informant in a safe house not too far from here," she explained to Bob. He's the one who gave us all the intelligence on the camp."

"Much of which was inaccurate," Bob added, not hiding the anger in his voice. "If we'd known the camp was larger than we'd been told, we would have taken more men. We weren't even told about the sentries."

Diana nodded. "You'll take Bob to the safe house," she ordered Hammond. "Let him speak with Borgman. See if he's been hiding anything else."

There was a pause. When Hammond didn't respond, Diana snapped at him.

"That's a direct order."

"Well, that's going to be a bit difficult," Hammond said, in a low voice. "Borgman's gone."

"What?" Diana exclaimed, looking aghast at Hammond.

"The safe house keeper's gone, too, so we think Borgman must have somehow paid the guy off," Hammond explained.

"You should have stayed on site. This mission was far too important! You let him get out, giving him the potential to warn the FARC that we were coming?!"

"He clearly didn't; the attack was a success," argued Carter.

"Stay out of this if you know what's good for you," Diana snapped at him. "This was Nick's responsibility.

"It was hardly a success," Bob piped up. "We completed the mission despite the shoddy intelligence we'd been given. Now our team leader's missing. I'd hardly call that a success."

"So where is Borgman now?" Diana asked, irritated.

When no one answered her, Diana picked a photo up off her desk, stuck it on the whiteboard next to Hart's picture and scrawled MIA across it in a black marker pen.

"Wait," said Bob, looking at the picture. "That's your

Dutchman?"

"Yes, why?" said Diana, spinning round to face him.

"I saw him," Bob explained. "He was in the camp hours before the attack. He was drinking with the FARC commander."

"And you didn't wonder who he was?" asked Diana, incredulous. "Or think to mention this when you walked into my office a few moments ago?"

"We had a mission and orders to follow," Bob retorted, getting to his feet and facing Diana square on. "We had to complete that mission, never mind wonder who the party guests were."

"Right," Diana said, meeting his stare square on and nodding. "And there's the difference between an SAS soldier and an intelligence officer. One does, the other thinks."

"What? Like your team here?" Bob batted back to her with a nod of his head towards Hammond and Carter.

No one spoke for a minute. Everyone seemed extremely deflated all of a sudden; the atmosphere in the room was bleak.

"Right," Diana said eventually, looking up at Hammond and Carter. "You two can say goodbye to Bogotá for a while."

"You're firing us?!" Hammond spluttered. "You can't! You never gave us a direct order to stay in the safe house with Borgman after the interrogation."

"No, I'm not firing you," said Diana, smiling. "Although in a second you might wish I was."

She stood up and walked around to the front of her desk. She leaned back against it and folded her arms over her chest. She looked almost smug.

"You two will go back in with the SAS team. They're going back into the jungle. Their mission is to bring back their leader. Yours is to find a giant Dutchman. Now, that is a direct order."

"Hold on a minute," Bob piped up, whilst Hammond and Carter processed what Diana had just said, "I haven't agreed to that. I'm not prepared to take outside agencies with me as part of my team. They're not trained. I can't guarantee their safety. For all we know the place could be swarming with FARC reinforcements by now!"

Diana turned to him. "Please don't worry," she said, in a charming tone. "I won't hold you accountable should any harm come to these two."

CHAPTER TWELVE

VALENTINA'S FACE was set in a frown. For the third time that afternoon, Hart had opened his eyes to see the young girl observing him.

"You were having bad dreams I think," she said.

"I was?" Hart responded automatically, and then, in the next moment remembered, yes, he was. When was he not?

"Mr John, what was it in your dreams that made you so sad?"

"My friend died," Hart answered, without emotion.

"Mine, too," Valentina said, sadly.

That gave Hart perspective. No matter what he had experienced and witnessed in his life, it couldn't compare to seeing your friend's head blown off just in front of you at the age of ten. Having your friend's freshly spilt blood splattered across your face, moments before being grabbed by a complete stranger wielding a gun, then being carried away from your mother and everything you know had to trump anything he'd experienced.

"You're very brave," Hart muttered, for want of not knowing what else to say.

Valentina looked off into the distance. She took a deep breath in and then exhaled with a sigh. Neither spoke for a while, both lost inside their own traumatic memories for a moment.

Their reverie was finally broken by the sound of a giggling child. Valentina spun around and Hart looked up. Three or four young children were peering at them from outside. They had obviously climbed up the wooden frame of the house and were now lying on the platform just behind the drapes, peeking in under them. Valentina spoke sharply to them in their native language and they quickly disappeared. By the time she turned back around, Hart was sitting up, holding his head in his hands.

"No, no, no. You must rest. It will be dark in a few hours. We will stay here one more night until you are well."

"No, Valentina, it's too dangerous. We must move out within the hour. I feel much better now," Hart informed her, despite the fact that he looked anything but "much better".

"The medicine man—"

"I know," Hart said, gently but firmly. "But we can't stay here, Valentina. If anyone survived the attack, they'll be looking for you. We have to keep moving. Hopefully, my people will be looking for us and with any luck, they'll find us, but we can't risk staying put and waiting to be found."

Valentina observed him closely for a while. "Okay, we will see what the chief says. We cannot leave before we pay our respects to the chief. This is an important custom."

"Fine, but let's be quick about it," Hart said, impatiently, pulling on his shirt.

***

Juan was nervous. He'd lost the *rastro*. Of course, he couldn't tell Zamora this, it was more than his life was worth, but how long could he stall before he had to come up with something. What had gone wrong? He had followed the *rastro* to a stream. At first, he had wondered if the group ahead had crossed it to throw off any pursuers, but why now, when they could have done that by using an easier path further upstream? What if he'd missed something? Perhaps he had been too focused on the trail and hadn't paid enough attention to other factors. Tracking required varying different levels of attention, a constant refocusing between minute details on the track and the whole pattern of the environment around the trail; it involved both a detailed knowledge of the terrain and a deep understanding of human behaviour.

What Juan usually did when he lost a *rastro* was to stop for as long as was necessary to search for all possible signs, choosing every possible path through the jungle and checking each one. He didn't have the luxury of time now; he could almost feel Zamora breathing down his neck. He knew he had to make a decision soon. He needed a hypothesis, a working hypothesis. He would have to make assumptions based on his knowledge of these native indigenous people and their typical behaviour and add this to any practical evidence that he had available—practical evidence that was a little thin on the ground at this moment in time. However, as far as the hypothetical information went, Juan could use his knowledge to work out where the group might be heading, at what pace they were likely to travel, when and why they would make stops and for how long, and what their decisions might be based upon as they faced new obstacles in the jungle.

"What is it, Juan. Have you lost the *rastro*?" Zamora hissed at him, in a threatening tone. Juan jumped. He was frightened. Zamora's ruthlessness had always terrified him. He had to remain indispensable to his commander if he was to guarantee getting through this ordeal alive. He tried to stay calm.

"No, Patrón I have it. I am just working one more thing out to be sure."

"Well, you need to be sure quickly. We only have a few more hours before nightfall. Keep going," Zamora ordered him.

Saying a silent prayer, Juan took a deep breath and pointed

with his stick towards the opening that led through the jungle alongside the nearby stream, offering them what he hoped would be a safe passage through the jungle vegetation that continually fought against them. He led the way in a southerly direction; Zamora and his men followed.

***

Hart ate speedily. He was keen to get moving but he was famished and was grateful for the plate of food that was offered to him by one of the women. Valentina was also hungrily tucking into the white fish they had been served. As well as the fish, there was a selection of fruits on their plates. Hart didn't recognise most of it, but he trusted these people would know exactly what was and wasn't edible in this part of the jungle.

They sat with the other villagers on the ground outside the *casa communal*, the large ground-level structure in the village—a round hut with a sloping roof. Valentina had explained that every village had one of these communal meeting places where everyone would gather for important ceremonies such as marriages and funerals, and of course, greeting and saying goodbye to visitors.

Sat around the outside of the building were beautifully carved narrow canoes that had been dug out from a single large tree trunk. There were various sizes of vessels, ranging from a small fishing canoe that was less than six feet long and only a foot wide, that could only have held a child, to the larger communal boats carved from logs more than 40 feet long and easily four-feet wide. These looked as though they could have carried 20 people as well as a decent quantity of cargo. The boats were called *piraguas*, an adopted Spanish word, Valentina informed Hart. She explained that everyone in the tribe was expected to learn how to paddle and pole their boats into and against strong river currents.

Children would learn how to read the current of the river

from a very young age. The villagers depended on their *piraguas* for their livelihoods; the boats were used both for transportation and for fishing.

Finally, the meal seemed to be coming to an end. Hart looked around anxiously. Something was making his hair stand up on end. He felt as if he was being watched, which, of course, he could see he was... the villagers hadn't taken their eyes off him since he had emerged from the hut... but it was something else, something making him feel like he was under observation as if the trees around them had eyes. He was uneasy; his instinct told him they needed to move, fast. He insisted upon wearing his entire belt-kit to the meal, even though Valentina had argued with him that it might frighten the villagers and even anger the elders and the chief, but he wasn't taking any risks. If they were ambushed and he was caught out in the open unprepared, this would have been a huge waste of time, so before they had left the hut, Hart had gone through everything: he had his belt-kit, which contained spare magazines with extra ammunition, both his machete and combat knife, his 9mm Sig pistol and his damaged M16 and broken PRC radio.

A hush descended upon the gathering. A group of older children emerged from the *casa communal* that, unlike the other huts, was at ground level. They were carrying a large empty wooden throne, which they placed in the middle of the group. The throne was carved from fine wood, crested with several decorative carvings forming elegant depictions of hunting scenes and animals from the forest. Behind the children—following slowly—was a man who was undoubtedly the oldest person Hart had ever seen. He had to be at least 100 years old. He was completely bald, with skin that looked like worn leather, and he was tiny, too; he looked as though he had been pickled. The reverence of the other villagers clearly indicated that this was the chief.

Like the other villagers, he was dressed in a loincloth or an *anelia*, as the Emberá called it. The chief and the elders were covered with the black dyes of *Jagua*. Valentina whispered to Hart that this was a temporary form of skin decoration applied from the extract of the *Genipa Americana* fruit, also known as *Jagua*. Some designs were solid blocks of painting with small patches of skin showing through to help highlight the contrast. Others were elaborate patterns drawn with the thin tip of a bamboo stick. Each design had its own meaning.

Every villager was covered with intricate plastic bead necklaces and ornamental collars made with dozens of coins. Some wore wide bracelets and arm and ankle bands.

They helped the frail chief up onto the large throne, which made him look even smaller. Everyone was kneeling and bowing their heads to the chief. Valentina indicated to Hart that he should do the same. Silence and stillness descended over the group. Finally, the chief spoke in his native language. Valentina translated for Hart.

"He wants to ask me some questions," she whispered. "Shall I tell him everything that has happened to us?"

Hart pondered this for a few seconds. He knew that the FARC was the enemy of such indigenous people—they ransacked villages and recruited previously peaceful young men and women to train them up as soldiers—so it seemed safe enough to reiterate that he had rescued Valentina from a FARC camp and was guiding her to safety. After all, they had already shared this information with the four native hunters they'd met in the clearing and who had brought them to the village. The old chief probably wanted to verify what he'd been told when they had arrived the previous day, but Hart didn't want the chief to suggest that Valentina should stay with them.

"Okay," he whispered back. "But make sure he understands you have to stay with me. That it's dangerous for you to stay here, and that we have to leave as soon as possible."

Valentina nodded and approached the chief. She knelt before him and they spoke in hushed tones. Hart watched, feeling apprehensive, impatient and curious. After a few minutes, Valentina rose and returned to Hart. She knelt beside him.

"He will help us. He will tell the men who brought us here to lead us to the white woman who lives in the forbidden forest. She will be able to help us travel to the closest city from here, which is Quibdó. From there we can find a plane to take us to Bogotá."

"Okay. Great. When can we leave?" asked Hart, impatiently.

"In the morning," Valentina told him.

"No!" Hart said, a little too loudly. "No," he said again, in a softer, more hushed tone. "We have to leave NOW; we can't waste any more time. Tell the chief we're very grateful for his help, but we have to leave now." He stood up. There were gasps from the group; it was clearly not protocol to rise to your feet unless the chief had given his permission.

Hart hastily got back down to his knees and hissed at Valentina. "I'm serious, Valentina, we have to leave now."

Valentina frowned at him and bit her bottom lip. "Mr John," she said quietly and firmly. "These people feel I belong to them more than I belong to you. If you do not obey their wishes, they will not let me leave with you, they will keep me here."

Hart looked at her, then looked at the chief. Then he looked around the gathering at the faces of the villagers. For the moment, at least, he was defeated.

"Okay, okay, we'll stay," he said, despondently.

Valentina smiled. She turned to speak to the chief. What he said in reply was greeted with great cheers from the villagers, who all rose to their feet and started clapping their hands.

Hart looked around baffled.

"There will now be a celebration," Valentina explained.

"Why?" asked Hart

"Because you have saved my life and we will soon continue on our journey. There will be singing and dancing, wishing us safe passage," she said with a grin.

Hart looked at her, exasperated. The very last thing he felt like doing at this point in time was singing and dancing. Plus, if any surviving FARC soldiers were looking for them, this would be the very best way of attracting their attention. It was the worst idea possible, but he knew it would be futile to challenge the chief at this point: he just needed to stay on his guard.

Whilst the villagers started to dance to the sound of flutes, drums and turtle shells, Hart found a quiet spot under a small tree canopy and used the fading light to study his map. He estimated they were around six miles from the north-eastern edge of Utría National Park. He had a hunch that this was the "forbidden" forest the chief was referring to. He wondered if there might be friendly forces looking for him at the rangers' station—one of the operations designated ERV's—located on the Pacific coast at the western edge of the Utría National Park?

When Hart looked up and placed his map inside the side pocket of his camouflaged trousers, he saw Valentina dancing with the other villagers—some tribal dance that seemed to mimic the movements of animals. Beyond them, in the treeline around the village clearing, something caught his attention. What was it? A shape moved. Either a large animal was stalking the village, or Hart was going to have to extract himself and Valentina from the party early.

CHAPTER THIRTEEN

HE *RASTRO* had been heading in a south-easterly direction towards the Río Atrato for some time. They were getting ever closer to the boundary of the Utría National Park. Juan knew that the FARC Central High Command had agreed never to enter the park—all FARC soldiers were bound by this—if the *soldado sangriento* and the girl had managed to cross the park boundary, they would have escaped forever... unless Zamora wanted to risk his life by disobeying his superiors. Out of a strong sense of self-preservation, Juan chose not to share these thoughts with Zamora. It was late afternoon and he was growing concerned that they might have to stop for the night without having caught up with the *soldado sangriento* and Zamora's daughter. Just as his heart was growing heavy with fear, he heard it. The sound was unmistakable, and, with a huge sigh of relief, Juan stopped in his tracks, holding his right hand high above his head to signal for the others to stop.

"What? What is it, now?" whispered a frustrated Zamora.

"Can you hear it?" Juan hissed.

"What? No. I don't hear anything," Zamora replied.

"The drums," Juan said in an excited whisper.

The group fell completely silent and Zamora strained his ears. Eventually, he heard something. He wasn't totally convinced it was an external drumbeat rather than the sound of his own heart hammering inside his chest, but he was ready to grasp at straws at this point. He addressed the group.

"We follow Juan in a staggered file. If you see anything unusual or threatening, from here on in, fan out into attack formation and open fire on my command," Zamora ordered the men.

They pressed forward for another thirty minutes before Zamora heard, without question, the drums and other instruments. Then he heard the laughter and the voices of children singing. He moved up next to Juan, both men now stopping in their tracks as they got their first sighting, through the trees, of the clearance and the village in its centre.

Zamora ordered his men to spread out along the north-eastern edge of the clearing and to observe the village from a safe distance. It would be dark within an hour. That's when they would strike. He himself got down onto the ground next to Juan and started crawling forward. Juan stayed by his side.

"Not too close, Patrón. Surprise is our strongest weapon," Juan warned him.

Zamora knew this, of course, but he had to be certain. He had to know if she was there. He looked over the crowd of dancing villagers. Then he saw him.

Sitting outside of the group, alone, was the *soldado sangriento*! A minute later, a girl had come running up to him, pulling his arm, obviously trying to persuade him to dance. The *soldado sangriento* resisted.

Zamora knew before the girl even turned her head... when she turned it was confirmed... it was his daughter, Valentina!

***

There was a bright flash, followed by a deafening explosion. Hart was thrown backwards with a tremendous force. He landed on his bad shoulder and could not help but cry out in pain. His whole upper torso burned, but he had no time to think about it. He rolled onto his front and lay on the ground observing what had happened. The music had abruptly stopped as soon as the first explosion had happened. Some villagers were already running around, screaming; others were standing frozen to the spot, stunned. Valentina was lying on the ground beside Hart, shaken but still conscious. Hart heard the first round of gunfire. Crouching low, Hart reached out and grabbed Valentina's ankle, pulling her towards him as she struggled and screamed. She finally looked around and saw that it was Hart holding her. She squirmed towards him and clung to his hand.

"Hold tight," he told her. "We're getting out of here. Run, now!" Valentina nodded. They got to their feet and Hart expertly steered her through the villagers who were running around in a blind panic. He had to get them out of the killing zone as fast as possible. Judging that the gunfire seemed to be coming from the north-eastern corner of the clearing, Hart headed in the opposite direction.

He needed to put as much distance between them and the camp as he could. Although the darkness that had now fallen would conceal them, it would also make any escape into the dense secondary jungle surrounding them almost suicidal, but they had no choice.

Not until they were well behind the cover of the trees, did they dare to stop running and look back at the now burning village. Valentina huddled into Hart, her body shaking. As they watched, Zamora came striding into the village, walking among the bodies... his face furious. Valentina saw him and grabbed Hart's hand tightly.

"My father," she whispered.

"Yes," said Hart, grimly, recognising Zamora from the J2 intelligence photos he had been shown during the briefing in Bogotá.

"He is killing the people who helped us," Valentina exclaimed, woefully.

"Now we know he's alive and looking for you, we're in even more danger." Hart looked down at Valentina's face, which was illuminated by the fire that was now taking hold throughout the village. Her eyes were hard.

"We have to go back. We have to try and save some of the villagers," Valentina screamed, tears beginning to roll down her cheeks.

"We can't. It's too dangerous. We just can't risk it, Valentina," Hart said, darkly.

Valentina spun around to look him closely in the face. "Do you really have no feelings? They helped us and now they need our help," Valentina sobbed. "What is wrong with you? Why do we sit here wasting time? Are you really such a bad man with no feelings?" "Yes, probably a bad man," he said, instinctively. Adding suddenly, "Trying my best to save your life."

"We can't stay here and allow my father and his men to kill everybody in the village," Valentina hissed.
"We don't have time for this," Hart hissed back, exasperated. "We have to go now!"

"Please help them," pleaded Valentina, taking Hart's hand again and squeezing it tightly. "They don't deserve this."

Hart stared at her. She was very convincing, but he shook it off. "Come on," he said. "We have to go. It's too late to save the village. We can only try and save ourselves now." Valentina reluctantly accepted Hart's logic.

Those within the village were being massacred by Zamora and his men, and there was nothing anybody could do to stop them. Hart knew the odds were heavily stacked against him; they would have to fight for their very survival. Attempting to navigate the jungle at night would prove dangerous and slow. The darkness was suffocating and robbed them of all their senses. They'd be extremely lucky if they managed to cover more than a couple of miles before daybreak.

***

Paola and Borgman had been making decent progress throughout the day since they had tracked Zamora and his men from the cave, and despite Borgman's ankle injury. She'd estimated that the group had left the cave only an hour before she and Borgman had arrived at its entrance. Borgman was still limping on his injured ankle but Paola had done her best to support him for long stretches. By nightfall, she had also heard the voices and music. There was clearly a tribal village up ahead. Maybe Zamora and his men had stopped there for the night. Perhaps she and Borgman could ambush and kill them as they slept.

As the sounds from the village grew louder, Paola realised that Borgman's progress through the jungle was now beginning to impede her a little too much. She wanted to carry out a thorough reconnaissance of the village before it got dark. She moved away from the *rastro* to reduce the possibility of running into Zamora and the other men should they happen to retrace their steps for any reason. She stopped by a cluster of nearby trees and instructed Borgman to take off his backpack and sit down and wait there for her return. She passed her own backpack to Borgman before heading off towards the north-western edge of the clearing surrounding the village. The light was fading fast and she moved as quickly as she dared whilst ensuring her movements would remain undetected. Finally, she found a place where she could lie on the jungle floor and inch her way through to the very edge of the treeline surrounding the clearing.

Paola, at last, had the village within her sights. She scanned the partying villagers for signs of Zamora, although it seemed highly unlikely there would be much merriment going on within the village if the FARC men were inside the village. It would make more sense that Zamora was waiting for a chance to attack and take their provisions. As if on cue with Paola's thoughts, an explosion lit up the gathering. Gunfire followed. The side wall of the large central hut caught fire and a few moments later, Paola saw them... Hart and Valentina racing towards the edge of the clearing!

CHAPTER FOURTEEN

BOB KING was seriously considering offloading their surplus cargo—by which he meant Hammond and Carter—after all, Diana Brooks had suggested they were dispensable.

The men were seriously hindering progress due to their lack of fitness and experience. Bob knew that, without them, he would be able to move at nearly twice the pace.

At 10 am that morning, a Black Hawk had dropped Bob, his team and the double act of Hammond and Carter near the site of the decimated FARC camp. They had found their way to the clearing surrounding the camp and Kav had quickly found Hart's trail. He had confirmed that a small person, presumably a child, was travelling with Hart. Like Hart, Bob had initially been unaware that there were any children in the camp—another fact the Dutchman had failed to mention perhaps. So, what was Hart up to? Trying to be the hero? Had he compromised his own safety to go on some rescue mission? Bob was secretly worried about Hart; he hadn't been the same since the incident with the Afghan kid in the Al Qaeda safe house.

With Kav leading, Bob close behind, and Mike and Jock bringing up the rear behind the cumbersome "cargo", they followed Hart's trail. Bob had ordered Hammond and Carter to stay close behind him in the middle of the patrol. He didn't trust them. Something just didn't add up. Had they let the Dutchman go? He couldn't quite put his finger on it, but his instincts told him that they were hiding something, and his instincts were rarely wrong.

Finally, they reached a small clearing. After spending some time walking back and forth and around the clearing, Kav called the men together to explain what he'd found.

"John and the kid definitely passed through here yesterday. They were met by four barefooted men, and then followed them. Sometime later, another group of five men came through this way and followed them. After that, two more people passed along the same route. One member of this last group is a large man, limping badly on his right leg. We're probably a good few hours behind these two by the looks of things."

Bob whistled softly. "Some party. Looks like we're the last to arrive. Well, boys, all the more reason to pick up the pace. Looks like we're not the only ones on John's trail."

***

Zamora had made his men search through the corpses before he was satisfied that his daughter and the *soldado sangriento* were not amongst them. The bloodshed had been barbaric, evil and cruel. The entire village still burned in a sea of red, yellow and orange. The cries of the villagers had echoed into the night. Zamora had watched as the flames ripped their way through the buildings surrounding him, plumes of smoke reaching desperately into the dark night's sky above as if trying to escape the blazing inferno below. Inside the burning *casa communal*, the bodies of the village chief and the elders were distinguishable only by the fact that the *Jagua* body paint they had worn had reacted to the fire and heat, inflicting third-degree burns and turning their skin waxy and white in colour. The chief had been abandoned and left sitting on his throne when the panic had first broken out throughout the tribe. He had been decapitated after being hit directly in the face by a GP-34 Russian made 40 mm semi-automatic grenade round that had dropped through the roof above him before exploding, killing him and all who sat around him, instantly.

The corpses were mangled and battered. They lay scattered on the ground, limbs at awkward angles and heads held in such a way that they couldn't be sleeping.

Outside the burning *casa communal*, lay many more corpses, once the repositories of people, now abandoned shells that would be left to rot in the open clearing. Some would be consumed by the jungle wildlife and others would simply decay, slowly giving up their flesh to the soil and showing their white bones to the sun.

The relief of not finding his daughter amongst the corpses had made Zamora feel lightheaded before the next wave of emotion—pure anger—engulfed him. He called the men to gather around. As Juan approached, he told Zamora that he was confident he had picked up the *rastro* of the *soldado sangriento* and his daughter at the south-western edge of the clearing. However, Juan assured Zamora that there was no way he could follow the trail in the dark. They would have to wait until first light before they continued to follow them.

Zamora had never felt so angry in his life. Someone had endangered his daughter's life and now she had disappeared again.

"Who fired the first grenade?" Zamora's voice trembled. No one met his murderous gaze. "Answer me!" he yelled.

Finally, Diego raised his hand. "Sorry, Patrón," he said, barely audible.

"Why did you do that, Diego?" Zamora questioned him, "When I had not given the order to do so? We needed to ensure my daughter's safety before we attacked?"

"I don't know," Diego squeaked.

"You endangered the life of my daughter? Now, because of your stupid actions, the *soldado sangriento* has escaped with her. Do you see what you have done?" Zamora screamed.

Diego nodded his head violently.

Zamora walked up close to him. Diego's head was bowed. As Zamora got within inches from him, Diego noticed that the commander had pulled his 9mm sidearm revolver from its holster. The young FARC soldier started to cry.

"Please, Patrón, I am so sorry for—" Before Diego could finish his sentence, Zamora fired two bullet rounds into the boy's forehead. A collective gasp rang out from the group as Diego's body slumped to the ground. Zamora turned to face his men.

"I won't have stupid men under my command! Anyone who endangers the life of my daughter will end up like this!" He kicked Diego's twitching body. Nobody moved or made a sound. "We rest now," Zamora continued, calmly. "We will sleep at the edge of the clearing here, concealed in the trees, in case anyone comes to investigate. If they do, we will eliminate them immediately. As soon as dawn breaks, we will continue to hunt and kill the *soldado sangriento* and get my daughter back." The men nodded silently and melted away into the treeline surrounding the clearing. Zamora stood over Diego's body and stared down at it for a full ten minutes before joining his men.

***

Hart and Valentina continued to push through the jungle in the darkness. For the first hour, their path had been partially lit by the light from the burning fires inside the village, but eventually the light had died as their distance from the village increased. Whilst the loss of that light was a huge hindrance, the peace that their distance from the village brought was welcomed. The screams and shouts that had rung through the trees had affected Hart more acutely than he could have anticipated. His sensitivity was heightened; it was as if every tortured voice came from right inside his head. This had not only set off his trembling hand again, but it seemed to have triggered a reaction along his entire right arm. His arm twitched as muscle spasms contracted from his shoulder to his fingertips. He gripped his M16 colt rifle tightly, desperately trying to stop the shaking.

From the mental picture, he'd memorised from the map, Hart knew they had to cross a river, a tributary belonging to the huge Río Atrato. He had no idea how deep or wide it was going to be, but he knew they had to get across it in order to reach the Utría National Park, which he hoped to reach by first light. Fortunately, as they continued onwards, the jungle was now becoming sparser in places, allowing some moonlight to shine through the canopy above, helping Hart identify the best route towards the awaiting tributary.

Eventually, Hart heard water. For a moment he thought he was imagining it, but it grew louder and louder until he was convinced, they'd found the river. He paused and turned to face Valentina. "I think we've reached the river. I'm pretty sure I have a rough idea of where we are. I'll risk checking my map and using my torch, once we reach the water," he announced.

"Good," replied Valentina's weary voice. "Maybe we can rest for a while after we cross it."

"Maybe," muttered Hart, with no intention of letting them rest and losing precious time. He had no idea how far behind Zamora and his men were. He assumed they would not have tried to follow in the dark, but he had no guarantee of that. He couldn't afford to lose a moment of time; he had to keep them moving and putting a river between them and their pursuers was a particularly welcome notion.

About ten minutes later they stood on the banks of the small tributary river. It flowed like time, always onward, always toward its destiny. It held a perfect consistency, an artery of blessed water. It fed this place, quenched the thirst of the mighty beings rooted in the rich soil nearby. Hart's spirits lifted in relief as he saw, by the watery reflection of the moonlight, that it was not nearly as wide as he had expected. It looked reasonably shallow; there were several rocks showing above the waterline, they would be able to cross it fairly easily without having to swim.

The moonlight splashed down its watery white-silver glow, as Valentina knelt by the river, scooping up and drinking the cool, dark water. Hart filled his water-bottle and added one of his few remaining purification tablets to it before drinking. With his stomach so unsettled, he didn't want to take any chances. Then the two of them started to wade, carefully, through the water. The moonlight's diffused glow, lighting the way, turning the jungle around them from pitch black to charcoal grey.

As soon as they'd made it across to the other side, Valentina slumped to the ground. She looked up at Hart.

"Mr John, we have to rest now."

Hart firmly pulled her to her feet. "I know you're tired," he told her, "But we can't take the risk. If your father and his men catch up to us, I'm dead and you're a prisoner in the FARC forever. We have to keep going."

"Okay," Valentina conceded in a tiny voice. They pushed on, heading in a south-easterly direction.

Hart consulted his map using his red-filtered torch. He calculated that they should only be a couple of hours from the park's boundary, so when after a short time, he heard the roar of fast-flowing water, he was confused. Had he made an error in identifying their correct position? They couldn't possibly be anywhere near the Río Atrato yet, but the sound grew louder and louder as they continued onwards, until finally, they broke through a treeline, encountering a wide, fast-flowing river. Hart stared at it in dismay as he realised that the shallow river, they had just crossed had not been the tributary that had been marked on the map, but simply a small stream that was unmarked. This was the tributary they had to cross. It looked huge—almost as wide as the Río Atrato itself! Now with the moonlight shining across its waters, Hart could clearly make out a torrent of white water flowing in a chaotic path, hurtling between large black threatening rocks. The roar of the water made communication between Hart and Valentina almost impossible. There would be no wading across this river; they would have to swim. It was hard to make out the far riverbank, especially now that the moon was now just beginning to disappear behind a build-up of clouds. He wiped his face from the incessant water spray that covered them both. Hart shuddered for a moment as he contemplated their next move. What unknown potential horrors lay beneath those depths? It was too dark and too dangerous to do a thorough investigation of the riverbank.

Hart removed his belt-kit, with the intention of using it as a floatation aid. He would place his rifle on top of it to keep it as dry as possible.

"Valentina, we're going to wade into the river, and I want you to climb on my back. We're going to swim across. I want you to clasp your hands together around my neck and whatever happens, don't let go!"

"Okay," Valentina replied in a barely audible whisper. She was exhausted.

Moments later, Hart was waist-deep in the fast-flowing water with Valentina's tired little body plastered to his back—her legs wrapped around his waist and her arms tight around his neck. He had no idea if they would survive this, but they had no choice but to try. The further they went downstream, the wider and faster the river would become, and he couldn't afford to waste time trying to travel upriver to see if it got any easier. It had to be done here and now... like this.

As Hart waded deeper into the dark waters, the current grabbed his legs and tried to pull him over. He fought back against it and kept moving forward until he was in up to his chest. He still couldn't make out the far riverbank. This was surely suicide!

"Brace yourself," Hart warned Valentina as he lowered his body into the water, keeping one hand firmly wrapped around the yoke of his belt-kit. He heard her gasp behind him as the water swept up to her chin. Then they were in and out of their depths, fighting for survival.

Hart swam a couple of strokes, but they were soon dragged under. He reached for the riverbed with his feet and pushed up. They surfaced and Valentina started coughing and spluttering, water had gone up her nose and she momentarily struggled to breathe.

This was going to be impossible.

They were swept along by the current; all the while, Hart struck out at an angle against it, trying to make some progress towards the far riverbank. Valentina's grip around his neck had tightened so much in her terror that, if he didn't drown, there was a good chance she'd strangle him to death. Unable to speak, he managed to push the thumb of his free hand under her clasped hands and give himself an inch of breathing space.

With one hand on his belt-kit and the other ensuring Valentina didn't throttle him, Hart had only the use of his legs. Swimming against the current was futile. At least they were been carried downstream towards the Río Atrato—the direction they needed to be heading, but how long would they survive this?

Hart kicked out with his legs again, trying to propel them towards the elusive far riverbank. On his second kick, his leg struck a hard object and he felt something grip his boot. They were pulled under again as Hart momentarily contemplated the terrifying prospect that there could be crocodiles present, even this far upstream. As he released his right hand from under Valentina's hands to reach down to try and free his boot from what he desperately hoped was just an entangled crop of thick reeds, he felt the little girl's hands slip from his neck.

Hart spun around and tried to grab Valentina's body, but he couldn't see anything and suddenly she was gone. He yanked his leg twice and it came free.

"Valentina!" Hart yelled into the darkness as he broke the surface and gasped for air, his heart pounding in his mouth. "Valentina!" He called out again, spitting out the water that sloshed inside his mouth. The fear of losing his young charge gave Hart a sudden burst of adrenalin and he kicked out with a renewed force. He soon noticed how much easier it was to move without Valentina strapped to his back, but where was she? He had to find her.

In the dark, Hart kicked his legs frantically, calling Valentina's name as often as he could, between taking gasps for breath. Finally, he thought he could make out the shadowy outline of some trees up ahead. He guessed he was about thirty metres or so from the opposite bank. This spurred him on, but he was still in a panic. Valentina could be anywhere. The current would have made light work of her tiny body. Hart stopped himself from thinking anymore and focused all his attention and energy on battling the turbulent waters and finding Valentina.

At one point his shin struck a sharp object and from the searing pain that followed, Hart assumed he was bleeding badly. A few times he misjudged the surface level of the water and ended up with a lungful of river water. He hoped there was still enough of the purification tablet in his system to kill anything before it killed him.

Finally, Hart's foot struck the riverbed again and a few seconds later he was able to stand up. He waded forward, still desperately calling Valentina's name.

Eventually, the water was only knee-deep, and Hart climbed up onto the riverbank and immediately fell onto all fours and vomited. A humming started up in his head and within a few seconds, everything suddenly went silent...

Hart had blacked out. Again.

CHAPTER FIFTEEN

ZAMORA RESTED but did not sleep. By the light of the burning fires, he sat on the treeline and studied his map. They were only a few miles from the boundary of the Utría National Park. It was likely that the *soldado sangriento* was heading there to find help from the park authorities; maybe he knew that the FARC leadership had long ago agreed not to carry out military objectives within the park boundaries and was counting on Zamora honouring this agreement. Zamora knew the risks of disobeying the FARC high command, but he had very little to lose now anyway. When he thought about it, surely these were exceptional circumstances; his crystallisation lab had been attacked and destroyed, and a foreign soldier had abducted his daughter... surely, he would be justified in entering the Utría National Park if necessary? Maybe he would be forgiven.

As dawn broke, one of Zamora's men approached him... it was Cesar; he had not spoken much during this expedition.

He was good at following orders and keeping himself out of the way.

"Patrón, I have information that may help us."

"What is it, Cesar?" Zamora asked, wearily.

"My nephew, Mateo, works for a logging company that is

clearing parts of the Utría National Park. He told me they have been constructing a small runway in the jungle to allow light aircraft to fly in and out of the area. This was some time ago, so it's possible that the runway has been built by now. The tribes in these parts know all about this runway. Maybe the villagers told the *soldado sangriento* to go there because they know we cannot enter the Park, and from the runway he can escape in a plane."

Zamora nodded, impressed with Cesar's line of thinking. "Do you know the exact location?" Zamora asked, his hopes beginning to rise.

"I think I could find it, with Juan's help," Cesar assured him.

Zamora looked down at the map. "We are roughly six miles from the park boundary. Around here," Zamora said, pointing.

Cesar studied the map and then pointed to a spot on the south-eastern boundary of the park.

"This is where I think the runway is," he said.

Zamora nodded, thoughtfully, looking at the map. Then he looked up at Cesar. "Tell the men to pack up," he said, with urgency. "We leave immediately. The *soldado sangriento* already has a big head start on us."

***

Hart was lying on the floor in the safe house and the boy with half a face was shaking him. Behind the boy, Hart could see Paddy standing over him, shaking his head, telling the boy that Hart was dead and that there was no point in shaking him, but Hart knew he wasn't dead. The boy kept shaking him. Hart could clearly hear his voice almost screaming, "Wake up, wake up, wake up! Mr John, please wake up!"

Something was wrong, the boy's voice sounded too young. Hart opened his eyes. Valentina was shaking him, staring down at him, her eyes filled with tears. Even though she noticed Hart open his eyes, she kept shaking him and pleading with him.

"Wake up, Mr John. Please wake up, please wake up!"

Hart reached up and took Valentina's shoulders gently. "I'm here, I'm awake. Valentina, it's okay. Thank God, you're okay. I thought I'd lost you!"

Valentina threw herself at Hart's chest. He wrapped an arm around her as she sobbed. "I thought you were dead! I really, really thought you were dead," she sobbed.

"I'm okay. Everything's okay," Hart said to her as soothingly as he knew how.

His exposure to children had been limited, but a natural instinct kicked in and he held Valentina gently in his arms until she stopped crying.

When she had eventually calmed down, Valentina knelt beside him. He sat up slowly and looked at her... her big brown eyes suddenly looked so sad and frightened that she looked far more vulnerable than she had seemed before.

"I need you. So, you cannot die. You have to promise me to stay alive and get us to safety. Okay? Do you understand? You have to promise," She started to cry again.

Hart nodded. "I promise to do my best to stay alive and get us both out of here safely."

Reassured, Valentina lay down beside Hart and closed her eyes. "I'm so tired," she whispered.

"Okay," said Hart, gently. "We'll move further up this bank and rest in the treeline over there for a few minutes."

The river continued to flow past with confidence, a mass of powerful water moving forward with purpose. The unrelenting water spray covered the muddy riverbank. Swamp-like vegetation and old, rotting trees crept towards the river's edge creating slimy pools of debris from the withered leaves and twigs. Above the mass of water and slightly further up the bank, stood the giant trees of the jungle forest, lining the riverbank and offering an almost impenetrable barrier into its interior. Their trunks gnarled, and twisted, with a massive girth, and interlacing roots protruded from the soil in great loops and ridges. Each tree cast an ominous silhouette in the darkness, as if they had been drawn with charcoal as a warning towards unwelcome travellers.

Hart knew that, even if he wanted to, he didn't have the capacity to go on. His legs were numb; they felt like lumps of dead flesh. He took Valentina's hand and struggled up the steep sloping muddy riverbank towards the treeline, before lying back down in his soaking clothes. Within seconds, his whole body started to tremble. Soon he was shaking uncontrollably. Feeling this, Valentina urgently sat up again and looked at him, alarmed.

"Mr John! What's wrong with you? Why are you all shaky like this?"

Hart wanted to sit up, he wanted to stop shaking, he wanted to answer her, but all he could do was curl tighter into a ball. The images were coming thick and fast now. In the safe house, outside the safe house, the blasts of the grenades and the imaginary sight of Paddy's dead body being kicked around by the Taliban soldiers.

The nightmare wouldn't stop. He couldn't stop it. All the while, he was aware of Valentina's voice as if it was trying to reach him through a portal from another world.

"You're really scaring me now, Mr John. Please stop it," Valentina pleaded.

Hart found he had no control over his body. It was terrifying. Finally, by focusing his mind completely on becoming still and pushing the images away, Hart managed to stop the shaking. He looked up at Valentina who was shocked and scared. She deserved some explanation. Why shield her from the truth after what she'd been through? She had already proved herself as brave as any soldier he knew.

"I'm sorry, Valentina. I don't know exactly what's wrong with me but sometimes I get very shaky. I can't control it. Sometimes it makes me sick."

"You have some sickness?" asked Valentina.

Hart shook his head. "Well, not a normal sickness. I think it might be something that happened to me before. Before I came here. When I was in a different place, trying to rescue a man."

"What happened to you before you came here? How has it made you sick?" Valentina asked.

"I killed a child," Hart said, fighting the stabbing pains in his chest. "It was an accident. He shouldn't have been there. It was a place for soldiers, not for children. He was in the wrong place at the wrong time."

Valentina shrugged her shoulders. "You know something," she said. "Sometimes children get mixed up with soldiers. It's not their choice." Hart nodded.

"I know, but I still feel bad for having to kill him." He failed to mention the clinical way in which he'd had to end the young boy's life. "Then my friend died. Another soldier. I feel like I should have done more to save him."

Valentina nodded and patted Hart's arm. "It's okay, Mr John, I'm sure you did as much as you could. You're a good man. Sometimes people die and there is nothing we can do. This happened to some of my mother's friends. There was nothing she could do."

Hart looked at this wise companion and decided he had told her enough. There was no need to tell her everything. He didn't have to tell her about Kevin.

Valentina lay down again next to Hart. He took his cue from her and lay back down, too, desperate for some rest now.

"Mr John, tell me a story whilst we rest," Valentina asked.

"I'm sorry, Valentina, I don't know any stories," Hart said.

They lay in silence for a few moments until Valentina spoke again. "Okay, then I will tell you a story," she said. "I will tell you the story about the Star-lighters. It's my favourite story. My mamá told me this story many, many times. It is all about the children who do not have anywhere to go, and they are lifted into the sky and given a very important job. They become the Star-lighters. It is their job to light the stars at night. Sometimes they don't feel like lighting all the stars and they pull the clouds across the sky, and behind the clouds, they play. They can never come back to earth, but you can't feel sad for the Star-lighters because when they lived here, they were not happy children, they were very unhappy. In the sky, they are always happy. So, they are the lucky ones. They will never be unhappy again. I am a lucky girl because I have a good mamá who always looks after me and makes me happy. She told me if I ever felt unhappy, I could close my eyes and imagine playing in the sky... with the Star-lighters.

I could just close my eyes... and I'd be happy."

Hart closed his eyes.

***

Paola stared up at the stars, thinking about the story of the Star-lighters she had made up and had repeatedly told her daughter over the years; she remembered what comfort it had brought both of them. Having watched Zamora and his men destroy the jungle village she was unable to sleep. She couldn't risk ambushing Zamora, even if she did gather the courage to take him on under the noses of his own men. She couldn't risk getting killed herself and not being able to ensure that Valentina made it to safety. She deduced that her only option was to continue to track Zamora, only attacking him if caught up with Valentina and the British soldier.

What if Zamora caught up with them and killed the soldier, and then took Valentina back? With what her daughter knew, without her mother to protect her, Valentina would not be safe in the FARC. She knew too much for any female, let alone a child. Whilst she believed that Zamora, no matter how sadistic he was, would never harm his own child, what about the FARC commanders higher up the chain? They would never risk leaving Valentina alive.

Paola shuddered.

A few metres away Borgman was breathing deeply. He was asleep. Paola was in two minds about whether to carry on alone and leave him. He was not much use to her. There was something about him she didn't like or trust, but she thought it prudent to maintain the status quo for the time being.

CHAPTER SIXTEEN

B OB KING was hearing voices. A couple of hours ago they'd stopped for the night. Kav had followed Hart's trail assiduously as far as he felt he could go before the light failed. The ground had swerved into a narrow valley. Through it ran a small stream that they had followed for most of the afternoon, it seemed like the perfect place to stop for the night. From the narrow corridor of this jungle valley, they could see small shrubs growing on either side of what was almost a gorge. The jungle had been the heart of this world but now they felt they were deep inside its soul.

Bob had ordered the men into an all-round defensive circle, facing outwards, so that they would be able to watch for any surprise attack that might come before night fell and the blanket of darkness finally descended upon them until the morning. They would then take turns sleeping and keeping watch throughout the night. Although he had forbidden any naked flames—which meant they had only eaten cold rations—Bob had conceded to hammocks being erected rather than sleeping on the jungle floor in a 'hard routine' scenario. Having a hammock and an overhead 'Basha' to sleep under was a welcome concession, especially to Hammond and Carter who were still struggling with the harsh conditions in the jungle. The noises that had fascinated both men earlier in the day now felt threatening to them.

The vines had taken on the appearance of snakes and every shadow had now become a potential crouching Jaguar in search of a fresh kill. Bob had considered making them sleep on the jungle floor to punish them for their slow progress. As it was, they'd been clueless about hanging their hammocks and Bob had ended up hanging them himself before retiring to his own hammock.

Kav took the first watch.

An hour after nightfall, the rain began. It wasn't just rain; it was a downpour as heavy as any of the men had ever witnessed. It was as if a waterfall had just been turned on. The drops struck the jungle floor like they were bullet rounds being fired from above. The trees offered no shelter, droplets the size of almonds smashed their way through the foliage above. Bob had been unable to sleep. He knew he needed to rest but found he was unable to still his mind and had taken to listening to the rain, as well as the distant racket of the nocturnal animals in the tree canopy above. The noises came from every direction, rustling, squeaks, clicks, bird song and mammalian calls.

Suddenly, Bob realised he wasn't just listening to the sounds of the animals, which mingled with the sounds of Jock's snoring; he could also hear faint voices. At first, he couldn't make out whether they were coming from within the group or from further beyond, so he decided to investigate.

Bob slid out of his hammock, gathered his belt-kit and M16 and silently crept off towards Kav, who was sheltered nearby underneath a waterproof camouflaged Basha shelter. Bob was doing his best to avoid slipping on the rain-soaked ground which was quickly becoming a sea of thick wet mud. He called out to Kav through the drumming sound of the rain, warning of his imminent approach. A red-filtered torch answered, briefly flickering on and off, assisting Bob through the shroud of darkness that surrounded both men.

Moments later Bob's face appeared under the Basha. "Kav,

can you hear those fucking voices?" Bob hissed. "I think it's coming from those two idiots we're having to babysit. What a pair of absolute fucking wankers. I just wanted to make sure one of them hadn't got out of his hammock for a piss and got lost in the dark and was now bothering you."

"Yea, I've heard them too. Those fuckers will get us all killed out here. Do you want me to go over there and sort them out? I can give them both a swift punch to the head if you want?" Kav offered, a little too eagerly.

"No, it's okay. I'll go over there myself and tell them to keep it down and wind their necks in," Bob replied, with a frustrated edge to his voice. "I'll relive you shortly and let you get some shut-eye." Bob turned and headed off towards the direction of Hammond and Carter.

As he approached through the darkness, he pinpointed the voices; they sounded more urgent, even though they were hushed beneath the noise of the rain.

Bob decided to move closer to try and listen more clearly to what the men were discussing. Using the noise from the downpour to silence his approach, he stopped just a few metres from Hammond and Carter.

At first, the conversation seemed to be simply the two men complaining about their female boss. What he heard them say about Diana Brooks, Bob couldn't disagree with. He laughed silently and inwardly to think of how she would fare herself in these conditions. However, the subject matter soon turned more disconcerting. Bob strained to hear exactly what they were saying.

"Just keep your eyes on the prize, mate! We play it cool here and we'll be back in Bogotá picking up payment from the Colombians in no time." That was Hammond's voice, Bob deduced.

"I was ready to walk when she said she was sending us out here. What if Borgman's dead already? How do we get paid then?" Carter hissed.

"We had no choice. She would have shipped us back to

London without severance if we'd refused. Just sit tight," warned Hammond.

"I don't know if I can handle another day of this bullshit," Carter moaned.

"Well, we don't have a choice. Don't fucking bail on me now. If we do go down, we'll go down together. We have to stick it out!" Hammond whispered, beginning to sound exasperated.

"Okay, okay," Carter agreed. "But we go back to the FARC and ask for more money for this. We didn't sign up for this shit."

Bob had heard enough. He clenched his left fist around the stock of his M16 as tightly as he could, almost trying to snap it and channel his anger. He gritted his teeth in an effort to remain silent. It took all his inner strength to suppress the rage he felt. He badly wanted to kill both men then and there, though he knew visceral reactions were seldom helpful and productive. Instead, he would have to let go of his rage and use logic. He had to think smart.

After allowing himself time to calm down sufficiently, Bob finally shouted out through the noise of the heavy downpour. "Guys, for fuck sake, keep the noise down. Go to sleep. You were worse than useless today. I don't want you falling apart and compromising us tomorrow. Get some rest. Do I make myself clear?"

There was a pregnant pause before both men grunted sounds of consent.

Bob made his way back over to Kav and discreetly shared what he'd just overheard the two men discussing. Bob insisted that Kav kept the information to himself until he'd had a chance to speak with Jock and Mike in the morning and decided how best to deal with Hammond and Carter.

For the next couple of hours after taking over sentry duty, Bob turned over in his head what he had heard. So, they were on the take from the FARC. That made sense. Bob hadn't trusted them from the outset. Now he'd confirmed his suspicions. What would happen if they met a FARC patrol and Hammond and Carter decided to cash in their goodwill with them; these men were a liability. Bob was still livid. He needed to get rid of them as soon as possible. He'd find a place to dump them off; he felt justified. They were holding them back. Nothing would give him more relief. If they survived until they were picked up, he would then turn them in and expose them for what they were. C'est la vie when you become a dirty traitor. He wouldn't give it another thought.

CHAPTER SEVENTEEN

A SENSE OF PEACE enveloped John Hart as he gained consciousness after a very brief rest. It was a strange sensation as if his mind was a clean slate and clear of all thoughts. He felt as though he was floating, suspended in the ether and in a different dimension. The pleasant feeling only lasted another few brief seconds before reality crashed in around him. With the sounds of the jungle reaching his ears and the small figure huddled against him. He opened his eyes.

Dawn sent shimmering rays over the jungle, the eastern sky filled with blended colours of pinks, yellows, and pale oranges. A mere glimpse of heaven that would quickly fade into blue. The colours of the foliage returned to green and the air surrounding them had already started to warm up as if someone had just turned on a modern convection oven. It was the perfect dawn, one to be savoured instead of squandered. Now though, he had to get up; they had to get moving. Under this radiant beauty a new day had come, new possibilities, a fresh page yet to be written.

"Valentina," he whispered, shaking her shoulder gently. "Valentina, come on, wake up. We have to get going."

As Valentina pulled her tired little body off the jungle floor and stretched her limbs, Hart took out his map to consult it. They were still about three miles from the border of the Utría National Park, and now that they had crossed the river it looked as if there were no more major obstacles in their path. If they were lucky and they moved at a decent pace, they might reach the northern border of the park in a few hours. Hart checked his watch. It was almost 6 am. Hopefully, Zamora and his men were only just leaving the village, and they still had to cross the river. Hart estimated that this gave them a good few hours head start, but they still couldn't afford to waste any time.

As he got to his feet, Hart realised he ached from head to toe. His shoulder throbbed and he hoped that it hadn't become infected. He didn't have time to check. They were both hungry and weak, but they had to keep moving.

"Okay, Mr John, let's go," Valentina said, gently.

Hart marvelled at her stoicism. The way his body was feeling, he couldn't even begin to imagine how she was feeling. They had both been tossed around in the river and their clothes were still soaking wet. He put his hand on her shoulder and gave it a gentle reassuring squeeze. He was out of words. She too. Valentina nodded at him and gave him a weak smile.

They set off through the jungle.

Rather than head southwards and take the direct route towards the park, Hart decided they should stick to the riverbank and follow the tributary to the Río Atrato and then follow the main river south to the park boundary. Although this would entail them making two sides of a triangle, at least they were guaranteed a relatively easy path. The jungle looked dense and it would prove slow going taking the direct route, whereas along the riverbank the vegetation appeared to be fairly forgiving and sparse in some areas. Choosing this route also meant that he wouldn't have to keep checking their location; they could navigate by following the path of the rivers. Hart felt weak, and any advantage that could be gained from taking an easier route would prove vital in surviving this ordeal.

***

Zamora had woken his men before dawn by kicking them. In the early morning light, Juan had taken up the *rastro* and the other men had followed... the mood was sombre after the demise of Diego. Juan pushed all thoughts of the FARC leadership's response to a group of their soldiers entering the Utría National Park far from his mind. They would be severely punished for sure, but at that moment he couldn't think of these things, because punishment at the hands of Zamora for losing the *soldado sangriento* and his daughter would be far worse.

Fortunately for Juan, the *soldado sangriento* had not been able to be too careful when escaping the village and there was plenty of clues and broken branches to help guide him. Juan was impressed that the *soldado sangriento* had managed to make any progress at all. The jungle could become quite impassable at night. Whilst he was sure that the pair were probably much further ahead than Zamora was willing to believe, it was essential that Juan continued to ensure Zamora believed that it was possible for them to close the gap.

He had a moment of nervous uncertainty when they reached a shallow river and it took him a while to pick up the trail again when they reached the other side, but when he finally did, they made quick progress right up to the moment when they reached the main tributary river that ran into the Río Atrato. At this point, Juan's heart sank. The pair had definitely gone into the river! The *rastro* stopped at the bank, but the current was so strong it would have swept them downriver several hundred metres; maybe even as far as the Río Atrato, which flowed northwards towards where they had started out from. In fact, Juan was doubtful if they'd made it across in one piece at all. He silently prayed that his tracking didn't end with the sighting of a couple of corpses lying on the riverbank. If it did, he was sure there would be more corpses joining them and thrown on to the heap. He kept these thoughts to himself as Zamora began barking out orders for the group to begin entering the fast-flowing river.

Without mentioning he was terrified of the water, having seen a crocodile bite a man's leg clean off when he was a child, Juan dutifully followed behind Colm and Cesar as instructed by Zamora. He shuddered as he watched Cesar prepare to enter the river. At 39 years old, Cesar was the oldest and least fit member of their group. He'd gained weight in the four years since his wife had died. She had been an officer in the FARC, very beautiful and was one of Zamora's favourite victims. The rumour was that she had started to refuse Zamora's advances and Zamora had killed her in a fit of rage. Cesar had never spoken out about the incident if indeed it was true. He had simply retreated into himself, but there was a dark glint in his eye whenever he was around Zamora.

Before he was fully submerged, Juan watched in horror as Zamora's body was pulled under the raging torrent of water. The water spray was constant, reducing his vision to only just a few feet. He had lost sight of Zamora. Juan dared hope for a moment, that his tyrannical boss might be lost forever. Finally, Juan spotted Zamora. He had surfaced, coughing and spluttering. He had somehow found a foothold and was beginning to wade out towards the other side.

Moments later, Juan was also being pulled under.

Remembering what he'd been taught by his father, he did his best not to fight against the current but to work with it as he struggled to half swim and half walk along the riverbed, holding his breath for as long as he could whilst submerged. By the time he resurfaced, he could hear Cesar screaming behind him, but he kept pushing forward. It was each man for himself in situations like these. Juan had one purpose and one purpose only: to reach the far bank that he saw looming in front of him.

It wasn't until he'd pulled himself all the way out of the river that Juan looked back to see where the rest of the group were. He was shocked to see how much further downstream he had travelled than anyone else. He was also aware that there was a commotion going on upriver.

Exhausted, Juan trudged back towards the other men. As he drew closer, he realised they were pulling an unconscious Cesar out of the river. The big man was barely alive, he had struck his head against rocks, blood now covered almost his entire face.

***

It was shortly before 9 am when they arrived at what Hart believed was the north-east corner of the Utría National Park. There were no distinctive posts or large fences to mark the boundary, but Hart's calculations, based on his map and the time they had been on the move, told him they were probably now just entering the park.

Valentina looked completely drained and exhausted. Hart told her to rest beside a nearby enormous mahogany tree whilst he had a quick look around for any buildings or definite tracks. She gratefully sank to the ground, curled up and closed her eyes.

Hart almost immediately came across a well-defined dirt track. Using his compass, Hart calculated that the track was heading south-west. There didn't seem to be any other signs of civilization.

When Hart returned to Valentina, she was fast asleep. Taking in what a pathetic, pitiful sight she cut, still dressed in her wet, filthy t-shirt and shorts, looking worryingly weak and frail, Hart decided to give her a few more minutes rest before they continued following the track he had just discovered. With any luck, they would come across a park official, or even the mysterious 'white woman' the village chief had spoken of, who would hopefully take them to Quibdó. He felt a certain sense of relief at having made it this far and reaching the park in one piece and still very much alive.

***

Hammond yelped like a dog when he hit the ground after Bob kicked him out of his hammock. A moment later, Carter was also scrambling across the jungle floor having been rudely awakened.

"Hey! What the fuck are you doing?" Carter yelled at Bob.

"Get packed up. We're moving out," Bob told them, plainly.

"But it's still dark," Hammond protested.

"Won't be in ten minutes," Bob replied, sharply. "Now pack up your stuff or you'll be staying here by yourselves."

A few moments earlier, Bob had discretely spoken with Jock and Mike, recounting the conversation he'd overheard between Hammond and Carter just hours earlier. Both SAS men had immediately wanted to take decisive action against the two traitors but had finally relented after hearing how Bob planned to off-load both men at the first available opportunity, leaving Hammond and Carter to take their chances surviving in the jungle on their own—survival chances that were slim at best. Once Bob and his team eventually returned to the British Embassy, he would report both men to Diana Brooks. After sharing the news, Bob was confident there would be no recovery party coming to look for Hammond and Carter anytime soon.

True to his word, ten minutes later the group left the narrow valley by the stream, with Kav leading in a south-easterly direction.

The group trudged on for just over an hour in absolute silence, pushing their way through the dense, suffocating undergrowth, fighting for air, which now hung heavy, moist and still. It was still early morning by the time they were within sight of the clearing that lay just 20 metres ahead of them. Kav stopped abruptly and Bob grabbed Hammond and Carter, pulling them aggressively to the ground. Even from where they were lying, Bob could smell the bloodshed. His heart sank as he imagined the devastation that they were about to witness.

Indicating to Hammond and Carter that they should stay put, Bob followed Kav who crawled forward on his stomach towards the edge of the clearing. They peered out from amongst the trees at the remnants of the native village. The majority of the huts had been burnt and levelled to the ground.

Only the large main building in the centre of the clearing retained a few of its walls, although it looked as though the roof had been blown in. Corpses lay scattered all over the place.

The silence was eerie; there were clearly no survivors. The sour stench of faeces radiated from the village, beckoning flies to cautiously hover and feast upon the bodies.

"Let's hope John's not amongst that lot," Kav whispered. Bob didn't answer; he didn't want to entertain the idea.

Once they were reasonably satisfied that whoever had carried out this horrific attack had long since gone, and there was no sign of life around them, Bob stood up and motioned for the rest of his SAS team to slowly follow him into the village. Hammond and Carter were to remain by the treeline until the search had been completed. As they moved into the open clearance, each member of the SAS team continued to scan for any remaining human presence. What they came across was a horrific sight. Men, women, and children had been shot, stabbed and burnt alive. The acrid smell of burning flesh and death hung thick in the air. There was an uncomfortable silence; even the animals in the surrounding jungle had gone quiet, as if in a mark of respect.

Bob instructed the men to check over every single body, praying that no one identified Hart and the girl.

It was with a great sense of relief that Mike and Jock returned to Bob thirty minutes later to confirm that they were both sure Hart was not amongst the dead.

The child they could not be so certain about. Although they had a vague idea of what she'd been wearing, none of them could accurately remember her face with any detail. They had only briefly seen her from a distance just before the FARC camp attack. Mike and

Jock had also found a dead FARC soldier lying near the centre of the village. Half his face had already been eaten away during the night, but it looked like he had been shot in the head at close range.

To add to the good news that Hart's body had not been sighted, Kav returned to the group to confirm that he had managed to pick up Hart's trail on the edge of the clearing. He led the group over to the area he'd been studying.

"See this," Kav pointing to the imprint of a large boot print next to a smaller sized imprint. "This is definitely John and the girl. By the width of these imprints and how recent they look, I'd say they were definitely travelling in a hurry."

"Can you tell how long ago they left the village?" Bob asked.

"I'd say these footprints are no older than roughly twelve hours, so perhaps around dusk last night," Kav speculated. "They would have fled the attack and probably started out in the dark."

"What about tracks left by whoever carried out the attack on the village?" Bob asked, gravely.

"Yes, here," said Kav pointing at the ground around the first footprints. There were several fresh footprints clearly visible in the soft muddy ground. "They left just a few hours ago. Must have waited until first light to follow them. The first group of men is now only four, not five. The other group, the twosome, also followed shortly afterwards."

Mike pointed behind them towards the village. "Yea, Jock and I found one of the FARC fuckers over there with half his face eaten away. Looks like he'd been shot in the head at close range."

Bob nodded. "Which means, hopefully, John managed to put a little distance between himself and this lot following."

"But also, between him and us," piped up Jock. Bob nodded ruefully. He took a few steps away from the group and then turned to face them.

"So, here's what we've got so far, boys. John left the FARC camp with the girl. At some point, he's encountered a group of natives who've led him to this village. Meanwhile, another group, we'll assume it's the FARC, due to the one lying over there forming part of a wildlife dinner menu, tracked John to the village. He escaped as they launched the attack on the village."

"And the last group? The duo?" asked Mike. Bob frowned, puzzled.

"Who the fuck knows? Could be another FARC faction?" Bob brushed it off; this was of little concern to him at that moment. He instructed Jock to go and fetch Hammond and Carter from the nearby treeline and then the group continued on their way.

***

Hart and Valentina were following what felt like the road to nowhere. Hart began to gently hum to himself, the song belonging to the popular Talking Heads band, '*Road to Nowhere*'. They were beginning to overheat as the sun was now almost directly overhead and there was no nearby tree cover to protect them. The road had clearly been used as a logging road, no doubt transporting an enormous number of felled trees through the Utría National Park towards the Pacific highway some 40 miles away. The jungle vegetation had been stripped and cleared away long ago, the remnants of felled trees lay rotting or drying out in the sun along the roadside. Their bark beginning to curl, ridges raised and silvery in the late morning sun. How far the road stretched before it arrived at any town or village, was anyone's guess. There was nothing marked on Hart's map. He had to hope that if they followed the road for long enough, they would eventually come across park employees working in the jungle.

The clear path should have made their progress quicker, but the early effects of heat exhaustion were beginning to slow them down. Valentina had already been forced to stop twice and Hart was beginning to seriously worry. Out in the open with no jungle canopy to protect them, the sun was an oppressive presence that continued to sap their energy. If they didn't find help soon, he would be forced to leave the track and seek refuge in the nearby trees. This would slow them down even further and probably allow their pursuers to catch up. Hart wasn't sure they were going to make it.

So, when they came across a narrow trail leading off into the jungle with visible
tyre marks on it, suggesting a vehicle had driven along it fairly recently, Hart didn't hesitate. They had nothing to lose. They would follow the narrow trail and pray that it would lead them to the owner of the vehicle. It was the first sign of western civilization Hart had seen since entering the jungle two days previously. Hart also welcomed the good fortune that the trail was protected and directly under the canopy of the trees again, which would give them some much-needed shade from the midday sun. The trail was intertwined with thick tree roots. The light beamed through the tree foliage, covering them and everything around them in a warm green light. The trail swerved back and forth unpredictably with mighty trees arching over it. The trail looked fairly well used and clear. As they made their way along the trail, Hart studied the vehicle tracks. He was sure it was a substantial 4x4 type. Perhaps a Jeep or a Land Rover.

His hopes were raised even further when he finally spotted a small jungle clearing up ahead, and a small hut eventually came into view in the centre of the clearing. There was a vehicle was parked outside the hut. As Hart had guessed, it was a Land Rover Discovery, although it was old and beaten up. He looked at Valentina and she smiled at him. They hardly dared hope that the worst was really over.

As they approached the hut, they noticed that it had been well cared for. The hut sat like a timid mouse under the sprawling giant trees surrounding it. It was made entirely of wood and there was a small garden to one side that was full of tropical flowers, trees, and plants. This looked like someone's home. Not wanting to take any chances, Hart reached for his 9mm Sig pistol and slowly took off the safety catch. He motioned to Valentina to shelter beside the Land Rover whilst he investigated further.

As Hart slowly approached the hut, a voice rang out, making him jump.

"Who's there? I have a gun. I am not afraid to use it. Don't try anything. I will shoot you if I have to." Whoever it was, spoke in poor broken Spanish.

Hart replied in fluent Spanish. "I'm sorry, we didn't mean to alarm you. I'm a soldier. I'm British and travelling with this young girl. We are being followed by FARC soldiers and need help urgently."

"My Spanish is not very good. Did you say you are British?" the woman spoke again, this time in English.

"Yes," replied Hart in English. "Are you American?" enquired Hart.

"Canadian," she said, after a short pause. "Okay, I am putting my gun down and opening the door now. Please show me your hands before I come out."

Hart put his pistol away and held up his hands. The door to the hut opened and a woman looked out. She checked that Hart was unarmed and then emerged. She was dressed in large, baggy clothes and her long grey hair was matted, almost into dreadlocks. She looked completely unkempt and Hart estimated she was probably in her mid-50s, although if someone had given her a bath and a haircut, perhaps she might have passed for 45.

The woman smiled at Hart. "I don't often get visitors out here. You scared me."

"I'm sorry," Hart said. "As I said, I'm British, and with the Army. I have a young girl with me. I need to get her to safety." He turned and walked back towards the Land Rover. "Valentina, you can come out into the open now. It's safe." Valentina walked out slowly from behind the Land Rover.

"Why, hello, child. Do you speak English?" the woman asked her. Valentina nodded but her shyness prevented her from speaking. "Valentina. That's a beautiful name. My name is Amelia."

"I like your name, too," Valentina eventually said, suddenly warming to Amelia and walking right up to her. "This man is Mr

John. He is a good man and helping me."

"Well, Valentina, you and John look like you need some food and rest. Please come inside and make yourselves at home?"

Valentina and Hart followed Amelia inside. Whilst there was little in the way of furniture—a wooden bed, a small table and two chairs, a small stove and some basic cooking and washing facilities—everything was very neat, everything except for a pile of books and papers that were precariously piled up in the corner of the room.

"I'm a conservationist," Amelia explained, seeing both Hart and Valentina staring at the books. "I'm studying everything about the natural wildlife and vegetation in this part of the rainforest. I've lived here for two years, recording endless information about every species of flora and fauna."

As she spoke, Amelia put some bowls of fruit, nuts and vegetables on the table as well as a plate of dried meat and fish. "Please, dip in and help yourselves."

Hart and Valentina fell on the food hungrily. Amelia poured them both glasses of water that they practically inhaled. Meeting Amelia for the first time, they had not stopped to think about how hungry and thirsty they were.

"We are very grateful," Hart said, not caring that he spoke with a mouth full of some very delicious berries. "But we cannot stay here too long. We must get to the park office where I hope someone can help us. Failing that, Quibdó will do."

"The park office is on the coast and several hours drive away," Amelia informed him. "I have a better suggestion. Not far from here there's a small airstrip. There's a light aircraft there, it transports workers and brings in supplies. I'm sure you would be able to hitch a lift and persuade the pilot to fly you to Bogotá, where I assume you need to go."

Hart wanted to throw his arms around Amelia and kiss her. They were saved. They were going to make it. He was sure of it.

CHAPTER EIGHTEEN

Z AMORA had allowed his men precious little time to recover from their river crossing. They were now pushing forward along the riverbank as fast as ever, with Juan in the lead. The mood amongst the group was low and Juan was exhausted; he had lost the *rastro* a couple of times, only picking it up each time through sheer luck. At times, he pretended he was on a definite track when really, he was just following the riverbank, praying that the *soldado sangriento* had done the same.

As the group continued heading southwards, following the Río Atrato towards the Utría National Park, Zamora began to lose patience, plus the late morning sun was starting to bite and give him a headache. They were more exposed on the riverbank, and although this allowed them to scoop water up to cool their heads occasionally, the heat and the humidity made their journey almost unbearable.

After a few more minutes, Juan stopped once again to inspect the ground. Zamora finally snapped. He walked up to the hunched figure of Juan, lifted his leg and kicked the side of Juan's head with brutal force. Juan instantly fell down the riverbank, landing awkwardly and almost falling into the river. He was barely conscious and held his head, screaming out in agony. Zamora walked towards the waterline, reaching down and dragged Juan back up the riverbank before kicking him again, this time in the ribs and even more savagely.

"This is not a game!" Zamora screamed. "My daughter's life is at risk. If anything happens to her, I will hold you personally responsible and kill you in the most painful way you could ever imagine!" Zamora continued to kick Juan in the stomach and ribs as he spoke every fifth or sixth word. Juan could do nothing but curl up into a ball, trying to shield himself from the full impact of Zamora's savage attack.

Suddenly, Zamora was grabbed from behind and pulled away from Juan. Zamora whipped around, furious, his hand flying towards his sidearm. He hesitated when he saw Colm standing before him and, at 6' 4", towering over him.

"What are you doing?" Zamora screamed like a petulant child. "I will discipline my men any way I see fit. You will not interfere." Colm stepped right up to Zamora.

The other men cowered in fear. Colm, the measured one was going to speak, and speak up to Zamora.

"I couldn't care less about what you do to your men, but this one's the only tracker in the group. If we lose him, we're fucked. If you're that heated up, go find a monkey to shoot, but don't kill the guide. I don't know about you, but I fucking want to get out of here alive. If we lose him," Colm gave a quick nod towards where Juan lay semi-conscious on the ground, "We could be lost for days and die out here."

Zamora and Colm continued to stare at each other. The other men were rooted to the spot; nobody dared move. They all assumed Colm's fate was sealed. After a few uncomfortable moments, however, a smile slowly appeared on Zamora's face. He turned and walked a few paces into the jungle, got out his Russian made pistol and shot a brightly coloured parrot that was perched nearby on a branch about ten feet above the ground. The parrot fell, the strike mark on the bird was eternal, a scar from the bullet round that had instantly taken the bird's life. There was silence, save for Juan's groans as Colm helped him to his feet.

Zamora turned to Colm. "Do you see how I shot that parrot? If you ever challenge me in front of my men like that again, I will aim and shoot at your head like it's a parrot in a tree." Zamora aimed his gun at Colm's head to demonstrate before adding, "Do we understand each other, Irishman?"

"One hundred percent," Colm replied, slowly and coldly.

***

Amelia watched Hart and Valentina devour the food she served them and drink the reviving coffee she'd brewed. For several minutes all that could be heard in the little hut in the middle of the Colombian jungle were the sounds of Hart and Valentina eating and drinking.

"What happened to your shoulder," Amelia asked Hart, finally.

"I was shot," he informed her, between mouthfuls of food.

"Who cleaned it up and dressed it?" Amelia enquired.

"Some old witch doctor we met in the jungle," Hart quipped. Valentina frowned at him but was too busy eating to speak.

"Sorry," Hart mumbled, noting Valentina's frown. "Don't mean to be flippant. He probably saved my life."

"I should perhaps take a quick look at it," Amelia suggested, moving over to a shelf and taking down a wooden box. "I have a few basic medical supplies."

Hart turned his chair to her and sat patiently whilst she removed the primitive dressing that had been applied, cleaned the wound with antiseptic and redressed it. "Is that a Scottish accent I detect?"

"Yes," Hart informed her, as she applied the antiseptic. "I'm originally from Glasgow."

"My father's side of the family is from Scotland. My grandfather moved over to Toronto after the war, in 1948. My parents met in Toronto and moved to a town called Newmarket, just north of Toronto. That's where I was raised."

"Never been to Canada," Hart admitted.

"It's a beautiful country," Amelia said, softly. "Although I don't miss it... too many bad memories back there. I'm much happier here."

"What kind of wildlife and vegetation do you study exactly?" Hart asked, diplomatically changing the subject.

"I mostly track endangered birds. We've recorded nearly 2,000 species of birds' native to the Colombian jungle. We're particularly worried about the parrots. They're threatened by loss of habitat due to deforestation in these parts, as well as a lucrative trafficking trade. They're hard to breed in captivity. They're emotional and stubborn creatures. It wasn't too far from here, in the Amazonian jungle that the *Spix Macaw* population dwindled to just one. We'll see that happen to some of the populations in Colombia if we're not too careful."

"I had a *papagayo*; he was my friend," Valentina blurted out. "He had red and green wings and tail, but his head and shoulders were the colour of the sky. He flew away on my birthday last year and never came back."

"That sounds like a blue-headed *pinous*." Amelia said, gently. "They're rare here in the Chocó. Did he have some pink on his throat here?" Valentina nodded, enthusiastically, and Amelia smiled. "Then your friend was a *rubrigularis*. They are very beautiful." Valentina smiled, but it was clear she was fighting her emotions as she recalled far away memories. Hart took this as his cue to get moving.

"We're really very grateful for your hospitality," Hart said, standing up. "But we must get moving. The people who are following us could be less than an hour or so behind us for all we know."

Of course," Amelia said, "Let me get my car keys and we'll hit the road. I'll take you to the airstrip. If we have no luck there, then I'll drive you to Quibdó. That's the closest town; it's just over 20 miles away. You'll be able to make a call from there and ask your people to come and get you."

Hart walked outside whilst Amelia found her keys. The jungle was baking hot and almost completely still. A few nearby birds called out whilst pecking for grubs. There was the occasional movement of mammals, mostly small, sometimes not. Distant chattering and squawking could be heard, but apart from that, there was a general hush, as if the jungle was taking a much-needed midday siesta. Hart suddenly felt a wave of tiredness sweep over him. He closed his eyes for a few seconds. They sprung open again as he felt something touch his hand. He looked down. Valentina had taken his hand. She held onto it tight.

"I think this is a good woman. She will take us somewhere safe, yes?"

Hart nodded and gave Valentina a weak smile.

As they drove through the jungle, Amelia asked a few questions about Valentina. Hart avoided giving too much information away. He made it sound as though he and Valentina had crossed paths by chance - that fate had thrown them together and he was trying to get her to safety as they assumed her mother had been killed in the camp raid.

"Forgive me if I'm asking too many questions," Amelia said, sensing there was more to the story, but deciding not to push Hart for any further information. "I don't get to speak to many people out here, just an old American guy called Hank, who also works for the conservation agency. He delivers my food and water supplies to the Utría National Park headquarters on the coast once a month. I drive there to submit my research and recommendations and collect the supplies. That's the only chance I get to speak English."

They fell silent for a moment. Suddenly Amelia looked at Hart, something had just occurred to her.

"Do you have any money?" she asked him.

"A few dollars," he replied. I wasn't expecting to be in the jungle for more than a day at most."

Keeping one hand on the steering wheel, Amelia's reached

inside her shirt and pulled out a pouch that was attached to a cord around her neck. She niftily unbuttoned it with one hand and pulled out five one-hundred-dollar bill notes.

She handed them to Hart. "That's five hundred, American, that should easily buy you a passage to Bogotá." Hart didn't take the offered cash.

"I can't take that from you. That's a lot of money," he said, hesitantly.

"Take it!" Amelia urged him. "What do I need it for? Everything I need is provided for me. I just keep a little cash hanging around in case of emergencies, and correct me if I'm not wrong, but this is an emergency. You never know when you might need it to save your life. In this part of the world, your life's always on a knife's edge. I'd hate not to use this money to save someone," laughed Amelia.

Before Hart could protest again, a little hand reached forward from the back seat and grabbed the cash out of Amelia's hand. Hart whipped around to see Valentina staring at the money, her face lit up with awe.

"Thank you, lady," Valentina said with reverence. "You are kind, a very kind lady."

Hart frowned. He didn't know how to express his gratitude. He was beginning to shake. A familiar stirring was starting in his stomach; he tasted acid in his mouth.

"I'm sorry," he said suddenly. "I need you to stop, now. I'm going to be sick."

Amelia pulled over immediately. Hart jumped out just in time. He bent over double and with one violent contraction, all the undigested food that Amelia had earlier prepared for them propelled into the air. He heaved again and once more the contents of his stomach splattered across the ground at the side of the track. Hart wiped at his mouth, acidic residue forming a shiny patch on his sleeve.

Sorry about that," he said, climbing back into the Land Rover. "I'm okay, I feel better for that. We can carry on now."

Amelia looked at him, concerned. "I hope it was nothing I gave you."

"No, no," said Hart. Then Valentina piped up from the rear.

"He is very sick because he hurt a boy soldier in another country and then his friend died." Hart looked over at Amelia who didn't take her eyes off the road in front of them.

"I see. I think that would make anyone very sick," Amelia said.

***

Kav's face was intently focussed on the ground as he studied the point where Hart and Valentina had crossed the river. Finally, he looked up at Bob. "John and the girl definitely crossed the river at this point here, Bob. So did the group of four following them, but it looks like the other group of two decided to head upriver, presumably looking for an easier crossing point place." He stood up and faced Bob. "What do you think?" he asked, looking at the white water cascaded past a series of rocky outcrops in front of them. A plume of water vapour hung over the riverbank. As with the previous groups who had passed by this point, had their clothes not already been soaked from the oppressive humidity, the water spray from the river would have drenched them as if they'd been caught in a heavy rainstorm.

"Should we try and cross here or head upriver?" Kav suggested.

Bob frowned. "My personal choice would be to go upriver," he addressed the group as a whole, "But we don't have the time. I think we've got to hope that if John with a young girl in tow, managed to make it across, then we can, too."

"We don't even know if they made it across, they could be ten feet under for all we know," Carter said, gruffly. Bob ignored him.

"Prepare your kit, guys, we'll start to make the crossing in a couple of minutes."

"You have got to be fucking joking," Hammond shouted out, stepping forward. "That's just suicide. I'm not going in there."

"Not a problem," Bob replied, calmly. "You two can stay here. Suits us fine. I'm sick of you both. We'll send someone to pick you up in a day or so." Bob turned his attention to preparing his kit for the crossing.

After a few minutes, Bob looked up to see that Hammond and Carter hadn't moved. They were both ashen faced, assuming they were caught between a rock and a hard place in the worst possible way, convinced that they were about to face their demise one way or another.

Bob finally suggested. "I'm prepared to leave you here with a few days' rations. I'll make sure you get picked up once this shit show is over?"

Hammond and Carter looked at each other for a split second before Hammond spoke for the two of them. "Okay, we'll stay here," he said, shakily.

"Hold on," said Carter. "If they don't make it across, we're totally fucked. No one knows we're here; there will be no rescue party."

"Good point," Hammond agreed after thinking it through for a moment longer. "Okay, we're going to cross with you, but let's see one of you cross first, so we know it's at least possible."

Bob shook his head, exasperated and half hoping the pair of them drowned in the river like the rats they were. He sighed to himself as he continued making his preparations to cross the river. Each man took off his belt-kit and attached it to the back of their lightweight Bergens, ensuring both were fully waterproofed and everything was correctly sealed. In the jungle, once equipment became wet it was almost impossible to get it dry again due to the extreme humidity in the air. Damp equipment would rot very quickly and a man with rotting equipment would not survive very long in this brutal habitat. They then secured their rifles to their belt-kit and double-checked that their weapons couldn't be detached and become lost in the river.

Once they were satisfied that all their equipment was secure and waterproofed, Bob told Mike and Jock to cross first. The current almost immediately gripped the legs of each man as they lowered themselves into the ferocious, fast-flowing river, threatening to destabilise them. They seemed unfazed; they had faced far tougher challenges whilst serving with the SAS in other parts of the world. They defied the swelling rapids around them as they glided across the river, using the current and protruding rocks to their advantage. It took them less than ten minutes to cross.

Hammond and Carter looked mildly impressed and reassured... until Bob turned to them, grinning, and said, "Right, your turn."

Unlike Mike and Jock before them, Bob and Kav had a terrifying experience crossing the river. It wasn't the current or the rocky terrain that hindered them, it was Hammond and Carter trying to grab on to the two SAS men for support. It took them twice as long as the advance party to get across. Whilst they were greeted with the good news that Kav had picked up the trail again, Bob was almost apoplectic.

"You could have got us killed!" he shouted at Hammond and Carter. "You're the biggest pair of wankers I've ever come across. We almost drowned out there because of you two fucking idiots." He was panting with exhaustion and anger. Hammond and Carter were on their hands and knees recovering from the crossing.

"Jock, give them two days rations, we're leaving these two here."

Hammond looked up at Bob, terrified. He still hadn't caught his breath. Bob rounded on him before he could even open his mouth.

"You were more than happy to stay over there, which would have saved us time and avoided Kav and me swallowing half the fucking river," he practically spat at Hammond. "So, that's it! I'm finished dragging your arses along. You stay. No fucking discussion." He looked up at his team. "Two minutes, guys, and then we move out."

Hammond and Carter sat, speechless, on the riverbank as Jock unpacked some rations for them.

Finally, Carter looked at Bob and spoke in an apologetic voice. "You will get someone to come and pick us up in a day or so?"

"Didn't I fucking tell you I would, prick," Bob muttered, still fuming.

When the men had finished rearranging their equipment, checking that their weapons were water-free and working properly, they set off. Whilst they were uplifted by the fact that they now knew that Hart and the girl hadn't drowned, their urgency was also ramped up by the news that the group of four following Hart had also made it across.

They had no idea how far the two groups ahead had travelled and couldn't afford to waste another second.

***

Paola had gambled that there would be an easier crossing point just upriver where it would hopefully be less fast flowing and much shallower. Her instinct had proved correct. She and Borgman had successfully crossed the river without any problems. They were now making their way back down the river following the far bank, Paola searching for the point where she could pick up the *rastro* again. Suddenly Paola held her arm out to stop Borgman.

"Listen," she hissed. They stood, still and silent, listening for the noise that Paola had heard. Just up ahead around the river bend, they could both now make out the distinct sound of voices speaking English. Paola and Borgman inched forward until they, at last, saw two men sitting on the riverbank. It sounded as though they were arguing about equally sharing their food.

She motioned to Borgman to stay put whilst she investigated further. Paola crept into the nearby trees, staying out of sight. She continued to stealthily move forward, knowing how to approach without making any noise. The roar of the river would assist her and cover the sound of her final approach.

Finally, having positioned herself behind a tree, Paola spoke sharply. "Don't move. I have a gun."

Hammond and Carter spun around and looked to see where the voice had come from. "Don't shoot. We're unarmed," Hammond blurted out.

"Put your hands on your head and stand up slowly," Paola instructed both men.

The two men did exactly as they were told. Only when they were upstanding with their hands firmly clasped on their heads did Paola emerge from the jungle, her AK47 pointing straight ahead of her. Keeping her weapon aimed at them, Paola drew closer still to the men.

"Who are you and what are you doing here?" she asked them, sharply.

Hammond took in Paola's FARC uniform. "We were kidnapped, but we managed to escape and we're now waiting to be rescued," Hammond replied.

"Bullshit," snapped Paola, quickly moving forward and continuing to aim her AK47 directly at Hammond's head. He capitulated immediately.

"Okay, okay," he said in a strained voice. "We were travelling with some men. They were from the British Army. One of their team got left behind in the jungle and they brought us with them to try and help rescue their man. We're from the British Embassy."

"So why did they leave you behind?" Paola asked. "By any chance, were they part of an attack on a FARC camp north of here a couple of days ago?"

"I don't know. They left us behind because we were slowing them up. We weren't involved in any camp attack; we just pass on information," Carter said suddenly. "Ask him." He looked behind Paola and she turned to see that Borgman had followed her along the riverbank. He held his AK47 down by his side in a relaxed fashion, which told her that Borgman didn't see these men as a threat.

"What does he mean?" she asked Borgman, turning back to look at Hammond and Carter again.

"It's true, these men are with the British Embassy in Colombia. I shared some information about Zamora and the camp. These men are my contacts. I gave them information about the camp in exchange for my freedom. They forced me to work for them when I got busted trying to move goods from Colombia to Europe."

"Goods?" Paola asked. Borgman nodded.
She looked at him for a long time, assessing the situation.

"Okay," said Paola finally, pointedly putting away her AK47. "So, now you two are coming with us." She walked forward to Hammond. "My name is Paola." She held out her hand. With a little hesitation, Hammond slowly took his right hand off his head and took her offered hand.

"Nick," he said, shakily. "And this is Joe."

"Okay, Nick and Joe," Paola said, plainly. "You will join us. You can place your food rations in our backpacks to take with you. We may need some help. Your Dutch friend here may also need some help, he has a bad ankle. If your British friends do not overcome the group of men, we are following up ahead, we will have to do it and we will need as much help as we can get."

Hammond and Carter stared at Borgman; whose face was impassive. He was suddenly aware that, whilst he temporarily needed Paola for her expertise in tracking in order to get to Zamora, ultimately, he would have to get rid of her; she now knew too much. Whether he needed Carter and Hammond alive or dead he wasn't sure yet. The British wouldn't have sent them into the jungle unless the men were indispensable. Then again, as Paola had pointed out, to overcome Zamora and his men, they would need all the help they could get, so it was prudent to make the British men believe that he would be loyal to them.

Borgman looked closely at Paola. Her face gave nothing away.

The dynamic within the group was acutely charged.

Technically they were all enemies, but for the time being, they were dependent on each other for survival. Everyone held their cards close to their chests.

CHAPTER NINETEEN

ART still felt weak after emptying the contents of his stomach onto the jungle floor, and the bumpy ride along the logging road wasn't helping him feel any better.

Valentina sat on the back seat struggling to keep her eyes open; she would drift off for a few seconds, her head lolling forward, and then wake with a start as they hit another bump in the road. Amelia, clearly starved of conversation, chatted away about the various flora and fauna of the area. Hart attempted to sound interested, to be polite—after all, he felt completely indebted to Amelia, her extraordinary generosity had probably saved their lives, but this was hardly the time to be learning about the mating habits of monkeys.

Finally, they emerged into an enormous man-made clearing, Hart scanned the clearing and his heart leapt as he spotted a small light aircraft parked at the far end of what looked like a poorly made runway. It was the sort of plane that would barely have been noticed flying in this part of the world. It looked like a tin can with wings. Maybe some thirty years ago it had passed as the cutting edge of micro-aeroplane engineering, but now it looked more like a battered steel coffin waiting to pitch its human cargo into the hungry jungle below.

The only building visible was a white portacabin, towards which Amelia was now driving. There was also a selection of tree-cutting machinery lying around, a couple of JCB diggers and a small generator. The place looked deserted.

"Doesn't look like anyone's home," Hart mumbled, suddenly feeling a little deflated. Amelia shook her head and smiled at him.

"There will be someone on site. He'll be inside. I just hope it's the pilot and he's sober," she said. Hart threw her an alarmed look.

Amelia parked the Land Rover next to the portacabin. Hart looked into the back seat. Valentina was asleep; he figured there was no point in waking her until he had assessed the situation and considered their options. She was still clutching the five hundred dollars that she had eagerly taken from Amelia. Hart gently prized the bills out of her hand and put them in his pocket.

Hart and Amelia got out and Amelia walked up to the portacabin door. She stood to one side of it and knocked gently. Like everything in the clearing, the portacabin had the look of a poorly planned enterprise gone badly wrong. The metal walls, once white, were rusting and covered in dirt and moss that clung to the iron roof.

"Hola! Rodrgio?" she called out.

"¿Quién es?" a muffled deep voice replied. Hart heard the sound of a TV or radio playing from inside.

"It's Amelia. The Canadian parrot lady." She turned to Hart. "That's what he likes to call me," she said with a chuckle.

They heard the sound of the metal iron door opening to reveal a short man with a round unshaven face, who Hart thought looked more typically Mexican than Colombian.

"Amelia! How are you, cariña? It has been so long!" he cried, in perfect English, beaming. His smile faltered when he spotted Hart. "Who's this? You brought a friend with you?"

"This is my friend John," Amelia said. "He's a soldier from the UK and needs your help. He rescued a little girl from the FARC and now needs to get her to Bogotá straight away."

"A soldier from the UK, here? That's something I don't come across every day. You're a long way from home, friend. So how can I help?" Rodrigo asked, puzzled.

"Your plane," Amelia said, "Would you take them to Bogotá?"

Rodrigo laughed. "My friend, I cannot just leave. I have men working in the Jungle right now. What if something happens and I need to take them to the hospital?"

Hart listened carefully to Rodrigo to see if he could detect any signs that he'd been drinking. The man appeared to be in full control of his faculties but through the open door, Hart could see a couple of bottles of beer and a large bottle of tequila sat on a nearby table. Beyond that, he could see six camp beds, strewn with clothes and toiletries. The stench of stale sweat that comes from a group of men living together in a hot and humid confined space for a long period of time wafted out.

"I can wait here until you return," Amelia suggested. "If anything happens, I can drive them to the park headquarters for medical help."

"Or I can fly the plane myself," offered Hart. "If you have someone in Bogotá who can fly it back."

"I want to help, I really do, but it's just impossible," Rodrigo said in a friendly tone. "Why don't you take them to the park office?" He asked Amelia. "They will be safe there."

"We don't have time," Hart explained, in a sombre tone. He took the money Amelia had given him out of his pocket. "I can give you five hundred dollars. It's all I have."

Rodrigo stared at the money for a moment. Then he looked up at Hart. His eyes flicked to Amelia, then back to Hart and then back to Amelia. Before he could speak, a small voice caught everyone's attention.

"Mr John?"

Hart and Amelia turned around. Valentina was standing

behind them. Imagining seeing her through the eyes of Rodrigo, Hart realised she cut a distraught and sorry figure. She was filthy, her dirty clothes were torn, and her body looked broken, she was hunched over with tiredness.

Okay," said Rodrigo. Hart spun around to look at him. He nodded. "We'll go."

There was a moment whilst Hart wondered if Rodrigo was going to take them as a goodwill gesture. He was just about to hand the money back to Amelia when Rodrigo held out his hand for it. Hart pressed the money into the man's hand, suddenly kicking himself for not keeping some back. He hadn't even tried to bargain with the man. However, he couldn't think about it for long, Rodrigo was urging them to follow him.

"Come, quickly. If I am caught, I lose my job." He marched off towards the plane, calling back to Amelia. "I will be gone no more than two hours. If anyone radios or arrives on-site, tell them I had to pick up some emergency supplies from Bogotá."

Hart looked at Amelia and put his hand on her arm. "I don't know how to thank you—" he began. She put both hands on his shoulder, turned him around and pushed him in the direction of the plane.

"Go! Quick. Both of you, before he changes his mind and you lose both your ride and the money."

Valentina followed Hart and then stopped as if she had suddenly remembered something. She quickly turned and ran back towards Amelia and hugged her tightly. "Thank you, kind lady. Thank you. You will have a long and happy life because you were so kind to me."

"Bless you, my dear," Amelia said softly, hugging Valentina back. She prized Valentina's tiny body off her and looked her in the eyes.

"I've already had a long and happy life, and I wish you the same," she said, a little emotion creeping into her voice. "Now, go."

Valentina ran after Hart and Rodrigo who had almost reached

the plane.

***

Paola continued to track the SAS group, now just ahead of them. She had managed to close the gap between them, but also understood the importance of maintaining a safe distance. She had no idea what kind of reception they would receive if they were spotted. She wanted to have the best possible chance of helping Valentina, so it was important to stay out of sight until it was absolutely necessary to make their presence known.

Hammond and Carter followed behind her and Borgman, bringing up the rear. No one had spoken for some time. All she had heard behind her for the past hour or so was the deep breathing of unfit middle-aged men. Suddenly something snapped behind her.

"Fuck!" a voice cried out.
Paola spun around. Carter had tripped over a branch and it had broken as he fell. It looked as though his ankle was bleeding.

"Okay, that's it," he shouted at her. "I'm not going any fucking further. I need a break. Fuck this bullshit."

"Keep your voice down," Paola hissed at him. Hammond approached her.

"Come on, we need a break," he panted at her. "Just a short one. We're not used to this humid weather. Remember, we live in Bogotá."

"Where you obviously do no exercise," Paola muttered back, irritated. "Okay, okay, we take five minutes. Just five minutes, okay. Then we go." Hammond sank to the ground. "I will fetch some water," Paola said, without hiding the disdain in her voice. She collected Hammond and Carter's water-bottles' and looked over at Borgman, who was squatting close to the ground examining something of interest. Sensing her eyes on him, he looked up.

"Here, look at this!" Paola walked over to him and looked

down. "Is this blood?" he asked her.

She glanced at the spot he was pointing at on a thick exposed tree root and shrugged her shoulders. "It could be, though it doesn't look very fresh. It is dried up."

Paola squatted down and studied the spot with more interest. Eventually, she nodded knowingly before slowly turned and shook her head sadly. She stood up.

"There was a fight here, recently. Look the body fell there and rolled towards the river. It was pulled along the ground, probably the man was kicked," she announced.

"What does this mean?" Borgman asked, solemnly.

"Tempers are becoming more unpredictable up ahead and we must reach Zamora before he gets to my daughter." Paola said, darkly, before turning to go down to the water's edge to fill the water-bottles'. "We leave in two minutes," she called back to the men.

***

Zamora's group followed the tyre tracks that had recently been left behind by the 4x4 vehicle along the logging road. Juan had barely managed to stand up after the savage beating he'd received from Zamora, and was now doing his very best to try and follow the *rastro* up to the small jungle-hut at a decent pace to avoid yet another brutal attack from Zamora, who he sensed was waiting for the slightest excuse to finish off what he'd started.

Thankfully, after arriving at the empty hut, Juan was able to confirm that there were no foot tracks leading away from the small hut. The vehicle would offer the *soldado sangriento* a good head start, but at least now there would be no more delays trying to work out which way he had gone. Juan had also confirmed the vehicle had headed in the direction towards where Cesar believed a new runway had been constructed recently, and that the logging road took a circuitous route towards that part of the jungle.

Juan took a very brief moment to study the map, identifying an alternative trail through the jungle which he believed would offer a shorter and quicker route, allowing the group and chance to catch up with the 4x4 jeep. There was now a real chance that they could reach the runway before the *soldado sangriento* managed to get himself and Valentina airborne. Even if they arrived a few minutes behind, perhaps there would be no plane parked there anyway. Or maybe the pilot would refuse to fly them out of the jungle. The blood practically boiled in Zamora's veins as he thought about what he would do to the man who had taken his daughter from him.

***

Unencumbered by Carter and Hammond, Bob and his team had made excellent progress. They had reached the northern border of the Utría National Park an hour or so ago and were now at the junction of the logging road and the narrow jungle trail that led to Amelia's small hut.

Since identifying the place where Valentina had earlier sat down to rest, Kav had been carefully scrutinising the ground for some time. After the good progress they'd made over the past couple of hours, Bob was now growing irritated.

"Kav, can we get moving? What's the problem?" he asked, impatiently.

"Okay," said Kav, standing up. "Here's what I think happened. John and the girl definitely headed up this narrow track. The group of four followed, heading up the track after them. Then this is where things become interesting. It's only a theory mind, but I believe there's a strong chance John and the girl either commandeered a 4x4 vehicle somewhere along that track, or they've managed to find someone with a 4x4 to give them a lift," Kav suggested.

"What? What makes you think John managed to find a 4x4

from somewhere up that track, Kav?" Bob asked, sounding slightly sceptical at this theory.

Kav pointed towards the ground. "Because these 4x4 tracks you can see here, have recently been left shortly after John and the girl headed along the track. They show a direction of travel coming back down the track towards us and then heading west down the wider logging track. The group of four also came back down the track shortly afterwards and followed them up this logging road. There's no sign of John and the girl coming back down the track on foot, so I'm assuming they must have been travelling in the 4x4."

"Okay, all we can do for now is to keep following the FARC group ahead and make sure John and the girl manage to get out of here in one piece without those fuckers up ahead catching up with them," Bob suggested.

"Christ, some fucking party this is going to be," quipped Jock as they set off down the logging road at a slightly faster pace than before.

***

Roughly twenty minutes after Bob and his men had taken the decision to continue following the FARC men up ahead, who she assumed were in turn following the 4x4 vehicle they believed to be carrying the soldier and her daughter, Paola and Borgman arrived at the very same spot, with Hammond and Carter lagging a little way behind.

Paola quickly made the same assumptions that the men in front had made. However, Paola knew something the SAS men in front didn't know.

"This road eventually splits in two directions. The first takes you towards the Pacific coast and the other heads off through the jungle before joining the Río Atrato and following the river to Quibdó. That must be where they are going," she told the exhausted men. "There's an ancient hunting trail that runs nearby the river. It eventually joins the road further south. I remember discovering it some years ago whilst out on patrol. I couldn't follow it because the trail eventually entered this park, but I'm sure if we can find it and follow it south, we may be able to gain on them up ahead. Come, follow me."

She turned towards the river hoping to pick up the ancient hunting trail.

The weary men followed.

CHAPTER TWENTY

A S THEY approached the aircraft, Hart identified that it was an old Cessna 208B Caravan; it was in poor shape, as he had initially suspected when first spotting it as they had driven into the man-made clearing. The body of the plane, as well as the windows down the side of it, were covered in dust and dirt. The cockpit window had, at least, been wiped down but was only marginally cleaner than the rest of the aircraft.

Rodrigo had climbed inside ahead of them. Hart lifted Valentina up and then climbed in through the side door. He placed his M16 colt on the floor beside his seat but opted to keep wearing his belt-kit until they were safely in the cruise—he accepted that old habits die hard. Inside, he noticed that two or three rows of passenger seats at the back of the plane had been removed to allow a large space to hold cargo. Large straps lay across the floor that would presumably be used to secure the load. At the front, behind the two cockpit seats, there were three rows of passenger seats, with two seats per row and space between them to get to the cockpit. So, along with the two pilot seats up front, the plane could carry six passengers and a reasonable amount of cargo.

Rodrigo was in the cockpit beginning his checks. In his hand, he held a small red coloured book. He was going through his checks, repeating them to himself out loud. He got up and walked back to the main door.

"Sit. Get buckled up," he said, indicating the seats with a quick nod of his head. "I will do the external inspection. I'll be back in just a few minutes," He then lowered out of the door and swung himself under the plane.

Valentina gingerly got into a seat. She looked up at Hart terrified. "How can such a big thing get into the air?" she asked. Hart noticed she was trembling. Of course, the poor girl had never been on a plane before.

He knelt beside her. "It doesn't matter how big something is," he explained. "I've been on planes far bigger than this. It matters how powerful it is, how strong it is." Valentina looked none the wiser. Hart took her hand. "Look at you," he said, gently. "Look how small you are, yet, you're probably stronger inside than many big men. What you've done, what you've been through with me during the last couple of days... well, there are even some soldiers—big, tall, strong men—who could not have done what you have done." Although she made no sound, big tears formed in Valentina's eyes and rolled down her cheeks. Hart was struck dumb; he couldn't find any words.

"We are leaving the jungle now," she said in the smallest voice Hart had ever heard. "This is my home. This is where I was born and have lived all my life. Who will I be now?"

Hart took Valentina's hand in his right hand. "It's just a place, Valentina. Your home is wherever you are, wherever your heart lies." "But my heart is here, with my mother, in the jungle," Valentina sobbed. Hart shook his head.

Her words were cutting through him. "No, your heart is always with you. Never forget that."

Valentina nodded as Rodrigo climbed back in and closed and secured the latch on the exit door. He was so focused he didn't notice Valentina's state. Hart strapped himself into the seat beside Valentina. She took his hand and held it tightly. Hart listened to Rodrigo running through his endless list of safety checks. Whilst it was costing them precious time, the pilot's diligence was reassuring.

"Parking brake, set. Switches, off. Ignition, norm. Circuit breakers, check. In. Fuel tank selectors, both on. Radar, off. Air conditioner, off. Inverter, off. Wing flaps, set 1st stage..."

At last, Rodrigo fired the engine into life. Valentina jumped and grasped Hart's hand more tightly. Rodrigo looked back at them. He pointed to the headsets on the armrests of the seats and motioned for them to put them on so that he could speak to them clearly above the roar of the engine. Hart helped Valentina on with her headset and then put his own on.

"Check her belt," Rodrigo instructed Hart through the earpieces. He then saw the terror on Valentina's face. *"No te preocupes, pequeña. Soy el piloto más seguro en toda Colombia,"* he said with a big smile.

Finally, Rodrigo released the handbrake before speaking again into his microphone.

"We will taxi for a short distance and then stop whilst I carry out some power checks. Don't be alarmed. The engine noise will increase whilst I apply full-throttle power for a few seconds before pulling it back again. Once I'm happy that the power checks are within the safety limits, we'll taxi to the far side of the runway and I'll manoeuvre the aircraft to face directly down the centre of our runway. Be prepared, it will be a very short take-off and extremely bumpy. Hang on tight!"

The aircraft finally lurched forwards and bumped along the rough surface of the jungle clearing before coming to a stop at the far end of the runway where Rodrigo carried out the power checks as promised. The noise was deafening, and Valentina gripped Hart's arm with both hands. He tried offering her some calming words but wasn't sure she would hear him above the racket and Rodrigo's voice continuing his checks.

"Flight controls, full, free, correct. Flight instruments, check, set. Fuel boost, check, normal. Fuel tanks, check, both on. Fuel quantity, checked. Fuel shutoff, check, fully on. Elevator, aileron, rudder trim, set for take-off. Over speed governor, check 1750 within limits."

Hart stared out of the dust-covered windows. From their position perpendicular to the runway, it looked much shorter than it had before, and he was suddenly concerned whether they were going to clear the tops of the trees at the edge of the clearing. They must have been over one-hundred-feet tall at least. It was almost as if the trees were daring them to try and escape the jungle, offering one last obstacle to stop them from reaching freedom.

Having completed his power checks, Rodrigo released the aircraft's handbrake and allowed the aircraft to lunge forward under his control, steering it around and lining it up facing down the centre of the short, man-made runway.

There, Rodrigo carried out his final checks for a short field take-off. "Flaps, twenty degrees. Power set for take-off. Annunciators, check. Brakes, release. Rotate, seventy knots."

At last, Rodrigo applied the full throttle whilst keeping his feet firmly on the brake paddles. The aircraft lurched forward violently. The brakes kept the plane in check as the engine power quickly built to a climax. Suddenly, and without warning, Rodrigo took his feet off the brakes and the aircraft tore down the runway like a wild animal unleashed, the sudden force pushing Hart and Valentina back into their seats. Although they were strapped down; all three occupants were thrown around as the aircraft bumped its way towards the edge of the clearing.

They accelerated at an incredible rate. From Hart's point of view, through the cockpit window, it looked as though the enormous trees at the edge of the clearing were racing towards them. For a few moments Hart grew convinced they were not going to make it. Surely there wasn't enough room to take off and clear those trees, but nor was there time to apply the brakes if Rodrigo now had second thoughts; they were now past the point of no return.

Anger raged through Hart's veins. After everything they'd been through, were they really going to die in a pointless plane crash because the pilot had misjudged the take-off. Bile rose in his throat, all the usual faces of people he'd lost in the past suddenly flooded through his mind. He was aware of Valentina's nails digging into his arm. The pain was a relief.

As the aircraft at last lifted up into the air, Hart held his breath. Through his headset all he could hear was Valentina screaming and Rodrigo swearing.

"*Vamos muchacha. Vamos perra. No, me falles ahora...!*" Rodrigo yelled at the old plane. It almost felt as if they were in a vertical climb, the angle of ascent was incredibly steep.

Suddenly, there was a scraping sound beneath them, and the aircraft shook violently for a moment. Hart realising that the treetops had scraped the underside of the aircraft, but... they were clear.

Rodrigo turned around and punched the air with his fist. He was grinning like a Cheshire Cat.

"Wow, amigos! That was fucking close. I nearly shit my pants! I didn't think we were going to make it, I truly didn't! This old girl needs a serious engine overhaul and power check."

"No kidding!" Hart shouted back, extremely worried, but also truly thankful to have survived such a dangerous and potentially fatal take-off.

"I'll have her checked out when we arrive in Bogotá," Rodrigo assured Hart, not that it would affect Hart and Valentina. "The worst is over now. Just relax. This old girl can travel at almost two hundred miles per hour in the cruise. I'll have you on the ground in Bogotá in just over an hour."

As shaken as he was, Hart couldn't help but release a huge sigh of relief. He looked at Valentina's face; all the blood had drained from her face and her teeth were chattering. Hart looked down in the well between his seat and the window. There were some old canvas bags down there, presumably used to cover goods in the back before they were strapped down. He threw the bags over Valentina's shoulders and rubbed her. She was freezing; she was going into shock. As they banked to the left, Hart looked through Valentina's window. Through the dust he could see there was a stunning view of the jungle below and the Río Atrato meandering through the trees. The aerial view beneath them was incredible, a network of vast tributaries, the mighty river and the jungle, all interconnected and working together.

No sooner had Hart's pulse returned to somewhere close to normal than the engine gave its first alarming splutter. Valentina screamed and grabbed Hart with both arms.

"Mr John, make it stop! I want to get off!"

Before Hart could speak to reassure her, the engine spluttered again before cutting out altogether and then an eerie silence hung around them. For a split-second, Rodrigo didn't move. The aircraft seemed to hang in mid-air, still aloft from momentum. In the next moment, everything changed. The aircraft pitched violently, Rodrigo started pushing forward the control column in an attempt to build up some lifesaving airspeed, whilst continuously swearing in Spanish. Valentina began screaming again and Hart started breathing again. They were plummeting towards the ground.

The plane's propellers ceased to slice through the thick jungle air that was heavy with moisture and the scent of the dense vegetation below. The jungle prepared to receive and welcome them into its deadly embrace. The plane behaved like an amusement park ride, only nobody was probably getting off this ride alive. There were no parachutes, and even if there were, there were not high enough and there was no time to use them, in seconds the plane would become a fireball in the trees. All that would remain would be a mess of mangled metal.

Rodrigo was doing his very best to correct the spiral dive that they were now in. He closed the power throttle and placed the flaps up. He then applied full opposite rudder to try and stop the spin, which he succeeded in doing, but the aircraft was still on a deadly dive downwards. Finally, he centralised the rudder, levelled the wings and pulled the aircraft gently up out of the dive seconds before they hit the jungle floor. Rodrigo had somehow managed to get the aircraft flying straight and level again at just 400 feet above the ground. He configured the aircraft into a glide attitude, applied full flaps and cut off the fuel supply from the tanks before switching the master switch off and all aircraft avionics.

"I'm going to try and land her in the river," he called back to Hart, sounding surprisingly calm. "Unbuckle yourselves and unlatch the main exit door. Force it open before we hit the water. We have about twenty seconds until impact!"

Hart was already out of his seat. He unbuckled Valentina, lifted her out and held her shaking body with his left arm whilst he fought with the latch on the exit door.

"Come on! For fuck's sake, open!" he screamed at it. It was stuck.

***

Zamora and his men had heard the aircraft's engine fire up. They had raced through the jungle and charged into the man-made clearing just in time to see the plane lift up in its dramatic almost vertical ascent. They all let out a collective gasp as the landing gear tore through the tops of the treeline. Zamora let out a cry like a strangled animal. He threw his AK47 onto the ground and spun around, his eyes searching for Colm.

"Give me the fucking RPG now. I'm going to blast that bastard out of the sky!"

"You can't," reasoned Colm. Your daughter is on that plane!"

Zamora charged at Colm and tried to grab his backpack. "I'd rather she died than be taken from me by some fucking foreign *Hijueputa!*"

Colm wrestled with Zamora, but the Colombian was crazed with rage and wrenched the backpack from him. He got the rocket launcher out and began loading it.

Wait, look!" It was Juan.

Zamora looked up to see what Juan was pointing at. He watched aghast as he saw what had stopped all the men in their tracks.

The plane was stuttering. In the distance they all heard the engine cut out and watched as the aircraft began spinning and falling out of the sky.

"Noooo!" Zamora screamed. Despite his actions a few moments earlier, he was suddenly stricken with grief at the thought of Valentina's impending death. Moments before the plane reached the top of the jungle trees in the distance, it swept out of the dive and glided up, but only briefly. The men watched as it lost height again and headed towards the ground and finally out of sight.

"The river," Colm shouted. "He'll try to bring it down in the river. There's a chance."

At that point, Zamora suddenly realised they were not the only ones who had been watching the fate of this plane. There was someone sitting in a Land Rover parked next to the old steel portacabin. The engine started and the Land Rover began to drive off. Zamora picked up his AK47 and took aim.

"Stop him! We need that fucking vehicle"

He ran at the Land Rover as it sped away towards the runway, which was also towards the direction of the river. The other men followed his lead and ran towards the Land Rover shooting. A few of their bullet rounds bounced off the back of the vehicle and one shattered the rear window, but it didn't stop, the Land Rover carried on driving, reaching the bumpy runway and bouncing down it at full speed.

Although it seemed fairly futile, Zamora and his men gave chase.

***

Bob and his team were less than a few miles behind Zamora by the time they heard the aircraft.

Kav heard it first. He was in the lead. He stopped and raised his hand to stop the others. "Listen." They did, and all heard the distant roar of the plane as it took off.

"Well, I'll be damned," Bob muttered, shaking his head. "I'll bet you anything our man is on that plane."

"Where's he found a plane in the middle of the bloody jungle?" asked Jock.

"You know John," Bob said, smiling. "He'd find a white sandy beach in Alaska, with a couple of beautiful women selling his favourite ice cream."

They all looked up and saw the plane emerge from the treetops. They stood there watching its assent as it climbed higher across the blue afternoon sky and towards the fragments of scattered cloud waiting above.

"Nice of him to wait for us," said Jock. As he did, the plane's engine gave its first heavy splutter.

"That didn't sound good," Mike almost whispered, a second before the engine cut out completely and they watched the plane start to fall back to earth.

"Jesus!" exclaimed Bob. "That's going headfirst into the trees."
The men watched, feeling painfully helpless as the plane dropped, spun and then levelled out again. They watched as it glided onwards, gradually sinking below the treeline. They listened, with heavy hearts for the inevitable explosion, but there wasn't one.

"Come on!" Kav shouted, racing forward. Let's hope they've landed in the river, there's no time to waste!" Bob, Jock and Mike followed; adrenaline giving them renewed strength.

***

Paola, Borgman, Hammond and Carter had easily found the ancient hunting trail that ran alongside the Río Atrato. Despite its close proximity to the river, the ground didn't appear to be too muddy or treacherous. The trail managed to stave off the abundant green mass of vegetation that advanced and threatened to swallow it up, vines as thick as a man's arm hung lazily above them. The trail had afforded the group smooth progress along its route, despite the stagnant air being filled with flies and other bugs swarming above their heads. They could see water snakes worming their way through the muddy, brown waters in the river below, disappearing as quickly as they had appeared. Bulbous, unblinking eyes belonging to bullfrogs watched them from the thick reeds, as they passed nearby. Around a sharp bend, the Río Atrato looked to be picking up speed, a wide section of rocky rapids making it a dangerous prospect for anyone foolhardy enough to consider crossing the river at this particular point.

Carter had become over-confident with every step; their quick progress had lifted his spirits. He had become completely oblivious to the ever-present dangers that surrounded them. After turning the bend in the river, he roughly pushed past Paola to take over the lead.

"Let me take a turn leading, you're beginning to slow up," Carter shouted, as he pushed passed Paola, grinning. "This is not a game. Get back here behind me. I will lead the way. You have no experience of the hidden dangers and don't understand the jungle," Paola snapped at him.

Carter ignored her and continued to run just ahead of the group as if he was an excited schoolboy on a school outing. Moments later, almost instantaneously, Carter appeared to drop down into a large dip in the trail. A split second later, a scream from deep within Carter forced its way from his mouth, it was the kind of scream that made Paola's blood run cold, it tore through her like a great shard of glass.

Carter had run headlong straight into a wide stretch of deep quicksand. It stretched across the entire trail, reaching around him in all directions. He could never have known that quicksand within this part of the jungle was formed when water struggled to escape the saturated loose sandy ground, creating a liquefied soil that was unable to support any weight. The saturated sediment had appeared solid to Carter's untrained eye until a sudden change in pressure had revealed its true liquid form. The quicksand was a spongy, fluid-like texture, swallowing up objects that fell into its deadly mixture. They would sink to the level at which their weight was equal to the weight of the quicksand, in Carter's case, this would be well below his own body height.

Carter was frantically pounding the quicksand around him, clawing at it like a possessed animal, trying in vain to pull himself out. It was useless. He realised with horror that he was in a deadly embrace and sinking deeper into the spongy texture. The more he moved the deeper he sank. He was petrified and sobbing loudly, begging and screaming for the others to come to his aid and rescue him.

There was nothing Paola or the others could do to save him; all they could do was look on in horror as mere spectators. Carter was too far out into the middle of the quicksand and well out of reach. Had he not run into the quicksand's lethal embrace; they might have had a chance of recovering him. Now they watched as Carter was slowly sucked under the warm, wet sand. He felt the loneliness and despair of self-pity. His flaying arms had by now been consumed by the quicksand, disappearing below the surface as if a tight-fitting pair of handcuffs had been placed on him. The surface of the quicksand now reached his chin. It felt as if he was floating in thick porridge. He was gasping, taking deep breaths as if preparing to hold his breath underwater. Moments later, Carter was pulled down once again, the surface now reached his eye level. He stared wildly at Paola, tears in his eyes, unable to speak or breath anymore. Then with one final deadly pull, he was gone, sucked below the quicksand for eternity.

Darkness enveloped Carter. The sand having completed its deadly embrace around him, filling him with helpless deep dread. He was still being pulled down; he held his breath for as long as he could. Red and black dots danced in front of his closed eyes. His heart was still beating rapidly in panic. The urgency for air was more critical than ever. There were now no more red blotches in his field of vision. They had been replaced with an eternity of blackness.

The only sign that Carter had ever fallen prey to the quicksand was the air-bubbles that now rose and appeared on the spongy surface.

The group stood staring at the quicksand for a few moments in disbelief until Paola broke the atmosphere and gathered them. "We have to keep moving. We must try to move around the quicksand and re-join the trail further up ahead." Paola responded, in a determined but hushed tone. "Follow me and keep up."

Around thirty minutes later they successfully managed to navigate around the quicksand. Moments later, after re-joining the trail, Paola recognised the unmistakable noise of a plane taxing in the far distance, its unnaturally loud engine noise tearing and cutting through the dense, suffocating undergrowth of the jungle towards them, like a beast charging just moments before the kill.

They picked up the pace, hoping to catch a glimpse of the plane through the mass of trees ahead. Finally, they spotted the plane reaching up towards the skies above, before watching with stricken feelings as the plane conducted its aerial acrobatics.

"My baby, my baby," Paola cried as they watched.

"We don't know she's on the plane, it could be anyone," Borgman tried to reassure her.

But Paola knew.

CHAPTER TWENTY-ONE

W ITHOUT a second to spare, Hart managed to force the latch on the plane's exit door undone. He picked up his M16 colt from the floor beside his seat and swung it across his back, then grabbed one of the straps beside the door and wrapped it around his wrist before flinging himself back into his seat. He kept his left arm around Valentina, who was curled into a ball on his lap with her face pressed into his chest and her body trembling violently and braced himself for the impact.

Rodrigo continued to fill the air with expletives as he struggled to control the aircraft. Finally, there was an almighty jolt as they hit the surface of the water. The plane jerked a couple of times as it skimmed along the river as if it was a flat-edged stone being thrown across the surface of the water. The front propeller pushed under the water and pulled the aircraft to the right. The port wing struck a rock causing the rear of the plane to flip up into the air. Hart and Valentina were thrown forward and would have landed on the back of the pilot's chair had Hart not been holding onto the strap. Valentina's screams were drowned out as a large submerged rock smashed through the cockpit window.

Hart watched, helplessly, as a torrent of muddy river water

poured into the cockpit, the weight of it pinning Rodrigo to his seat and scuppering the pilot's chance of survival. Within seconds the cockpit was completely submerged, and the water was rapidly rising up Hart's legs. He looked up. The exit door had slammed shut as they had flipped up, but it was still unlatched.

"Valentina," Hart shouted above the roar of the water and the crunching of the plane as pieces began breaking up. "In a minute I need you to take a deep breath. We'll be underwater. I'll have to let go of you so I can get the door open. Hold onto me as tightly as you can. As soon as that door is open, we'll swim up. We have to wait until the door is submerged under the water or we can't swim free. Okay."

"Okay," Valentina shouted before screaming as the water rushed up her legs until she was waist deep. Hart willed the water to rise quickly so they wouldn't be submerged for too long. The longer they were under, the more chance that Valentina would panic.

When the water reached his chest and Valentina's body was almost completely submerged, he said, "Right. Are you ready? Remember, you've got to take a big breath. Inhale as much air as you can. Don't worry. Try to stay calm."

"Yes," Valentina called back to him, making an attempt at sounding brave but unable to disguise the terror in her voice.

The water carried them higher up the aircraft until they were level with the exit door. Hart let go of the strap and put his hand on the exit door, ready to push it open as soon as the water pressure equalised. He knew he'd have to hold tight onto the handle to prevent them from being carried further up the aircraft as the water level continued to rise.

It was time.

"One, two, three, and... now!" Hart called out just before both their faces disappeared under the murky rising water. They had both taken a large breath, Hart just hoped it would be enough to sustain them until they escaped from the doomed sinking plane.

There were a few excruciating moments whilst they waited for the water to cover the exit door. The silt in the turbid water and the rapid movement of it meant it was impossible to see anything. Finally, Hart gave the door a push. To his relief, it moved. He pushed harder and it fully opened. He could feel Valentina's hands gripping his shirt. He reached down and pulled her body up and pushed it through the door, praising the child for keeping calm and marvelling at her self-control. He pulled his own body through the door.

They ascended quickly but the current was strong, and they were soon swept downstream away from the sinking plane. Hart had managed to grab Valentina's T-shirt as they swam up towards the surface.

On reaching the surface, he shouted at her. "Hold onto me and don't let go!"

The riverbank was only 40 metres away, but it might as well have been 100 the way Hart was feeling. With the last of his reserve energy, he struck out towards the riverbank with Valentina holding onto his shirt and kicking with the little strength she had left.

At last, Hart reached down with his feet and found he could stand on the riverbed. He looked down for a moment and missed the fact that they were approaching some rocks sticking out of the river. Before he could stop her, Valentina, who had flipped onto her back and was kicking her way towards the riverbank, collided with the rock. She immediately let go of Hart and her body sank beneath the water. Hart reached down and grabbed what felt like an ankle or wrist, but it was suddenly yanked out of his grip.

"No! No, no, no!" he cried out. Searching frantically in the murky water with his hands and legs. "Valentina! Fuck…, where are you?!" He waded along the riverbed, his eyes scanning the water desperately. After everything they'd been through, especially during the last hour, there was no way he was losing her to the Río Atrato now.

"Come on, come on, where the hell are you?" he panted as he waded downstream, frantically digging in the water with his arms, searching for Valentina's body. Up ahead another crop of rocks jutted above the surface. Praying that Valentina had been washed towards the rocks and stopped in their path, Hart took a dive with his arms outstretched before him. After a few moments, he felt something soft and smooth. He grabbed at it with all his remaining strength; it was Valentina's leg. He pulled her up and out of the water, threw her body onto his shoulders, and waded out on to the riverbank as fast as he could.

Hart lay Valentina on the ground, on her back. Now that they were on land, he could see that Valentina's head was bleeding heavily. The cut was at the top of her forehead and blood was running down either side of her hairline. Quickly, Hart removed his MI6 and belt-kit and shirt, ripping the sleeve. He tied the material tightly around Valentina's head, which temporarily stemmed the blood flow. He anxiously calculated the chance of her being alive, considering she had smashed her head against the rocks with considerable force and had been submerged for quite some time, but he couldn't allow himself to consider that she may be dead. He realised, he cared about this child. He cared about her more than he'd cared about anybody or anything in a very long time. He knew loss. He'd lost the two people in the world he loved the most. Now he felt those familiar stabbing pains in his heart, the weight behind his eyes and the metallic taste in his mouth.

Fearfully, Hart bent down and placed his ear next to Valentina's nose and mouth, hoping to feel her breath on his cheek. Nothing. He looked to see if her chest was moving. It was still. He checked her pulse. Nothing. Trying his best to stay calm, Hart placed her head down the slope facing towards the riverbank to try and drain any river water from her lungs before then commencing CPR.

Hart then tilted Valentina's head back, lifted her chin and pinched her nose closed. He took a normal breath and covered Valentina's mouth with his to create an airtight seal. He gave two one-second breaths and watched her chest rise as he forced the air into her lungs. He followed this with 30 chest compressions. Hart continued the cycle of heart compressions and mouth-to-mouth resuscitation on autopilot. Outwardly, he managed to stay calm, but inside he was crashing fast. Finally, at last, Valentina's body jerked as she coughed and spluttered and then threw up the brown river water.

Hart couldn't help crying out in relief. He rolled Valentina onto her side as she continued to gasp for air. As her breathing stabilised, she started to cry. This was a good sign. He had been pushing the thought from his mind, but he knew there was a risk she'd suffered brain damage. She would be, at best, severely concussed.

"Valentina, can you hear me?" He knelt over her body, stroking her head.

"Mr John, Mr John!" She said, struggling through her sobs.

"It's okay, you're okay," Hart said, trying his best to soothe her.

"The plane... we crash... I think I die," she spluttered.

"It's okay. Stay calm. Everything's okay. We got out. We're safe now."

Valentina was shivering. Hart replaced his ripped shirt and lay down next to her and although his clothes were wet, he wrapped his body around her to try and offer her some sort of warmth. She was in shock. So was he, but he had to now stay strong for her!

He had no idea where they were or how they were going to get to Quibdó. They had thankfully come out of the river on the same side as the clearing where they had taken off from. Maybe he could get there and find one of the loggers or return to Amelia's house and secure a lift to the Park's main office on the coast, but what about Zamora and the FARC group? Where were they? Presumably, they were close enough to have seen the plane go down. With any luck, they would assume that all the occupants had died.

Hart knew that he had to give Valentina a little time to recover but then they had to get going. He couldn't afford to waste a moment of time. Apart from anything else now, he had to get Valentina to a hospital urgently. She may have internal bleeding, as well as the head injury. He needed a little rest too; he was going to have to carry Valentina from this point onwards. She was far too weak to stand up, let alone walk.

As soon as Valentina had stopped shaking, and her sobbing had subsided into more of a whimper, Hart sat up and put on his belt-kit and took his waterproof map out of his pocket. He looked upriver to see if he could detect any signs of the plane wreckage, but there was nothing. The surface of the water hid all evidence beneath its depths. There was no visible sign that the plane had ever existed.

Hart studied the map, but locating their position was an educated guess. He had no idea how far they had flown south before the aircraft had come out of the spin. For all he knew they could be back level with the northern boundary of the Utría National Park; he prayed they were further south than that. Worst case scenario, they were still at least 20 km from Quibdó, but he hoped it was more like 10 or 15. Could he really carry Valentina that far?

Valentina groaned beside him. She was trying to sit up. Hart helped her, but before she was upright, her eyes rolled back into her head and she flopped into his arms.

"Valentina!" Hart cried, alarmed. He gently shook her, but she was unconscious. He felt her pulse and checked she was breathing. He had to get her to a hospital as soon as possible. He pulled himself up, the adrenalin giving him extra strength, picked up his M16 and lifted Valentina onto his shoulders. He wanted to get clear of the exposed riverbank in case the FARC group had seen the plane come down and were now heading in the direction of the crash site. He needed the cover and safety of the jungle again.

Much to Hart's surprise and relief, after trudging a short distance into the jungle, he came across another logging track. He couldn't believe his luck; this was surely the road to Quibdó. Even if it didn't lead them to Quibdó, it would lead somewhere—hopefully somewhere with people and a phone so that he could call for help.

They had only been walking for about twenty minutes when Hart heard the unmistakable sound of a vehicle approaching behind him at high speed. His heart leapt into his throat. Whoever was driving, was in a hurry, and he had to stop them. He'd take it by force if necessary. He had to get to Quibdó as soon as he could; this could mean the difference between life and death for Valentina.

As the sound drew closer, Hart made a snap decision. He left the track and placed Valentina gently down, hidden behind a nearby large tree. He then returned back to the track and squatted by a bunch of smaller trees, his hands tightly gripping his colt, waiting with anticipation.

Finally, a vehicle came into view. Hart's spirits soared as he recognised Amelia's Land Rover. He jumped into the road, waving his arms wildly. The Land Rover braked hard in front of him.

"Thank god!" Hart called out, racing to the driver's door. "I can't believe you found us."

"Where's Valentina?" asked Amelia, deeply alarmed.

"Beneath that huge tree, just over there. She's alive, but only just."

"Go get her and get in!" Amelia screamed, as if in pain.

Hart didn't hesitate. He ran back to the tree, scooped Valentina up and carried her back to the vehicle. It was only when he had opened the rear passenger door and secured Valentina across the back seat that he saw the blood covering the back of the driver's seat. He then spotted the small bullet hole, around the level of Amelia's chest. She was holding the steering wheel with her left hand only. Her right arm drooped, limply at her side. She looked pale.

"What happened?" Hart asked, dumbfounded.

"The FARC soldiers... they reached the runway as you were taking off," Amelia said, weakly. Her head now lolled slightly to one side. "You drive..."

Hart finished strapping Valentina into the back seat and shut the rear door behind him and quickly hurried around to the driver's door.

"Okay, let's get you out of there."

He helped Amelia get into the passenger seat. She had clearly lost a lot of blood and was extremely weak. Hart now had two casualties on his hands.

"Listen to me, closely," Amelia said, grabbing Hart's hand. "I don't know how long I can stay awake. This track will take you to Quibdó. Don't go to the police. They will take Valentina. Go straight to the cathedral. The priest there will help you. He will send for a doctor without alerting the authorities. You might be able to call from there, too, and get your people to pick you up. You can drop me at the hospital on the way. It's on the main road along the riverfront and just along from the cathedral. You can't miss them. The cathedral is in a small plaza."

Hart climbed into the driver's seat. "Okay but hold on. We're not too far away now."

"We're about an hour away," Amelia said, slurring her words now. Hart pressed his foot down hard on the accelerator.

The Land Rover's wheels spun in the mud for a moment before finding traction and the vehicle finally leapt forward. They drove for a few minutes, Hart constantly checking to see if Amelia was still conscious and whipping his head around to see if Valentina was showing any signs of coming round.

Amelia was beginning to look extremely pale. She was shivering. "I don't feel too good," she said suddenly, sounding like she was about to lose consciousness.

"Shit!" Hart said. He slowed down and brought the vehicle to a stop. He got out and quickly opened the passenger door to check on Amelia.

"Don't stop," Amelia mumbled.

"I need to look at you," Hart said, sternly.

"No... there's nothing you can do," Amelia mumbled, trying to push him away. Hart ignored her and gently tipped her body forward. He lifted her shirt and saw that there was a bullet hole in her back, just under her right shoulder blade. It must have punctured her lung. It was a miracle she had got as far as she had. Whilst he held her, Amelia's body was going cold. She continued to shiver.

"Please..." she weakly pleaded with Hart. "Keep driving. Get the girl to safety. Don't waste any more time. She's young; her life is precious."

Hart was torn. There was nothing he could do for her; he knew it. He settled Amelia comfortably in her seat again and then climbed back into the driver's seat and drove on.

As he raced down the logging track, Hart watched Amelia, as the life literally slipped out of her. She smiled at him.

"You're a very handsome man, with a good soul."

"I don't know about that," Hart mumbled.

"I do," Amelia said, calmly. "But you're sad. You seem lost." Hart said nothing.

"You'll find your path again."
Hart couldn't look at her anymore.

Amelia whispered. "Follow your path." Just before she lost consciousness she added, barely audibly, "Stay alive."

Then she died.

Hart drove on deep in thought. The only path he planned on following right now was the one that led directly to Quibdó, whilst aiming to do his very best to make sure he and Valentina both stayed alive. Hart allowed himself a moment to let out all the grief he was feeling and had stored up over the years. He let out a roar that would have startled a lion. He hadn't said enough to Amelia; he hadn't thanked her. She had saved their lives. His hands gripped the steering wheel and he stamped on the accelerator, driving the Land Rover as fast as he dared given the uneven surface of the logging track. He had to get Valentina to Quibdó; he wasn't going to lose another person he had grown to deeply care about.

CHAPTER TWENTY-TWO

Z AMORA STARED hard at the ground where Juan was pointing out the footprints. They had followed the tracks of the Land Rover from the runway and now Juan had stopped to study the ground where he said the vehicle had suddenly braked. He also discovered that it had picked up another passenger. Juan had been walking around the area for quite some time. Zamora was getting impatient again.

"Come on, tell me what you are seeing!" he barked at Juan.

"Patrón, the tracks appear to belong to the *soldado sangriento*. Look here, his strides are wide and purposeful, like those belonging to a runner," Juan pointed out. "He ran along the track towards where we stand now. The vehicle braked hard and stopped here. The *soldado sangriento* then ran towards that lone tree over there and picked something up," Juan pointed towards the lone tree in the near distance that stood still in the late afternoon air. "His tracks are closer and deeper over there, showing he was carrying something heavy. He then walked back towards the waiting vehicle," Juan informed Zamora, nervously.

"Is that it? Don't you see anything else? Could that something he picked up by the tree over there, have been my daughter?"

Zamora, asked, getting frantic.

"There is something else I've spotted. I believe the *soldado sangriento* swapped places with the driver, before driving off. Also, I've spotted blood on the ground. Someone is injured. I just can't be certain who the blood belongs to?" Juan admitted.

Zamora rounded on him instantly. "What the fuck do you mean, you can't be certain who is injured? For your sake, you better start working it out within the next few minutes if you know what's good for you," Zamora threatened.

Juan was once again fearful for his life. He continued nervously, pointing towards the lone tree. "Patrón, please forgive me. I've spotted traces of blood on the ground over there by the tree, but also significant traces of blood mixed in with the mud right here. If you look down closely you can just about make it out." Juan and Zamora squatted for a closer inspection, a squelching sound coming from the mud beneath their boots.

"I can't say for sure if the blood belongs to *soldado sangriento* or the driver of the vehicle, but as I've spotted blood by the tree, I'm sure it must belong to the *soldado sangriento*. I just can't work out why he would drive the vehicle if he was injured?" Juan instantly wished he had kept the final thought to himself.

Zamora stared at the lone tree in the near distance. It stood out from its surroundings and the nearby riverbank, bathed in bright angelic light. Its branches hung low with the weight of the *Borojó* fruit that grew from its branches in abundance. The dark round fruit had a reputation in Colombia as being a natural Viagra. The branches looked like a mother's arms when she returned home laden with gifts.

Finally, Zamora spoke. Only this time, there was a dangerous edge to his voice. "If the heavy object the *soldado sangriento* picked up from the bottom of the tree could potentially be my daughter, is it not then possible that the blood you found might also potentially belong to my daughter?"

The air instantly turned electric; Colm and Cesar waited with bated breath for Juan's reply.

Juan chose his next words with care. "I'm afraid that is a possibility that cannot be ruled out, Patrón," Juan admitted. He didn't want to give Zamora false hope but at the same time, he dreaded to think what would become of them if the girl had been killed in the plane crash.

Juan quickly added. "The footprints are a little deeper here in this part of the mud, you see, he was definitely carrying something, which he put inside the vehicle. Of course, it could have been something he brought from the crash site."

Juan shuddered when he caught sight of the murderous stare that Zamora now fixed him with. He was inadvertently digging himself into a hole with every sentence. He looked away and continued, trying to repair the damage.

"They took off again at quite some speed. You can see here where the wheels have spun on the ground." He looked down the road in the direction that the Land Rover had taken, squinting, as if he hoped to catch a glimpse of the vehicle.

This road leads to Quibdó," Colm informed everyone, attempting to break the atmosphere.

"Yes! I know that!" Zamora snapped. "So, we go. We go now! We have already wasted far too much time."

Zamora turned and stared at Juan. "From what you've told me, I think my daughter must be dead. At best badly injured. Why else would the *soldado sangriento* be carrying her? Why would she not be walking?"

"I don't know, Patrón. Maybe she has injured her leg?" Juan muttered, terrified by Zamora's expression.

"You don't know much, do you?" Zamora said in a soft but threatening tone. "Because of what you don't know, we were delayed in reaching the runway. By now I could have my daughter back safely and the body of the *soldado sangriento* could be rotting on the floor of the jungle."

"I—" Juan started, and then thought better of it.
Zamora suddenly smiled.

"Here is the good news. I don't need your help anymore because we now know they are heading for Quibdó."

Juan's relief was short-lived. In a flash, Zamora raised his AK47 to waist height and fired half the gun's magazine into Juan's chest, killing him instantly. Every gunshot was one that stripped away Juan's very existence, which silenced him forever and closed his eyes for eternity. Every blast that cut through the oppressively humid air was a brutal touch from the Grim Reaper's scythe, taking possession of Juan's soul. His lifeless body crumpled to the ground. Zamora spun around and yelled at Colm and Cesar.

"I have never suffered fools and I will not start now. Nor do I accept failure. Now quick! Move! We have no time to lose!"

***

After watching the plane fall from the sky, Bob and his team had heard the distant gunfire of Zamora and his men shooting at the fleeing Land Rover. They had immediately raced along the narrow jungle track towards where they thought the gunfire had come from; some 500 metres ahead of them.

As they reached the edge of the runway clearing, they paused and became absolutely still. It seemed as if the jungle wildlife had collectively fallen silent again with them. In the distance, they could hear the faint sound of a vehicle speeding away and the muffled shouts of Zamora's group and the sound of sporadic gunfire as they presumably chased it. Moving around the edge of the clearing, keeping themselves concealed, they quickly made their way towards the logging track continuing to follow Zamora's group.

Less than 30 minutes later, Bob and his team were standing over Juan's body. His deathly pale skin was already beginning to pull tight against his bones. Bright scarlet blood drenching his shirt, a shirt that had been ripped apart by the dozen or more bullet rounds fired in anger. His eyes were wide-open eyes, staring bloody murder. Juan's body lay limply waiting to be consumed over the coming days by the wildlife hiding nearby in the trees.

Kav knelt down to inspect the empty ammunition casing that lay nearby. "Yep, 7.62 and probably from an AK-47. The other two men in the group stood over there.

The shooter was at very close range." Kav took a few steps back and then studied the tyre tracks more closely.

"Shit, this is confusing!" Kav admitted. "The vehicle we heard earlier in the distance is the one we've been following. It stopped right here. Looks like the driver briefly got out and was helped into the passenger seat. I think it's a woman. Either that, or it's a bloke with small feet," The other's laughed at this mild observation.

"It's too hard to say for sure; the mud's well and truly been churned up by those fuckers up ahead, but I think the other tracks might just belong to John. The boot tread looks similar. There's a lot of blood mixed in with the mud, so it's possible he could be in a bad way. Assuming he was on the plane we saw and survived. No sign of the girl though. The 4 x 4 took off down the track again at speed."

"So, you think there's a chance it could be John, and he's still alive?"

"Or maybe someone else," Jock suggested. "The pilot perhaps?"

Kav was already following a set of tracks that headed off towards the lone tree near the riverbank. He knelt down and studied the ground around the tree intently. After a few minutes, he stood up and shook his head.

"No, whoever got in the 4 x 4, also picked something up from the base of this tree. The tracks are clearer here. I'm sure they belong to John. He could have come over here to collect the girl?" he said, before adding, "Although, whether she's alive or dead is anyone's guess."

A sudden sombre moment descended on the group, taking them by surprise. Although none of them had met Valentina, they were obviously rooting for Hart, and if he was risking his life for this young girl, they couldn't help but have some emotional connection to her. They all felt somewhat saddened by the prospect that she might be dead.

"There's one other thing," added Kav. "I've spotted three new tracks back there on the logging road. Two I definitely recognise from before. They were the same tracks we followed to the tribal village and the one's that headed upstream at the river crossing. The woman and the guy with the limp. What's strange though, is they're now joined by a set of tracks that I don't recognise—a man. Somehow, all three have managed to pass us without being spotted. It's definitely them, and it looks like they're not too far ahead of us. Probably ten or fifteen minutes at most."

"Come on," said Bob suddenly. "At least there's a good chance John's still alive and has a set of wheels again. He should easily be able to outrun the other lot up ahead. It doesn't look like they're going to give up the chase anytime soon, so we're going to have to dig deep to close the gap and catch up with those fuckers. We'll then take them out before they get to John. My guess is John's heading for the nearest hospital. Has to be Quibdó. Let's go!"

***

Although Kav could never possibly guess their identities: Paola, Borgman and Hammond had been closer to the Río Atrato when they had watched the plane go down. They had quickly found the logging track and followed the Land Rover tracks. Having made all the same deductions as Juan, and with renewed hope that Valentina was still alive, Paola was now leading her group as fast as they could go, hot on the heels of Zamora and his men.

***

Hart had lost track of time. He had no idea if he'd been driving for ten minutes or more than an hour. His thoughts had been consumed in trying to work out what his next move would be. A sudden bump in the road that had nearly sent the Land Rover spinning onto its side brought him crashing back to the present moment. Amelia's body tipped over in the passenger seat beside him, her head almost ending up in Hart's lap. He instinctively pushed it away. He had seen enough corpses in his time to be unsentimental about the sight and feel of a body going into rigour mortis. Hart was confident he now had enough distance between himself and his pursuers to risk stopping the Land Rover to check on Valentina. He was deeply concerned about her condition, but she looked peaceful enough. He had to remain hopeful. From his medical training he knew that, if she was concussed, the longer she remained unconscious, the more danger she could be in. He knew if he could get her to Quibdó, someone would surely know better than him what to do with her.

After checking Valentina, Hart continued down the logging road. It was now beginning to grow dark and he was struggling to see ahead, but he had to keep his lights off for as long as possible. The last thing he wanted to do was help highlight his position to anyone who might be pursuing him further back down the logging road behind them.

At last, Hart started to see signs of civilization again. Through the trees in the fading light, he could see large wooden houses on stilts, as well as a few smaller shacks, dotted along the opposite eastern bank of the Río Atrato. The road suddenly made a sharp turn to the left, towards the river, and after another hundred metres or so the road finally led to a rickety old bridge. The top of the bridge was wooden, no doubt the rotting wooden planks had been cut from some of the nearby tall trees in the Jungle. The wooden slats were held together by ropes and anchored by large wooden stakes dug deep into the riverbank. Hart could see that the ropes had once been bright blue in colour, a long time ago, now they were a greenish brown. There were a few hints of the original rope colour shining through in the fading light, but generally the rope looked weak and dangerously frayed. The bridge was little more than a hastily erected structure.

Hart stared at the bridge, crestfallen. It looked as though it could barely take the weight of a couple of people, let alone two adults, a young girl, and a Land Rover. He stopped the Land Rover and turned off the engine for a moment whilst he contemplated and considered his options. There was no other road. It was either go on or go back, and the latter was out of the question. There was no other bridges insight. The river looked deep and was around 150 metres wide. Should he try to cross on foot, carrying Valentina? He quickly consulted his map in the poor light. His torch had given up all life after the latest dunk in the river. They were still a few miles from Quibdó and there were no other bridges marked on the map. This one wasn't marked on the map either, but he couldn't take the chance and hope that there were more bridges like this further along the river. Even if there were, how would he get the Land Rover to them anyway? The riverbank was completely impassable for a vehicle. This appeared to be at the end of the old loggers' track.

Hart knew that every indecisive minute could put Valentina's life in jeopardy. He came to a split decision. He would drop all the excess weight from the Land Rover and chance it. He had made it out of this river and one of its tributaries on two occasions now. If the worst came to the worst, he could do it again, but there was no point in not at least giving it a go.

Working as fast as he could, knowing he had already lost precious time in debating his next moves, Hart got out and opened the passenger door, unbuckling the seatbelt, he pulled Amelia's body out from the passenger seat and lay her on the ground.

"Goodbye, my good friend," he muttered. "Thanks for saving our lives. We won't ever forget you."

Next, Hart gingerly unbuckled Valentina and lifted her off the back seat and placed her in Amelia's now empty seat. He considered syphoning off some of the fuel—the gauge was showing they still had almost half a tank and they wouldn't need much to reach Quibdó. Hart decided against it, it would take far too long and leave him vulnerable if Zamora and his men were able to catch up with them.

Hart turned the ignition and started the Land Rover up again. He drove it forward and eased the front wheels onto the first wooden slat of the old bridge, holding his breath whilst he waited to see if the bridge would take the weight of the Land Rover's front axle, or whether they would plummet through the bridge into the fast-flowing dark waters below.

The rope holding up the bridge strained and creaked audibly, and the whole structure swung violently from side to side. Hart gently pressed the brake, allowing the bridge to get used to the weight of the Land Rover and settle. The bridge at last stopped moving, Hart eased off the brake and clutch and allowed the Land Rover to edge further along onto the next couple of wooden slats. He felt the back of the vehicle dip slightly and the bridge give another wobble. He knew both the front and rear wheels were now on the bridge, which miraculously seemed to be holding strong.

Breathing deeply, trying to keep himself calm, he waited for the bridge to settle once again before easing the Land Rover further across, almost wincing as they moved forward onto each new wooden slat, some of them creaking more loudly than others as they each took the weight that had to be close to two tonnes.

Suddenly, Hart heard one of the wooden slats snap as the rear wheels rolled off it. He noticed up ahead that there were two wooden slats missing, which left a gap of what looked like almost two feet. Hart had no idea whether the wheels of the Land Rover would be large enough to cross the gap, or whether they were about to plunge through the bridge and into the dark fast-moving water below. For the second time in less than a few hours, Hart prayed to whatever might be out there to help get them safely across.

Hart progressed as slowly as he dared whilst ensuring the Land Rover kept moving forward. He wanted to keep a little momentum up. Becoming stationary would increase the pressure on the slats. It was a desperately difficult juggling act, but he kept going, inch by inch, accelerating a fraction as they approached the missing slats.

By some miracle, they made it across and, as if delirious with relief, as the back wheels crossed over the gap, Hart pushed a little harder on the accelerator and moved rapidly over the remaining slats. He was dimly aware that there was some cracking and creaking going on behind him, and the bridge was swinging violently again. He now had a sudden burst of faith that told him to move the vehicle and get it across and off that bridge within the next few seconds.

He was right to have done so. No sooner had the back wheels reached solid ground, the ropes on the bridge finally snapped and the whole thing came apart, dropping in pieces into the river below.

Hart shook his head in disbelief. Glancing across at Valentina, he stepped on the accelerator and they lurched into the jungle along the barely visible track ahead of them. The trees formed a tunnel around them like a great dark snake, curving under the foliage that surrounded them. A few minutes later, as the jungle began to seriously thin out, Hart spotted the distant lights of the city. He almost wept with joy. They were only a mile or so away.

Only then did Amelia's words start to come back to him. Should he follow her instructions? She had warned him against going to the police or directly to the hospital. The city looked pretty big; it would surely have a decent hospital in it, but Amelia had told him to go straight to the cathedral and find the priest. Hart had around five minutes to think about it. He decided to trust Amelia.

What if there were FARC informants working in the hospital? He couldn't risk it. He'd rather Valentina died in his arms than be taken from him and handed back to Zamora and a life inside the FARC.

As they drew closer to Quibdó, Hart saw the cathedral looming up ahead. It looked large and imposing. Somehow, he'd expected something on a smaller scale, something quainter perhaps, but this was a building roughly three stories high.

Hart had turned the headlights on but had no idea what time it was. His watch hadn't worked since the plane crash, but the night was closing in quickly and there was a full moon. He drove through some minor streets to the north of the city before joining the main Carrera 1 road. This main road paralleled the Río Atrato, on the western edge of the city and led past the city's hospital. Hart noted its name as he drove past – Hospital San Franciso de Asis. In the distance, some four hundred metres further along the main road, stood the great cathedral. Hart smiled; it was also named San Franciso de Asis – it appeared to be a popular name in this part of the world.

Working out the best place to park, Hart decided to leave the Land Rover at the north side of the cathedral, just off the quiet Calle 26 street, where he believed it would be least conspicuous. There was an old-looking wooden side door entrance into the cathedral, it looked discrete and safe enough. This would be a preferable entranceway rather than going through the main doors where he would be sure to raise alarm if anyone saw him, dressed as he was— armed, carrying an unconscious young girl.

Hart could not leave his weapons in the Land Rover, so tried to conceal them as best he could. He swung his M16 colt over his shoulder, then removed his 9mm Sig sidearm from its hip holster and tucked it into the waistband of his trousers hidden under his shirt.

There had been a few people in the tree-covered plaza in front of the cathedral's main entrance as he had driven past, but the street on this side of the cathedral seemed to be deserted. Praying it would remain so for a few more minutes, Hart jumped out of the Land Rover and ran around to the passenger door. He scooped Valentina up into his arms and then ducked into the side door of the cathedral.

CHAPTER TWENTY-THREE

WHAT the fuck is this? Zamora was looking down at both the tyre tracks of the Land Rover and the discarded body of Amelia. It was obvious that the vehicle had driven up on to what had once been, a wooden rope bridge. The tyre tracks stopped on one of the remaining wooden slats... the rest of them had fallen into the fast-moving river below.

"It looks like they tried to drive across the bridge, but it collapsed," Colm offered, crouching down and inspecting the tracks in the poor visibility as night rapidly approached.

"I can see that!" Zamora snapped back. "But what kind of crazy fucking idiot would try to cross a bridge made of rope and wood in a heavy Land Rover?!" He stared at Cesar, who had not spoken a word since Juan had been killed. Now, however, Zamora really looked like he wanted an answer. Cesar opened his mouth to speak but Colm jumped in again, saving him.

"I think they may have managed to make it across before the bridge broke. Look, you can see here, where the frayed rope finally snapped. The way each thread is longer than the other means the bridge was straining under a heavy weight at the far end of the bridge, just before it broke."

"I pray the *Caremonda* made it across with my daughter. If not, there's a Land Rover at the bottom of this fucking river with both of them inside. There's no way we can know for sure until we reach Quibdó and check the city's hospital. This mother fucker is playing with us and now seriously beginning to test my patience!" Zamora screamed.

"We've got to get across as quickly as possible. It's going to be dark soon. We can't waste any more time," Colm ventured. "We can use the rope that's still attached to help anchor us against the river's current."

Without another word, Zamora started wading out into the river, holding onto the rope as he went. The river had swollen past the high marks of previous years, a torrent of unmeasurable force travelling on a constant path northward towards the Caribbean Sea. Colm and Cesar followed behind. The water rushed past their bodies, holding them firm in its clutches. They clung to the ropes as tightly as they could, avoiding being swept away under the dark waters that now tried to claim them.

***

The towering Cathedral of San Francisco de Asis was an imposing landmark and focal point in the small jungle city of Quibdó. The brightly lit cathedral was located within a small plaza that was lined with several trees, including two enormous palms. The cathedral shared the plaza with a white and gold-trimmed shrine, upon which stood a white statue of an eagle. Many came to worship at this shrine on their way into the cathedral.

The cathedral building was absolutely magnificent. It was gothic in design and the stone was painted a dark greenish-grey colour. Two tall steeple towers stood either side of the main double door entrance, which was made of ancient dark wood. The steeples had three separate viewing balconies, the first starting halfway up each steeple, with the highest one being right at the top. The steeple roofs were light grey, and cone-shaped, and overlooked the main entrance door, above which a large gothic concrete Christian Cross proudly hung. A line of tall pillars ran along the outside perimeter of the cathedral.

As Hart had entered through the wooden side door, noting it was scratched and dented and the doorknob had dulled with age, covered with greasy finger-marks. As he closed the swollen door behind him, it creaked and groaned. Once inside, he noticed that there were a few worshippers sitting in the pews along the back row. One of them looked at him and Hart immediately rearranged Valentina's body so that she appeared more upright and her arms were draped over his shoulders, her head resting in the crook of his neck. This made her look more like a sleeping child than a potentially critically injured one.

The cathedral's side entrance had brought them into the building halfway along the far-right aisle. The inside of the cathedral was just as imposing as the outside. Hart suddenly realised he'd never actually been inside a cathedral before. He made a mental note and a promise to visit Hereford Cathedral if he ever managed to survive and get back to the UK in one piece. He'd been in plenty of churches in his time but never a place like this. He was thankful for the dark and gloomy atmosphere. The place seemed to be lit up entirely by candles. Hundreds and hundreds of candles flickered in sconces on the walls and in tall candelabras at the end of each pew. He could only just make out the pale brown polished tiles on the floor. Stone pillars at the far ends of each pew stretched up at least 100 feet and disappeared into the darkness before they presumably hit the ceiling, which was invisible in this low lighting.

Elaborate granite arches linked the pillars. Frescos along the walls depicted scenes from the life of Christ, and spaced between these were long, thin stained-glass windows.

As he made his way up towards the front of the cathedral, remaining hidden in the shadows, Hart got a whiff of incense. At the front of the cathedral, there was a decorated altar and behind this, Hart could just make out an extremely small wooden door that he presumed led to some kind of antechamber. He felt sure he'd find the priest out there. Before he had travelled more than a couple of steps, a figure stepped out from the shadows in front of him, making him jump and stop in his tracks. The man was dressed in dark robes. He smiled at Hart.

"Can I help you?" the man asked.

"Are you the priest?" Hart replied, in a whisper.

"I am Father Eduardo. What is your name?"

"Do you know Amelia? She lives in the jungle, just north of here?" Hart asked, quickly adding, "Lived..."

"I do. Has she sent you? Is she okay?"

Hart paused before answering. "I'm very sorry to tell you, but she died earlier today. I was in a plane crash this afternoon with her and this girl. We were being flown to Bogotá, but our plane got into trouble just after take-off and came down in the middle of the Río Atrato." Hart instinctively decided that he needed to keep the facts in short supply.

"The girl and I are the only survivors. I'm British, she's Colombian. Amelia and I rescued her from a FARC camp in the jungle. The girl's mother asked us to save her from the FARC," Hart offered, thinking that he might have embellished a little too much, but he was desperate. The words had just come out of him.

"Are you able to get a doctor to take a look at her? I don't want to risk taking her to the hospital. She and I both hate hospitals. I also need a telephone so I can call my people; they'll come and get us."

Fortunately, after processing the sad news of his Amelia's death, Father Eduardo seemed to take in everything Hart was saying and responded immediately.

"Come," he whispered urgently. "We will send for the doctor. Then I will ask Father Sebastian to help you make the phone call. We do not have a phone in the cathedral, but I can ask him to take you to his brother's gas station, it's very close by. There is a telephone there."

He ushered Hart towards the front of the cathedral and through the small wooden door behind the altar that Hart had correctly assumed led to an antechamber. The doorway had been there for generations yet went mostly unnoticed by those who visited the cathedral. Opening the wooden door, they entered a sparsely furnished room, stuffy even, where inside sat a younger-looking man also dressed in robes, accompanied by a couple of clergy boys. They were sat on a wooden bench beside a long wooden table that looked as if it had been there for centuries, the surface having the facial look of an old man – the lines like well-earned wrinkles. It was the sort of table surface that welcomed the eye and invited the hand to touch. They had been studying bibles. Father Eduardo spoke to one of the boys.

"Jesus, go and ask Doctor Sanchez to come here immediately. Tell him to talk to no one. He must bring his medical equipment. Tell him, there is a child who has been involved in an accident." The boy stood up and left the room without a word. "Come," he addressed Hart. "Bring the child over here."

The priest directed Hart to a small metal-framed bed in the far corner of the room. It was covered with a woollen blanket and a pillow that looked like it had seen better days. Hart gently laid Valentina down on the bed. Above it was paintings and faded tapestry panels on the wall.

"Father Sebastian. Our new friend here has been sent to us by the Canadian woman. You remember, Amelia? The one in the jungle who looked after the parrots?"

He turned to Hart. "She used to bring us some rare plants that grew in the jungle that are wonderful for drying and burning," he explained, sadly. Then he turned back to Father Sebastian. "I am sorry to tell you that she is now with God."

He paused, letting his words sink in. Then walked over and placed his hand on Father Sebastian's shoulder. "This man has rescued the girl from a FARC camp. Please take him to your brother's place. He needs to make an urgent call."

"I'd prefer to wait until the doctor comes, if that's okay," Hart said, looking from one priest to the other.

"Of course," said Father Sebastian. He fetched a jug of water and two glasses from the table and brought them over to Hart, who drank deeply before using some of the water to clean Valentina's face with a small cloth the younger priest had also offered him.

CHAPTER TWENTY-FOUR

Z AMORA hated Quibdó. The fact that it was the capital city of the Chocó Department, in western Colombia, annoyed him immensely. The majority of the city's 90,000 inhabitants were Afro Colombians and Zambo Colombians; Zamora hated these people with a passion; he saw them as filthy immigrants with no right to call themselves real Colombians. He had only ever visited the city twice and as far as he was concerned, this was twice too many. Now, as he jogged towards the lights of the city, with Colm and Cesar close behind, he hated the place even more for being the city where the *soldado sangriento* had potentially taken his daughter.

By the time Zamora, Colm and Cesar had successfully managed to reach the far riverbank without being torn from the rope they had desperately clung to, avoiding being swept away beneath the black torrent of water, the darkness of the night had almost completely surrounded everything. It ate up everything in their path, like a damp, thick, musty blanket, clinging to everything it touched. As soon as they had pulled themselves from the river like half-drowned rats, the light had been so poor that they had almost missed the tell-tale sign of Land Rover tracks on the muddy riverbank.

Colm had crouched down and used his torch to study the

tracks closely. After a few moments, he had looked up at Zamora, who had been standing directly over him. "There's no doubt about it, these tracks are fresh and definitely belong to the Land Rover. The crazy fucking bastard somehow managed to make it across."

A grin spread over Zamora's face, wide and open, showing his rotten yellow teeth in the poor light, he was ecstatic. The *soldado sangriento* and his daughter had managed to survive a plane crash a few hours earlier; presumably, they did not walk away completely unscathed. Now he knew for certain that they had survived the crossing. There was now real hope that his daughter was still alive.

A serious, thoughtful look suddenly appeared across Zamora's face. The *soldado sangriento* was smart, he would surely know that the hospital would be the first place Zamora would look for them. The hospital would also ask too many questions. No, that would not be a safe place for the *soldado sangriento* to seek help.

Then he looked up and the answer came to him as he saw in the far distance the lights from the city and the imposing cathedral. Of course! Zamora smiled to himself. If the *soldado sangriento* thought his life would be spared inside a place of worship, then he was gravely mistaken. He also wasn't as clever as Zamora had given him credit for. Either that, or he had completely underestimated how ruthless Zamora could be, especially when his daughter's life was at stake. They continued towards the jungle city, following the track that snaked through the trees and disappeared from sight into the blackness surrounding them. It was well worn but narrow and broken with knotted roots. Branches overhung making an archway as if welcoming them towards their destiny.

✳✳✳

"Can you tell me exactly what happened to her?" The short, rather rotund, softly spoken doctor asked Hart.

"We were in a plane crash earlier this afternoon. We had just taken off when we had some engine trouble and the plane came down in the Río Atrato. She was submerged for quite some time but was conscious when we started to swim towards the riverbank. As we reached the riverbank, she was dragged under. She hit her head hard against some rocks. I managed to get her breathing again, but she blacked out again and hasn't regained consciousness since then. That was a good few hours ago."

The doctor nodded and sat down on the bed next to Valentina to take her pulse. Hart felt a hand on his shoulder. He spun around rather more aggressively than necessary and made Father Eduardo jump.

"Sorry. I'm still a bit jumpy," Hart explained. Father Eduardo gave him a sympathetic smile.

"You should go with Father Sebastian now. You need to make your phone call and tell your people to come and get you. His brother's gas station is just in the next street. It will only take you a few minutes to get there."

Hart nodded. "Yes, thank you." Then he grabbed the doctor by the arm. "Do you think she's going to be okay?"

"I don't know, I have to do some checks. It would be better for me to take her to the hospital," the doctor said.

"No!" warned Hart and appealed to Father Eduardo, who nodded to reassure him.

"I will explain everything to the doctor," he said. "You go with Father Sebastian now. The girl will not be moved. I give you my word. She is safe here. Now go and make your call."

"Thank you," Hart said softly.

He walked towards the open door of the antechamber.

He paused for a moment and turned. "Her name's Valentina," Hart told the priest and doctor. "If she wakes up tell her that Mr John will be right back in a few minutes. Tell her she's safe and everything's going to be okay. Please don't mention Amelia." He followed Father Sebastian, saying a silent prayer for Valentina as he left the room. Maybe there was more hope of having it answered, considering where they were.

∗∗∗

"We have him! We have him!" Zamora hissed with sinister glee as they
approached from the northern end of the city and spotted the Land Rover parked next to the cathedral. He grabbed Cesar and shook him violently. "It's him! I'm sure of it! It's the vehicle. It's fucking definitely him."

In a moment of blind recklessness, Zamora ran towards the Land Rover. He could now see that the rear window had been shot out, with the rest of the vehicle riddled with bullet rounds. The once smooth metal bodywork had now been replaced with a rough and chipped exterior. It was a miracle that the woman left lying beside the bridge had been the only person to die. The realisation that his daughter could have been a casualty suddenly struck him like a drunken 'Hit and Run' driver. Incredibly, until now, he had not even considered the possibility. He had been in a state of almost perpetual blind rage over the last few days, his sole focus directed towards saving his daughter; all sensible reasoning had fallen by the wayside.

He had hoped to find his daughter inside the Land Rover. Colm and Cesar raced after him, crouching down and positioning themselves at either side of the small wooden side door to the cathedral, covering Zamora whilst he continued to search inside the Land Rover.

∗∗∗

Father Sebastian led Hart along a short corridor and out through the back door of the cathedral. They were halfway across the road when a movement further along the road caught Hart's attention. In the shadows he saw two figures crouching by the side door of the

234

cathedral and another figure standing by the open door to the Land Rover, searching inside.

"Shit!" Hart hissed, to himself, grabbing Father Sebastian and pulling him back towards the cathedral.

"What's wrong?" the young priest asked.

"Quiet!" Hart warned him as he hurried back to the back door of the cathedral.

Once they were out of sight, he explained.

"FARC soldiers – they've been following us. We need to hide the girl. Those bastards will kill anyone who gets in their way. We need to warn Father Eduardo and Doctor Sanchez."

***

Satisfied that there was no sign of his daughter inside the Land Rover and deeply disturbed by the sight of so much blood, praying that it didn't belong to Valentina, Zamora directed Colm to open the side door to the cathedral and lead the way inside.

Zamora and his men entered through the ancient wooden door and scanned the empty pews on either side of the cathedral, the last of the worshippers had fled through the main double door entrance after seeing Hart moments before. The men dropped their backpacks by the door and then slowly moved across the polished stone brown floor slabs, moving deeper inside the cathedral, their footsteps resonated in the otherwise eerily silence, swallowed whole by the cavernous timbered high ceiling. All three men held their deadly weapons at waist level, close into their bodies, their knuckles turning white as they made their way up the right-hand aisle. With eyes unblinking and scanning the vast interior, each man's trigger finger was poised to release a deadly reign of bullet rounds.

"Over there," Zamora whispered, as he nodded toward a side door.

The men approached the door, slowly and cautiously. Colm

and Cesar took positions either side of the wooden door whilst Zamora took cover behind a nearby pillar. He nodded to Colm and then, without making a sound and exercising the same care as if handling explosives, the Irishman turned the handle of the door. All three of them trained their guns on the door as Colm nudged the door open with his foot. The room was windowless and appeared empty of any furniture apart from the four tall candle stands in each corner of the room. Their light giving the room a much warmer and lighter feel than the cathedral's nave.

Zamora motioned to Colm and Cesar that they should go in to check. They followed his orders and seconds later emerged to confirm that there was no one hiding inside.

Zamora swore under this breath and spun around.

Where were they? Finally, he saw a stone spiral staircase on the opposite side of the cathedral, halfway along its length. He motioned for Colm and Cesar to follow him.

The men stealthily climbed the poorly lit staircase, their AK47's at the ready, once again. Winding up in a tight spiral, the inner part of each step was so narrow and pointed it was impossible to use. It curled around to the right with no handrail. The stones were cold, each step echoed across the cathedral. At the top of the stone staircase, they reached a long open balcony that looked as though it wrapped around the entire cathedral forming an upper mezzanine. Continuing to maintain silence, Zamora led his men along it. There were recesses along the back wall—a small window depicting a religious scene in stained glass in each one.

Suddenly, Zamora drew a sharp intake of breath. He pointed ahead of them. A small figure was lying, covered with what looked like a pile of religious robes, on a makeshift bed of blankets in one of the recesses.

"It's her!" Zamora hissed. He lurched across the room before anyone could stop him, dropping to his knees and grabbing at the heavy material covering the lifeless form beneath. His eyes bulged in an effort to acknowledge the sight before him. The acidic bile in his throat was forced down only by the burning rage now threatening to rip him apart. Books! He'd been tricked. They had dared to fuck with him. Hands trembling, he reached out and picked up a faded bible, its musty, stale smell filling his nostrils and fuelling his rage to boiling point.

"Agggh!" Zamora's roar tore through the air like a grenade exploding.

"Where is she?!" Zamora finally screamed at the top of his lungs.

"Safe!" Hart's voice called back from somewhere below. Zamora froze for a moment, shocked at Hart's brazen reply, and then leaned over the balcony.

"Show yourself, you coward! Shouted Zamora, desperately scanning below to try and identify where the voice had come from. Hart did not reply.

"Come on, *carechimba*, you know you have no chance. We are three and you are one," he shouted, indicating to Cesar and Colm that they should retrace their steps and go back down the stone spiral staircase.

"What makes you think I am only one?" Hart eventually responded, his voice echoing around them.

Zamora's head whipped round in the direction of where he thought Hart's voice had come from.

"You would not be hiding if you were not outnumbered," Zamora replied. From his vantage point on the far side of the cathedral, Hart remained silent as he watched Zamora join Colm and Cesar descending the staircase. He studied all three men carefully to assess their size and take note of the weapons they carried.

Zamora, Cesar, and Colm spread out, each of them covering an exit-way. Colm travelled the furthest distance, sticking close to outer wall of the cathedral and staying in the shadows as he made his way to cover the main double doors at the rear of the cathedral. Cesar went to the side door they had entered through and Zamora stayed near the stone staircase from where he could comfortably cover the centre of the cathedral.

"Where is my daughter, you *hijueputa*."

Still no reply.

"Give me my daughter, NOW!" he screamed.

"I honestly don't know," Hart finally replied. "I don't know what you're talking about. I've no idea where your daughter is. I can't help you. I'm just a radio operator who got separated from my team," Hart replied calmly.

"Liar!" Zamora yelled, clearly getting frustrated. "I saw you last night with my daughter in the Emberá village. I know exactly what you are. I know you have my daughter."

Hart could feel his pulse racing. The calmness he was portraying to Zamora was a front. He knew he was in a tight spot. He had no idea where the priests and the doctor had taken Valentina when he'd warned them that Zamora and his men were coming. They'd taken her up the stone spiral staircase and disappeared.

He'd panicked when he saw Zamora heading up there, which was why he'd called out to try and distract them, whilst at the same time hopefully warning the priests and the doctor of the impending danger approaching. He was stalling for time and prayed they were safe. Having succeeded in distracting Zamora and his men, Hart came up with the only bargaining tool he could think of. He couldn't take all three men on by himself; he needed to outsmart them.

"Okay, Zamora," Hart began with authority. "I'll give you your daughter, but only if let me go."

Angered by the fact his unseen adversary knew his name when he had no idea who this man was, Zamora lost his temper.

"Let me see her first," Zamora called out.

"I'm not able to do that. She's not here," Hart lied. "She was taken out of the cathedral when you arrived. She will be long gone by now."

"You're lying," Zamora screamed. "You did not have time to do that. We would have seen her."

"You have to believe me, Zamora. I spotted you checking my

Land Rover outside. She was moved from the cathedral whilst you were distracted," Hart called back. "Time is not on your side. As we speak, my people are coming for me. You can take your chances against them or I can take you to your daughter in exchange for letting me go."

"What are you talking about," Zamora snapped back. "How do your people even know where to find you? You have been running through the jungle for days' now with no help. How do they suddenly know where you are?"

"I telephoned them as soon as I arrived here in Quibdó," Hart lied.

"You are lying, again! If you keep treating me like a fool, I will kill you!" Zamora shouted. "A moment ago, you said you had no idea what I was talking about, claiming you didn't know my daughter. Now you are promising to take me to her. How can I trust you? How do I even know if she's alive?

"Believe what you want, Zamora." Hart called out, calmly. "Waiting here and doing nothing means you'll never get to see your daughter again. Letting me take you to her means we all get to walk away happy. You'll have your daughter and I get to stay alive. So, what's it going to be?"

For the first time in this exchange, Zamora was completely lost for words. The seconds ticked by whilst he tried to work out what his next best move might be. Hart was also trying to figure out a plan of his own. He glanced down at his 9mm Sig, wishing he had at least one more ally inside the building for support.

Whilst Zamora was considering his options, Hart found his way through the shadows, moving silently and stealthily, and staying close to the outer wall. He eventually reached the front altar and managed to conceal himself behind it. He waited, trying to steady his breathing, his hand clenching his 9mm Sig. He felt slightly vulnerable without his M16 colt rifle, having foolishly pushed it into the hands of the reluctant doctor after both Fathers' Eduardo and Sebastian had flatly refused to touch it. Hart had wanted them to have some sort of protection but had also believed the rifle might impede his ability to hide within the restricted confines of the cathedral. He was already regretting that decision!

They had left the room after him, Father Eduardo carrying Valentina and the doctor carrying Hart's rifle. Now all Hart could do was have faith that they were all safe somewhere and hope his 9mm Sig would be sufficient enough to help keep him alive.

Breathing deeply but silently, Hart waited. He knew he had to let Zamora make the next move.

Zamora's blood was boiling. The last thing he wanted to do was make deals with his despised enemy, the man he'd been hunting for two days, the man he desperately wanted to see spread out on the floor beneath him, with his life slowly and painfully draining out of him. He knew his choices were limited.

"Okay," Zamora called out, finally. "Tell me what you want me to do."

Hart hadn't been expecting Zamora to capitulate quite so easily. He hardly had a plan of his own worked out, but there was no time to lose. This was a deadly game of chess, and Hart was the pawn.

"Okay, but first, come out into the open where I can see all three of you, put your weapons on the ground and your hands on your heads." Hart directed.

"No, *Güevón*. You show yourself first," Zamora snapped back.

"No, Zamora," Hart steadily replied. "Remember, I have the upper hand here. I have your daughter and can take you to her."

"No," Zamora came back at him. "You come out into the open first."

Zamora pointed towards the altar, signalling to Colm and Cesar that he had at last identified where Hart was hiding. Colm and Cesar understood immediately and slowly began to make their way towards Hart, all the time ensuring they remained hidden from sight in the dark shadows of the cathedral.

Hart realised they had reached an impasse and that he had to try and continue to call the shots. "I will come out into the open and show myself, but only if we all lower our weapons together."

"Okay!" Zamora barked, clearly irritated. "Okay, okay, we will do it."

In the next few seconds, Zamora, Colm and Cesar nervously revealed themselves from the shadows and moved towards the centre of the cathedral. Hart crept out too, but stayed back, close by the altar.

After seeing Hart slowly emerge from behind the altar, all three FARC men raised and aimed their AK47's at him. Whilst he revealed his head, Hart kept his body shielded. He aimed his Sig at Zamora, assuming—and hoping—that he was the man to be most feared. The other two looked as though they wouldn't make an independent decision to end Hart's life. He knew he was outnumbered; he had no choice but to gamble and try to play it safe.

Before anyone could say another word, all four men were distracted by the sound of the cathedral's main door slowly creaking open. All four men immediately looked towards the huge double doors to see who was entering.

Silhouetted against the outside lights from the plaza, Hart saw three figures walk into the cathedral. The one in front was extremely tall and appeared to be carrying a weapon. The other two stood slightly behind him, one was armed and the other possibly not, Hart couldn't say for certain. Zamora blinked a few times to adjust his eyes to the change in light from outside. As his eyes readjusted, he could not believe what he was seeing. Could his eyes be deceiving him? Yes! It was, he was sure of it.

"Paola?" he exclaimed.

"Where is she?" Paola sobbed. "Where is Valentina? I just want my daughter back. Is she safe? Please tell me she's alive and safe."

"She's safe! She's alive!" Hart's voice echoed around the cathedral. It was filled with emotion; he was desperate to reassure this poor woman who had bravely sacrificed her daughter for a greater cause.

Paola almost collapsed with relief. She stumbled forward towards Zamora, throwing her backpack that hung from one shoulder, on to the floor. Her journey was almost over.

"I want to see her. Take me to her. Where is she?" she sobbed. Before she could take another step forward, a jubilant scream rang out from the balcony above, filling the entire cathedral. The scream was an adrenaline shot straight to the heart. It wasn't just any scream; it was Valentina.

She was running before her brain had even registered why. "Mamá, mamá, you're alive! I thought you were dead. I'm coming down."

Hart had looked up in horror, seeing that Valentina and Father Eduardo had come out of hiding and now stood in clear view on the balcony above.

Valentina had remained safe in the hiding place she shared with the two priests and the doctor until she had spotted Paola enter the cathedral with the two other men. Realising that her mother was still alive, Valentina had acted spontaneously, being sent into a state of total excitement and forgetting about any immediate danger she faced. Father Eduardo had pleaded with her to remain hidden and safe; sadly, the wise priest's words were ignored, having fallen on young deaf ears.

Valentina's footsteps could now be heard racing down the winding stone staircase, frantic to be reunited with her mother. Father Eduardo was in hot pursuit trying his very best to ensure his newly acquired charge remained safe from the clutches of the FARC.

Something strange had also overtaken Paola. As much as she hated Zamora, as much as he had been the source of all her pain—torturing her and trying to control her—she couldn't stand by and watch Zamora die. She lurched forward towards Zamora and her daughter. Valentina had successfully negotiated the staircase and was now running at full speed towards her mother.

Paola shouted with a mixture of joy and relief. Her outstretched arms ready to receive and embrace her daughter.

"Valentina, I love you so much!" she shouted.

She glanced across at Zamora. "Jose don't trust Borgman. He's going to kill you. He's not who you think he—"

She never got to finish her warning - two shots rang out in quick succession and struck Paola in the back. She fell forward, hitting the floor hard and landing on her side. Almost at once, a large red bloodstain appeared and spread across her back, the ebb and flow in time with her terrified heart. Her blood began to mingle with the brown polished stone floor. Her face was a picture of shock and absolute terror as she screamed out in agony.

After firing his weapon, Borgman had taken immediate cover behind the rear pew. Two more shots rang out in quick succession; then rapid-fire from another AK47. Zamora and Colm had also taken cover between the nearby pews. Cesar was not so lucky. He did not react fast enough and Borgman had dispatched him with his next two shots shortly after taking cover. Hammond also never stood a chance; without even knowing who he was, Zamora had killed him easily from his place of cover between the central pews.

Seeing her mother gunned down, Valentina had abruptly stopped running. She now stood frozen to the ground in severe shock, trying to take in the enormity of what had just happened. As the AK47 opened up once again, its rapid-fire jolted Valentina from the deep trauma of seeing her mother shot in the back. Instinctively, she ran forwards towards Paola, who was writhing on the floor in distress and shock, a rapidly growing pool of her own blood now spread across the cathedral floor.

When everyone was out of sight, Zamora erupted. "You bastard, Borgman! What have you done! What are you hiding? You piece of shit!"

There was no answer, and for a few moments, everything was still. The only sounds to be heard within the enormous cathedral came from Paola, who was moaning in pain, and Valentina, who was crying and trying to comfort her mother as best she could.

The next sound came from the rear of the cathedral. Borgman

had crawled back towards the main entrance and swung open the heavy wooden doors, escaping out into the night. Distance was all that mattered to Borgman. He wasn't stopping for anything. He was leaving Quibdó tonight, with all that he needed. The woman was nicely out of the picture, and if Zamora survived, he would deal with him at a later date.

"Run, you bastard," screamed Zamora. "Run as far as you can. I will find you soon enough and kill you!" His voice echoed through the cathedral.

Hart's bargaining chip in promising to return Valentina to Zamora was now well and truly dead in the water and worthless. He was in a tight spot and he knew it.

As if reading Hart's thoughts, Zamora shouted. "You thought you had some kind of advantage over me. I may have lost one of my men, but I still have my best soldier by my side, and my daughter has been returned to me," Zamora continued, darkly, as he inched his way out of the pew and towards where Paola and Valentina lay, checking that Colm was covering him from his position a few feet away.

"Show yourself, or I'll be forced to come after you," Zamora shouted.

He then stopped suddenly, as if a dark hidden force had just struck him directly in the centre of his chest with unimaginable power. Listening to the words Valentina now gently whispered to her mother, through almost uncontrollable sobs, inflicted more damage to Zamora's soul in that precise moment than any enemy could ever hope to achieve through torture.

His love for his daughter had been unconditional, but it was now being torn apart with every word Valentina spoke. They were words he had never thought possible—the words of a traitor!

On seeing her father and mother again, Valentina had instinctively run towards Paola, completely ignoring Zamora, almost as if he was insignificant to her. Zamora had always understood his daughter had an extremely close and special bond with her mother; something he had tried over the years to ignore and not become jealous of. Ignoring him under these unique set of circumstances was something he could easily forgive, especially considering what Valentina had been through over the last few days.

Now though, the words coming from his own daughter's mouth, this was something different. This was completely unforgivable! Each word was tearing down and destroying everything he had worked hard to build up over the years. It was as if a small demolition crane that had been sent in to tear down the strongest, sturdiest building imaginable, and it had done it with relative ease.

Valentina pleaded. "Mamá, please don't die. I need you, please stay alive. I can get you help. The doctor who helped me, he can help you too," pleaded Valentina. "When you're feeling better, Mr John will take us to his people. We can live a new life. Have a nice new home. Just you and I, together. I am going to tell Mr John's friends' all the things you told me. They will pay us lots of money. I will tell them about the secret bank accounts. Where the money is, and who it belongs to. I will also tell them about the secret recipe. Everything you taught me and asked me to remember. Mr John's friends will look after us and we can leave this place behind us, just you wait and see," Valentina smiled, trying her best to cradle Paola's head as she lay on her side.

Paola was so deep in ten shades of agony that she would be unreachable until she received proper medical attention and much-needed morphine.

Zamora had heard enough. "Valentina, come here, now. It's not safe for you out in the open. Come here and I will protect you," soothed Zamora, in a strained voice, trying his best to disguise the anger he felt inside at this unforgivable act of betrayal.

His tone had already betrayed him. Valentina's head spun around. "Never!" she shouted in anguish. "You have caused this. You are no father of mine. You are a beast! I saw what you did in the village. How could you kill those people? They were kind and just wanted to help me and Mr John. You are dead to me!"

This was too much for Zamora to take. It pushed him over the edge of reasoning. He threw all caution to the wind and dashed forward dragging Valentina to her feet and holding her tightly against his chest from behind, making her face Paola—he wanted her to witness what was about to happen to their daughter. He had lost all compassion. Slinging the AK47 across his back and reaching for his side-arm; the Russian made MP-443 Grach Pistol, he placed it to Valentina's head.

"You fucking spoiled little brat!" Zamora screamed in Valentina's ear. "I have sacrificed everything for you. How do you repay me, like this? You disrespect me and treat me like a dog." Looking towards Hart now, he continued. "Whatever this *hijueputa* has promised you it's not going to happen. Do you hear me? Your filthy whore of a mother has just killed you! Do you understand? You have left me with no choice!"

Despite having a gun held to her head, Valentina still attempted to try and free herself from Zamora's tight grip; but it was useless. He was too strong.

Whilst Father Sebastian and the doctor remained hidden upstairs, Father Eduardo knew he must try to reason with Zamora if there was any hope of de-escalating the situation. "Listen to me, my son. Now please, there's no need for this, this is the house of God. There must –"

As with Paola moments earlier, Father Eduardo's words were abruptly cut short. One single shot rang out. Zamora had had enough listening to reason, especially from some old priest. It was time for Father Eduardo to meet his God, in person. The bullet round struck Father Eduardo directly between his eyes, killing him instantly, before he even hit the ground. Zamora considered this an act of kindness—a swift death was always a charitable act in his opinion.

Hart knew he now had to act. He had to somehow save Valentina and Paola, but how to do it without exposing himself for long enough to be shot by one of the FARC men. Zamora had dragged Valentina back behind the central pews and the other remaining FARC soldier was no doubt gaining ground and moving closer and closer towards Hart through the shadows. Hart knew he had no moves left open to him; he had no bargaining power. His only hope was to try and make Zamora believe he was to be trusted. The only way to do that was by showing the FARC commander that he trusted him in turn.

"Okay, I'm coming out. There's been enough bloodshed around here for one evening," Hart said carefully. "I am placing my weapon down on the altar. In return, let your daughter go. You can have me instead." He slowly stood up and placed his Sig pistol on the altar between the golden candlesticks. There was something bizarrely sacrificial about the act, as if he was bargaining with God, making a moral exchange: his weapon for his life. Would this be it? Would God spare him now? Would a miracle happen?

With a strange sense of peace, Hart stood up to his full height.

"Okay, here I am Zamora, unarmed. Your advantage now: let your daughter go. Let's strike a deal where we all get to stay alive and walk away from this place with what we want."

Zamora remained motionless behind the pews, still holding his daughter tightly, his Grach Pistol ready and pointed at her head. As soon as Hart had stepped out into the open Zamora slowly changed his aim towards the man he had wanted to kill for many day's now. Appearing from the shadows behind Hart, was the surviving FARC soldier, the longhaired, bearded one. The situation did not feel good to Hart. He felt as though he had failed. He was suddenly sure he had been wrong to trust Zamora, but if this was how it was going to end, he knew he had done everything in his power to fulfil his obligation. Perhaps this was just plain Karma for what he'd done to the young boy in Afghanistan.

Despite the fact he was sure he was about to die, Hart suddenly felt calmer and more peaceful than he'd felt in years. The latent nausea had gone; he wasn't shaking. He was still and serene. It was as if he was being afforded one last feeling of wellbeing before he went on to feel nothing.

Then Zamora began his prelude to the inevitable. "So, Mr John. Do you believe you can talk your way out of this? Do you think you have allies coming to save you? Walk slowly towards me. I want to finally see you up close and personal."

Hart had no alternative. He did as Zamora instructed and slowly walked towards the man who in all likelihood was about to end his life. He looked at Valentina, the girl he'd tried so hard to save, but in the end, he had failed.

"That's close enough," instructed Zamora. "Stay exactly where you are and don't come any closer."

Hart now stood just 10 feet from Zamora and Valentina. He clenched his eyes shut, anticipating the pain that was about to come.

A shot rang out, and then another. Hart felt nothing.

At first, he wondered if death had come so instantly that he'd been spared the agony.

Then logic told him to open his eyes.

Zamora stood perfectly still, rooted to the spot, staring at Hart with a glazed expression. His mouth was open in some kind of disfigured half-smile. A look of complete shock was now etched across his face. His arms had released Valentina and now hung limply and motionless by his sides. His MP-443 Grach Pistol had fallen from his right hand and landed with a clatter on the cathedral stone floor. Valentina dared not look behind her, instead, she remained completely still and continued to stare straight ahead at Hart. At last, she made a sound again. It was more than crying; it was the kind of desolate sobbing that comes from a person drained of all hope.

The two shots had found their intended target – one penetrating between Zamora's upper chest and his left-hand shoulder, narrowly missing Valentina. The other driving directly through the right side of his skull taking some of his brains with it as it continued on its trajectory. Being hit at such close range by a high-powered rifle produced a horrific gaping mess. It was as if Zamora had been hit by an assortment of different weapons all at the same time.

In seconds the strength in Zamora's legs finally gave way. He dropped to the floor in a heap just behind Valentina. Death was coming to Zamora with slow rattling gasps. His breathing stopped for a second only to re-emerge like a drowning victim coming up for one last breath.

Zamora didn't fear Death, only where he would go. He had sinned so much and committed so many crimes against humanity, he would understand if God sent him to the pits of hell for eternity for the things he had done. He hadn't believed in God, but now, lying here staring at Death, he tightly clung on to the possibility of his existence. Would he be forgiven? Perhaps Zamora was just another innocent soul who had allowed himself to be persuaded by wrong things?

In his final moments fighting for breath, Zamora finally understood that Death was a shadow that lurked in the dark and was always there. He was the ghost that people feared. Death was nowhere near as merciful as Zamora had dreamed of it being. The pain that once burned like fire, had now faded away to an icy numbness. Black filled the edges of his vision and the only thing he could hear was his own heartbeat mixed with Valentina's distant sobs. His breath came in ragged, shallow gasps. Zamora was dead already; he just hadn't accepted it yet. His would be a painful death that befitted a man of Zamora's callousness and inability to show neither compassion nor empathy. At last, his heartbeat sounded for its final time. The world was at last rid of another psychopathic monster. Zamora was gone!

Valentina continued to sob, staring directly ahead, still not daring to move a muscle, she was sure the next shots about to be fired would be directed at her.

Behind Hart, the FARC soldier's AK47 was still smoking. He slowly lowered his weapon and approached Hart carefully.

"Don't be afraid, I am on your side," he began. "My name is—"

For the third time that evening, another conversation was abruptly cut short. A couple of shots, then another, and another. They just kept coming. The man hit the ground hard. Hart dived for cover behind the nearest pew.

After spotting Hart's Land Rover parked outside and witnessing Borgman leaving the cathedral in a hurry, Bob had ordered Jock and Kav to go after the Dutchman.

Bob and Mike had then crept silently inside the cathedral, arriving too late to stop the long-haired FARC soldier from firing his AK47, narrowly missing Hart and killing the other FARC soldier, who'd been holding the young girl. Bob was sure the FARC soldier had intended to kill Hart, but in error, had killed his colleague by mistake. Without hesitation, both SAS men had fired short controlled bursts from their M16's into the back of the remaining FARC soldier before he had a chance to deliver a second deadly burst from his AK47.

Hart was truly relieved to see his team; they had arrived just in time. Although, he had no idea what the hell was going on? He picked himself up and ran towards the FARC man who had shot Zamora and was now lying on the floor, rapidly losing consciousness.

"Who are you?!" he asked, desperately.

The man answered through short painful breaths. "Colm O'Leary. New IRA. Work for MI6. I report to London. Owen Bennett. Report my death to him, nobody else. Don't compromise our network."

As Hart was taking this in, Valentina had finally found the strength to move from the spot she'd been rooted to. She ran towards her wounded mother once again, trying her best to comfort her. Paola was also rapidly losing consciousness.

She looked horrified and shouted across at Colm. "You were

my mother's friend," she cried, "But you were also my father's friend."

Colm coughed up blood. "I loved your mother. Hated your father. Your mother's everything to me. Do what she tells you."

Valentina nodded, biting her lip to try and stop the tears that were streaming down her cheeks.

Then Colm was gone.

Valentina began to sob, again. Hart stood up and greeted Bob and Mike. He suddenly looked confused.

"I have to say, I wasn't planning on seeing you guys again. I was convinced I was on my own. How did you guys know I was here?"

"We've been trailing you for two days now, John. We're just sorry we didn't get here before all this shit went down. Looks like you handled it okay though," Bob said, respectfully.

Mike had picked up Hart's Sig pistol after retrieving it from the altar and handed it to him. Hart's attention immediately turned to Paola. He asked Bob to take a look at her whilst sending Mike to search the upper balcony to let the doctor and priest know that it was okay to come out of hiding.

Hart just hoped Paola's wounds weren't immediately life-threatening.

Valentina threw her arms around Hart and wept.
As he held the little dishevelled girl in his arms, he tried to hold back his own emotions. He was conscious that in a matter of days he would never see Valentina again. Assuming Paola would survive, he vowed not to leave Colombia until he knew she and her mother were safely taken care off.

Bob reported that Paola's wounds looked to be survivable. Moments later Mike returned with the doctor and the young priest. Taking in the scene before them, both men looked horrified. There was no time for sentiment. Hart instructed the doctor to quickly attend to Paola and her wounds.

Bob tried to pick Valentina up, but she clung to Hart.

"It's okay, Bob, let her stay with me for now. I've got her. Radio Kav and Jock and see how they're getting on? Hopefully, they've managed to catch up with the Dutchman. Then call for an immediate extraction and let's get out of here before the local authorities turn up and begin asking too many questions! With all the recent gunfire that's been going on around here, the local cops should be rolling up any minute now." Hart instructed.

The last two days had tested and pushed Hart to the limits of his very being. He was completely drained of energy. It was time to head back to Bogotá and leave some Embassy official to explain to the Colombia authorities why the Cathedral of San Francisco de Asis in Quibdó was now littered with corpses, including one belonging to the cathedral's senior priest. Holding Valentina, Hart stepped out through the large wooden double doors and into the warm night air of the plaza. Bob and Mike followed, carrying Paola. Their ordeal was now nearly over. Another mission almost complete.

Hart felt nothing!

CHAPTER TWENTY-FIVE

THE HELICOPTER ride back to Bogotá was a blur to Hart. Paola had been taken straight to the Hospital Universitario San Ignacio for an urgent operation, although it was sure she would survive and make a full recovery.

Borgman had managed to elude capture by making his way towards the nearby Río Atrato, where Kav and Jock's had found his hastily discarded AK47 half-buried in the muddy riverbank. They had followed his mud-trail towards the nearby Malecom Park & Gardens where he had literally vanished into thin air. Both men suspected that Borgman had probably managed to hail down a cab on the nearby Carrera 1 road and escape from the city. No doubt he would reappear soon enough, turning up like a bad penny.

After a brief medical examination, which included having the hole in his shoulder cleaned and stitched up properly, Hart had showered and fallen into a deep sleep. They had given him a room in the British Embassy next to Valentina's. Since arriving at the Embassy, Valentina had been cared for by Sarah Smith. Seeing her in this civilized, western environment suddenly made Valentina seem even younger and more vulnerable than ever.

When Hart woke at 10 am the next morning, having slept for a full six hours, Hart heard Valentina crying. He leapt out of bed and went to her room. Sarah was trying to console her.

"Mr John, Mr John!" she called out when she saw him. "I kept having a dream that my mother was dead. My old father was dead. Then you... you were dead too."

"I'm not dead, Valentina. Look, I'm here. I'm safe. You're safe. We made it. Your mother is being cared for and is now safe. She'll make a full recovery in no time. Everything is going to be okay."

The little girl looked up into his face. "When can I see my mother again? Where will we live?"

"You can hopefully visit your mother in hospital tomorrow," Sarah said gently. "We've also traced your mother's cousin. She lives just north of here in Pamploma, very near to the Venezuelan border. I'm told it's a very nice city. You and your mother will live with her until your mother has fully recovered from her injuries."

"But we want to live with you," Valentina said beseechingly to Hart.

"I'm sorry," he told her sombrely. "I have to go back to Britain."

"Will I ever see you again?" she asked.

Hart nodded and smiled. "Every night," he said, gently. "Before you fall asleep, when you close your eyes, you'll see me. And you'll know that I'm thinking of you."

"How can I do that?" Valentina asked him, urgently. "What if I forget what you look like?"

"When you really care for someone," Hart explained. "And they really care for you, too. It's impossible to forget what they look like."

"How do you know that?" Valentina pressed him, almost getting belligerent.

"Because," Hart began. "A long time ago, before you were even born, I saw someone I cared about for the last time. Even today, when I close my eyes..." Hart gently closed his eyes for effect. "I can see their face as clearly as if it was right in front of me."

"When you're ready," Sarah Smith said, in a hushed tone, breaking Hart's reverie and causing him to open his eyes. "Diana Brooks would like to see you and Valentina for an initial debriefing."

Hart and Valentina looked at each other. This was it. This was the moment they had put themselves in mortal danger for. Valentina was about to divulge all the information that could help close down a major international drug trafficking operation.

Two hours later, as Sarah Smith entered the office, where Diana Hart and Valentina had been sitting, Hart was more in awe of the little girl than he'd been of any person he'd ever met. The complex web of information that Valentina held inside her head was staggering. She had memorised names, numbers, countries, cities, codes and more. The information the British intelligence service now had at their disposal would surely lead to many, many arrests. Even some high profile, top-ranked political figures, some slightly too close to home for comfort. They would all be brought down by this information.

The only thing that bothered Hart was the way Diana had acted as if the victory had been hers alone. He was used to being taken for granted—being the unsung hero—that was all part of his job, but he didn't like how little credit Diana had given Valentina. Hart was now getting himself back into professional mode. The whole experience with Valentina had opened up places in his being that had been sealed up long ago. He needed to close down again, to protect himself. The nausea had returned that morning and, now that Valentina had left the office and he was sitting alone with Diana, it was almost as if the whole experience had been a bad dream. He was moving into that phase of detachment he felt after every operation.

He would forget it all in a matter of days. Or would he? Would he only succeed in pushing the events into the dark recesses of his mind, waiting for them to come back to haunt him like the recent events in Afghanistan had?

"You should be very pleased with yourself," Diana Brooks said, suddenly.

Hart stared at her for a moment. He found he had nothing to say. The vague attraction he'd felt for her only days before had now disappeared. He felt nothing. He didn't even want to be in her company anymore. He stood up.

"Do you know when we're due to fly back to London?" he asked her.

"You're booked onto a flight leaving for Madrid at 10 pm tonight," Diana said with a wry smile. "So, I thought you might like to join me for lunch. At my apartment perhaps?"

"Thank you," Hart said with a perfunctory smile. "But I need to debrief my men. We need to sort through our equipment and weapons, to ensure they're all packed up and ready to deploy back to Hereford."

Diana took the rejection in her stride but couldn't resist leaving a door ajar.

"You'll have my driver at your disposal if you change your mind. I'll be home for the rest of the afternoon." As if needing to explain herself she added, "I haven't left the office for the past 48 hours whilst you've been missing. I'm taking the rest of the day off."

Hart nodded, gave her a brief smile and left the room, walking away without looking back.

***

London was as busy as ever when Hart returned. The new Wembley Stadium had opened in March, a few months earlier, and now the city was preparing for the inaugural opening of the new London St Pancras railway station in a few months' time.

Hart had gone through several circuitous channels in order to secure a confidential meeting with Owen Bennett. He'd never actually met the man in the flesh before, although his reputation proceeded him. Now he was sitting alone in the office belonging to the Head of MI6, waiting for him to arrive. Hart surveyed the office. It was everything he expected: ostentatious, reassuringly expensive, and in one of the most exclusive parts of the city by the River Thames. Everything was tidy and organised. There was a large mahogany desk with three drawers on the left-hand side, an expensive leather swivel chair, the latest mac book pro, a floor to ceiling bookshelf with books neatly leaning against one another, a filing cabinet with paperwork neatly stacked on top, and a water dispenser with expensive-looking cups.

Hart looked out across the River Thames. As soon as he was done in this office, as soon as he'd delivered the message he'd come to give directly to Owen, he planned to head down to Broadstairs on the Kent coast where he'd rented a seaside cottage for two months. He may even take in a tour of the nearby Canterbury Cathedral to compare it with the cathedral in Quibdó. He was overdue some serious R&R. He wanted to switch off. He wanted to contemplate his future. He wasn't sure if he was cut out for the job anymore. The events in Colombia, on top of what he'd experienced in Afghanistan had shaken him to the core.

The vomiting and shaking had started up again as soon as he'd got on the plane back to the UK. He wasn't even sure if he could get through this meeting without needing to excuse himself.

Finally, Owen Bennett entered the office. He was a tall, exceptionally handsome man with a large over-enthusiastic grin. John stood up, subtly steadying himself on the side of the chair as a wave of nausea washed over him, as Owen approached him with an outstretched hand.

"John Hart, I presume," Owen said, in a deep voice that matched his extra firm handshake.

"Yes, sir," Hart said, gratefully freeing his hand from Owen's grip.

"Please, please, sit down," Owen continued, taking a seat behind his desk. "I believe you have some highly classified information to share with me. I've been briefed on your operation in Colombia. Excellent work, I must say."

"Thank you, sir," Hart mumbled. "My message concerns Colm O'Leary."

At the mention of the Irishman's name, Owen sat up straighter in his chair but said nothing. He let Hart continue. "I'm sorry to inform you, sir, Colm O'Leary was killed in the line of duty. He asked me to report his death to you, personally. At his request I did not include it in my report to the MI6 station head in Bogotá, or to my own superiors at Hereford. I trust that I have followed the correct protocol."

Owen said nothing. He seemed to be slightly lost. He simply stared at Hart.

"Sir?" Hart said finally.

"Sorry! Yes," Owen finally said, snapping out of his trance. "Thank you. Yes, you did the right thing. What was, um... how was his body disposed of?" Owen enquired, clearly trying to control his voice.

"He would have been disposed of in the clean-up operation, sir. Assumed the enemy, just another member of the FARC. I'm sure you're already aware, but there were also two British fatalities, one from your branch in Colombia and one from HMRC. The MI6 officer's body was flown back to the UK last week. We've been reliably informed that the HMRC officer died whilst running into some quicksand along the banks of the Río Atrato. It wasn't possible to recover the body. There was also a woman, Canadian citizen, who helped us enormously. Diana Brooks is arranging for the repatriation of her body."

Owen nodded. "Yes, I already know about the UK and Canadian fatalities. Though, Colm comes as a surprise and will be a hard man to replace," he said, softly. Hart got the distinct feeling that although Colm had been an MI6 operative, he had also been a personal friend of Owen's, but he said nothing.

"If there's nothing more, sir..." Hart asked. His hands poised on the armrests of the chair. He needed to get out of there in the next few seconds. He had that metallic taste in his mouth and was losing the feeling in his feet.

"Well, I'd be interested to ask you a few more questions, man to man. To understand more about this Borgman chap and his link to Chaplain, and where you think…" Owen began.

Hart was incapable of hearing anymore, let alone answering. At last, relieved of all official responsibility, having delivered Colm's message to the right man, it was as if Hart's body finally stopped holding out and gave in. The trembling started up and became overwhelming. A high- pitched whistling sound rang throughout his head, drowning out the sound of Owen's voice and Hart blacked out.

Again…

THE END

John Hart will return…in 'Minding Gold'

GLOSSARY

1. Al-Qaeda: A extremist Salafist militant organization founded in 1988 by Osama bin Laden. Al-Qaeda operates as a network of Islamic extremists and Salafist jihadists
2. Basha: Sleeping shelter
3. Bergen: Rucksack
4. Blue-on- Blue: Accidental strike on own forces
5. Belt-kit   Pouches a soldier wears on a belt to carry ammunition and survival equipment etc.
6. Block: A FARC military command unit responsible for one of the main operational regions
7. C-130:   Hercules aircraft used for military troop, vehicle and logistic transportation
8. Casevac: Casualty evacuation
9. C-26:   Surveillance aircraft
10. Comms: Communications
11. COBRA: Cabinet office briefing room
12. CO: Commanding Officer
13. DOP: Drop-off point
14. DZ: Drop zone
15. DSF   Officer commanding Special Forces: Director (generally a brigadier)
16. ERV: Emergency rendezvous
17. FMB: Forward mounting base for attack
18. FOB: Forward operating base
19. FARC: A guerrilla movement involved in the continuing Colombian armed conflict starting in 1964
20. FRV/FUP: Final Rendezvous Point/Forming Up Point
21. HE: High explosive

22.	Incoming:	Incoming enemy fire
23.	Int:	Intelligence
24.	IED:	Improvised explosive device
25.	JUNGLA:	Colombian Police specialist police unit. Set up by Britain's SAS in 1989, and trained by them, and the Americans
26.	J2:	The national level focal point for crisis intelligence support to military operations
27.	Kit:	Equipment
28.	LUP:	Lying-up point
29.	LMG:	Light Machine Gun
30.	MIA:	Missing in action
31.	MOD:	Ministry of Defence
32.	New IRA:	A dissident Irish republican paramilitary group which aims to bring about a united Ireland. It formed in 1997 following a split in the Provisional IRA
33.	OC:	Officer commanding
34.	OP:	Observation post
35.	PNGs:	Passive night goggles
36.	PTSD:	Post –traumatic stress disorder
37.	PM:	British Prime Minister
38.	Pressel:	Press to Talk (PTT) switch is usually mounted on one side of the radio handset
39.	PRC 319:	VHF radio
40.	QRF:	Quick reaction forces
41.	RTU:	Return to unit
42.	R & R:	Rest and recreation
43.	RHQ:	Regimental Headquarters
44.	RWW:	SAS Revolutionary Warfare Wing (RWW)
45.	RV:	Rendezvous (Meeting point)
46.	SF:	Special Forces
47.	Sit Rep:	Situation report
48.	SOP:	Standard operating procedure
49.	Sikorsky UH-60:	A four-blade, twin-engine, medium-lift utility helicopter manufactured by Sikorsky Aircraft. (Black Hawk)
50.	57th Front:	A FARC unit active along the Colombia-Panama border

WEAPONS

51.	AK 47:	Soviet-design 7.62mm short rifle
52.	Browning:	9mm pistol
53.	GP-34:	Russian 40mm grenade launcher. Connected to an AK-47 rifle launcher
54.	L2:	Hand grenade
55.	LMG:	A light machine gun designed to be employed by an individual soldier
56.	MP-443:	Russian standard military-issue side arm.
57.	M203:	Combination of 5.56mm automatic rifle (top barrel) and 40mm grenade
58.	M60D:	An American 7.62mm General Purpose Machine Gun (GPMG)
59.	M16 Colt:	A military rifle adapted from the ArmaLite AR-15 rifle for the United States military.
60.	M134:	A 7.62×51mm NATO six-barrel rotary machine gun with a high, sustained rate of fire. It features a Gatling-style rotating barrel assembly with an external power source, normally an electric motor.
61.	NSV:	A Russian made 12.7mm calibre heavy machine gun
62.	RPG7:	Soviet-made rocket launcher
63.	Sig:	Sigsauer 9mm pistol
64.	Stinger:	A Man-Portable Air-Defence System that operates as an infrared homing surface-to-air missile.
65.	81mm Mortar:	Medium range and weight mortar
66.	2 Para:	A battalion-sized formation of the Parachute Regiment, capable of a wide range of operational tasks.

ABOUT AUTHOR

Grayson Hardy was born and raised in Scotland. He joined the British army at 18 and served with an Infantry unit before successfully completing the rigorous SAS selection course to become a member of the UK's elite Special Forces. He now lives with his family on the outskirts of London and works as a security consultant, writer and investigative presenter.

 @RealGrayHardy

 @graysonhardyauthor

 https://www.facebook.com/TheJohnHartSeries

Printed in Poland
by Amazon Fulfillment
Poland Sp. z o.o., Wrocław

63895445R00162